Together We Evolve

Dear Helen,

with wild love & thanks,

Together

We

Evolve

Polly Roberts

Hermitage Press

CORNWALL

Disclaimer

This is a work of fiction. Names, characters, places, and incidents are either the product of the author's imagination or are used fictitiously, and any resemblance to actual persons, living or dead, businesses, companies, events or locales is entirely coincidental.

Published in Great Britain 2023
Hermitage Press Limited, Cornwall
hermitagepress.org

First Edition

Hardback edition: ISBN 9781739453534
Electronic edition: ISBN 9781739453541

A CIP catalogue record for this book is available from the British Library

Illustrations and sleeve art: Kim Stephens

Printed and bound by

TJ Books, Padstow, Cornwall

For Heron

At the top of the sand dune is a nest. A cluster of shingle weighs the centre of a ring of grasses where an oystercatcher made themselves king of the castle. Mating season is over and the nest has been abandoned, a few stray feathers left. The sand is cool. Maybe a mate was too rare to come by. Maybe they left in a rush.

The moon is out; the sun too. They balance on the horizon. Below them lies the sea, with white horses galloping across its body; life goes further when moving together.

This is our land, where we belong. Smell it: like generations of starfish, salt and chalk. Breathe. Are you ready to wade in?

A large bird swoops above our heads, another of our kind: grey, white, a misty shadow passed and gone. In recent years, it was only our ghosts who haunted these beaches. Yet here we are, back on our territory.

But our nests, too, have been abandoned: twigs across water all to show for weeks of gathering. It was the storm that ravaged them, wild winds tumbling carefully considered grasses as if only debris. Our shallow nesting grounds flooded until our long legs could no longer reach bottom.

We huddle on shore, wings held tight against our bodies, uneasy about what to do next. Our voices call out but are lost to the song of leaves from the trees at the top of the beach as they tap against one another in a gust of wind.

WINTER

1

The earth moves beneath me. It slips away as if I'm sitting on a parachute, someone pulling one end. The scenery's engulfed by a pounding glow: a halo that dilates and contracts. To see I have to squint. Am I squinting or wincing?

The earth steadies and I keep walking. Beside me is a tree, from its branches a bird takes flight – flickers of white – then it's gone.

And the ground moves again. Heat enters my toes and rises: a rush of warmth like I am a mug being filled with hot water. The water overflows and floods around my ankles, calling me to swim back to where I came from. Dad said we all began at sea.

But I can't swim.

The sky winds around me, squeezing then releasing – squeeze, then release. Black. Night's sky, consuming me headfirst; like a python it swallows me. Constriction then digestion. I'm trapped; I want to get out. It's too tight. Let me out. Squeeze.

Release. I'm gushing, slithering free. The force of the current carries me. I've been holding onto something – a shell. I found it in the stomach? Let go.

Throw the shell into the air. Kaleidoscopic air. Moving air. Earth is rotating on its axis. A huge, round ball with me balanced on its top, teetering. Whose idea was it to live on a round ball, one prone to flooding? I think Mum told me once, in one of her stories, of a big ship, some animals. I'm not seaworthy.

And squeeze.

I wake with the feeling something is wrong. With heavy breathing I lie, not yet returned from elsewhere. I'm a hovering subconscious overlooking my body. Inhabiting two places at once.

The bed moves beneath me. Everything dissolves, and I'm in the place where it hurts the most.

My forehead burns. Concentration shifts from the hurt to the point between my eyes: a throb, a pulse, a push – a third eye bursting through?

And again, my whole body burning, every cell fire – pressing against the confines of membrane, my skin.

'Sophia.'

'Pete.' My mouth shapes the word, but there's no sound. I'm in a capsule of concentrated air.

His eyes avoid mine. I want his reassuring face, one of his biology lessons on 'Why this makes sense.'

He says nothing. For too long: eyes half closed, as if he's going back to sleep.

He jumps up. 'Shit, shit, shit. Are you okay? Shit.' His hands shake. 'I'll get a bucket and some towels,' he says.

He still hasn't said everything's going to be alright.

I shuffle my legs over the side of the bed. My pyjama trousers are sodden, red, heavy. I pull them off, knickers

2

too. I fight a dizziness that wants to send me falling backwards, or else pull me upwards into the ether – to the heavens, where the baby must be headed – my baby – leaving me. Everyone's leaving me.

Dad said everything has to end. 'You know that, Sophia.' The baby wants to be there, where Dad is, not here with me.

Pete's at the door, awkward in his boxer shorts. His skinny legs buckle at the knees, like a toddler not strong enough to stand alone. He disappears.

And I'm groaning. A deep animal sound, an echo of a sound I didn't make. My heart races at this predator call; but it comes from within. Pete reappears at the door, holding a ridiculous bright red bucket. He hurries towards me. He pulls my hair back and plaits it like I taught him to when we first met. He loved my hair. He pauses with one warm hand on my back. And then prepares the blankets.

I imagined the birth many times: Pete holding my head, my hand, massaging my back, telling me I can do it. I hadn't imagined this. Pete holds the phone against his ear and speaks to a nurse. I can hear the crackle of her words; she tells him to take me to the hospital, they can make sure everything that must leave has left. She says the worst should be over. She says if the bleeding gets heavier, call again. Pete stares at the ceiling, his expression blank, I can't tell whether he's listening.

My stomach is tender, a kneaded dough that didn't rise. Am I missing a vital ingredient? The covers crinkle as I move; the noise makes me jump. I'd forgotten anything existed outside our shell, as my baby scrabbled to break it. Walking to the bathroom to run a bath involves stepping over the bucket: full of a pool of thick mucus. Can I throw it in the toilet? I'll bury it in the garden, pour it on the trees. I've been feeding it for three months so it must help something grow.

The taps drown out my thoughts. Pete's words muffle on the other side of the wall as he phones the hospital. I turn the taps off and climb into the bath. Images flash behind my closed eyes: white sheets, red buckets. In shallow waters, lingering on the edge of sleep, it's as if I'm beached on shore, waves gently lapping my sides, teasing to take me back.

'Sophia?' Pause. 'Can I come in?'

'Come in.'

'How do you feel?' Pete rests on the edge of the bath, dips his arm into the tepid water and takes my hand. I wait for him to scold me for lying in a cool bath. He doesn't.

'I feel good.' Relieved as normal sensations resume.

Pete looks absent, his skin pale except for dotted blood vessels by his eyes. 'I've phoned the hospital. They're expecting us: we need to leave soon. Are you hungry?'

'Just tired.'

Silence. He bites his lip, trying to find the words he's meant to say. His forehead twitches, like he's bothered by this inability to reason.

'I'd better get ready,' I say, standing up in the bath. The water has a pinking hue: the complexity of pregnancy rejected. It would make a beautiful photograph: swirls of absence.

Pete stands and wraps his arms around my naked body. He rests his head on my stomach. His body judders against mine as he holds back tears. 'It's alright; you're going to be alright,' he says.

2

Field Notes

Cabbage, Brassica oleracea capitata

Of the mustard family. A plant cultivated to
be eaten as a vegetable. Cabbages can be
red or green. They have thick outer leaves
that cover a head of younger ones.

Common Cabbage,

simple supplier of sustenance

I'll sustain you, if you'll sustain me

Easy.

I'll support your head

in my hands

as you rest in sleep.

I don't want for more or less,

only for trusting that your leaves support our

young.

You are sturdy, thick veined

to carry water far.

This is a practical arrangement,

well-practiced.

No want for more or less,

only for this continued bond.

Mum phones. I try to talk of life instead of death, but it's
like talking to a farmer whose sheep have been condemned

to slaughter. In the throes of lambing they'd shrug it off, but this farmer will have no lambs arriving.

Life cycles are cycles. They're meant to go: life, death, life, death. Life.

'How are you?' Mum asks. Hope hangs on the other end of the line, in the silence of her held breath. I manage vague offerings of a hand to hold through space, but I don't really want to hold her hand.

'It's too much,' I say after I hang up.

Pete's been sat on the sofa, half listening while flicking through the weekend newspaper.

'In what way?' His voice is tender: the usual pacifier.

'She can't bear that Dad's gone, and nothing of him will continue.'

'You're still here,' Pete says.

'Yes, her and I, stuck together like cement.' I picture our mixing. We form a single slab, a memorial stone.

Pete closes the paper. 'Come here.'

I collapse on his lap, falling between his open arms like a dead branch.

'Remember what the nurse said?' Pete starts, for the fiftieth time.

I remember they told me it was a miscarriage, like I'd held a rucksack upside down and let its contents fall out.

'Twenty-five percent of pregnancies terminate in a miscarriage. It's natural: a very normal outcome.' He repeats the nurse's clinical words.

Nothing about this feels natural.

He continues, 'It doesn't have to stay like this, love. We can try again.'

My stomach tightens.

'I'm shattered,' I say, and head upstairs.

In bed, I scan the swirls of our Artex ceiling in search of the spot where the brush stroke has gone wrong and the swirl is incomplete. Neil Young's, 'Natural Beauty' hums up from the living room below. The last time we listened to this track we had just moved back to Suffolk, we were pregnant and on our way to Southwold having visited Mum and Dad. Pete had held my hand while we drove, letting go only to change the gears. We were smiling as Neil sung how nature's wonders were to be preserved. I was thinking of our baby – the preservation of Dad. I want to ask Pete what he thinks he's doing, playing the same record from before all this happened as if nothing has changed.

The record's next track begins and the vibrations change. My pillow's wet with drool so I swap position. I am transported back; we are on the beach in Southwold, and Pete is holding his arms around my belly. I am saying how I want to see Dad as much as possible, and Pete is saying, 'That's why we're here.'

In June, Dad's two-year-old prostate cancer had been diagnosed as terminal. The news changed everything. We started to try for a child. Pete applied for a biology teaching post at a sixth-form college in Suffolk and, come September, we said goodbye to Falmouth. I was to bring the bloodline home.

'That's why we're here.' The words repeat in my mind. The reason has fallen to the outskirts of my memory, kicked around like a discarded ball. I want to reclaim it: 'Excuse me, that's mine, that's why I'm here. The baby doesn't matter, I'm here for Dad. Give me that back.'

But Dad's not here either.

Downstairs, the music ceases. Pete's voice calls instead, 'I'm going on a walk, fancy getting some fresh air?'

'It's raining.'

'Come on, Sophia.' His patience isn't insatiable.

He wraps me in warm clothes and bundles me into the car. He drives us out of Suffolk, as if crossing borders of land might cross borders of mind.

We follow the coastal road to Holkham. Pete points out the window to illustrate his endearing commentary, clearly designed to distract. 'Here, see? Pink-footed geese. Did you know, the adults fly over forty-five kilometres per hour. I'll slow down so you can get a good look. Do you see them? They're taking off over that field.'

I rest my hand on his leg.

He turns to me and beams. Encouraged, he keeps going. 'Can you hear that? An *ahng-unk* sound? Can you hear it?'

'Their brown breast feathers look soft,' I try.

Pete doesn't answer, then a moment later: 'Their breast feathers are actually a slight pink in colour.'

Outside the car, my lungs fill with sea air. The first gasp of salted wind takes me by surprise: heavy, as if I could choke on it. I pull my scarf over my nose and breathe in

11

the musty scent of mohair. My lungs protest at the contrast.

We walk the path that leads to the beach, sheltered by a forest of tall pines either side. I'm relieved by the darkness the pines cast, my shadow lost.

I've got Dad's sheepskin coat on. Dad had not only been the ranger for the Huntingdon estate, leaving the house every morning in his sturdy boots and fleece, but was the son of a botanist and a naturalist. He understood each landscape as well as the next, but he hadn't gone out much in his last days, so the coat acted as mediator. I would bring it to him soaked in the scent of the outside world he loved. I have Dad's height and the coat hangs the correct length, though its fit is loose. It is a skin to grow into. When I go, who will wear my skin?

The pine trees are still in growth and their needles shudder, parading the life around me as the wind brushes through them. The world is very much alive – the needles shimmy dark shades of green, not accepting their fate to fall. They taunt me.

I pause at the forest edge. 'You go ahead,' I say to Pete. 'I want to take in the view.' He lingers, apprehensive, then nods, and moves onwards down the sand dune towards the far-off shoreline. His red hat bobs up and down as he goes, his body lost to the wind as a shroud of sand particles circle up around him.

The collar of my coat flaps, snapping as it gets thrown one way and the other. Was that Dad calling from the beach below?

The beach sprawls open below me and fades into the distant horizon. The sea's lost to mist. The vast Norfolk sky stretches its pale pink mouth wide open, breathing steam over the landscape and swallowing up any distinguishing features. Pete's red hat stands out. He beckons for me to descend from the forest edge and join him on the white, empty sand.

I pull up my collar so I can't hear Dad's whisperings anymore and run down the steep incline from woodland to sea: from the edge of one ecosystem into the next. My heart skips a beat, my stomach left at the top as I cross into a new world. In this new world Pete stands waiting for me, and Dad's whispers are muffled by the towering sandbanks above.

Sand spins around my feet, skimming across the surface of the beach from me to Pete. The grains disappear at his feet, sinking into the wet sand.

'Sophia, come, look, there are lugworms.'

Pete holds his bare hand out to me. I take it. He uses the grip to pull me to him.

'See?'

'No.'

'Just there, the spirals of sand, like tubular mountains.'

'Oh yes. God, they're everywhere!'

The beach is covered in them: markings of the journeys of thousands of tiny worms, each burrowing to find their way. Families are under my feet, hiding from the world: some who prefer the dark, living alongside others whose eyes have closed to the light forever.

'I can't see the worms though,' I say.

'I just saw one, but it's gone again.' Pete glances at me, worried. I see it in his face, he's already searching for the next distraction, eyes scouting the sand for another discovery.

'You don't have to feel responsible for me. I don't need tending to.' I look at him until he stops scouring the earth and returns my gaze. His expression is guilty, then hurt, his eyebrows shifting into a frown. He knows it's not true.

The worms remind me of being on Dad's allotment, pulling long bodies from the ground. 'Careful, you'll burn their skin,' Dad would remind me.

When I poured the contents of my womb into a ditch by the tree in the garden, a long worm had wriggled across it, a friend to keep the buried foetus company.

'Sorry, I wasn't trying to,' Pete's voice trails off and he tidies his eyebrows back into their naturally raised position. 'Let's keep walking.' He puts his arm around my shoulder and kisses the top of my head. I remember Dad doing this, tucking my hair behind my ear before he did so.

Pete pulls out my camera and hands it to me, 'I grabbed this on the way out; I thought you might like to take some pictures.'

When we moved Pete encouraged me to set up my darkroom in the shed at the bottom of our new garden, but I knew the real job I was to take on was motherhood. I haven't been in the darkroom since the event. I take it reluctantly, pull off the lens cap and point the camera his way.

'No!' he cowers. I move rapidly up and down, trying to keep up with him as he dodges my line of view. He runs down the beach. He looks over his shoulder and waves, laughing.

I point the camera at the coast and peer through the viewfinder. Desolate: only murky greys, nothing worth photographing. Then a cloud must shift, because out of nowhere one line of sunshine casts itself across the water. It reveals an undulating surface, like a silk sheet being shaken, one person on either side. I face the camera downwards, still in the line of light, and my body rouses in remembrance of the joy in framing manageable pieces of this world. A hand is on my back. I look over my shoulder, still with the camera clasped against my eye. Pete is there, his face blurred through the lens. I find the focus and see his nose, the creases below his eye, the shadow of a strand of hair. He's handsome, slightly roughened from his run.

We walk on, the sky clearing and the blue of the sea showing itself as different to that of the sky above. We keep going until the light gives in and slides beneath the sea. Inside my stomach bubbles a secret excitement: I can go home and climb back into bed.

Pete offers to take us for dinner; he probably wants to go to one of the fancy places in Southwold town that Dad would've taken the piss out of, saying, 'All you need is a fresh fish and a fire.'

'Thanks, Pete, but actually I'm quite tired.' We walk to the car, him staring at his feet in disappointed silence.

On the drive home, I ask to stop by Dad's allotment to pick up a white cabbage for dinner. Technically the patch has been passed on to someone else, but there are still remnants of his last sown crop. We park the car beyond the entrance gates and walk through the patchwork of plots. When surrounded by dirt and earth, dilapidated sheds and the smell of vegetables, the mishmash of old glass windows propped over seedlings to make sun dens, I feel at home.

I lead Pete past the homemade tunnels: the trail of life – but life without people, without houses – a life of do-it-yourself and strong backs. Butterflies flutter about my stomach, fertilising old memories of this place where one bends and moves to a different rhythm: where hands get filthy and are meant to, where knees get stung and faces weather.

On Dad's allotment I had been a child digging, dressed only in my underwear. I peed in the corner by the rhubarb plant. I ate with dirty hands. We made fires, talked of whatever we pleased, encountered new things like grass snakes, aphids and slugs. We would face these new things, introduce ourselves to them, and test our relationship through trial and error.

The cabbage patch is a tidy line of bursting blooms. I squat by the largest cabbage, take my penknife to its throat, and behead it. I carry the white head back to the car, cradling it in my arms as if it's a sacrifice to the Gods. This is a practical arrangement. On the drive home to Cranston, the tight ball of leaves sits on my lap. In our kitchen, I will peel the larger leaves off, and make them responsible for holding steamed rice instead of younger siblings.

My camera sits on the dashboard, its lens staring at me as if to ask permission to photograph this beautiful specimen. I shake my head, not today. An abandoned notebook snags my attention instead. Pete had bought it for me to keep track of mileage for photography trips, fooling himself that these might become an actual career. I take a pen from the drinks holder and open the book, jot down some words, a remembered definition from Dad's gardening book and something else too. A rush runs up my spine as I do so, a familiar thread of creativity. Pete glances my way and I close the book quickly.

3

I settle on the musty armchair in the corner of the darkroom. The table light is on, and in my hand are the negatives from the trip Pete and I made to Holkham. Strings criss-cross and droop above my head, holding photographs I pegged out to dry weeks ago. I clearly didn't rinse the prints properly as they're streaked with chemicals. A white residue colours a pile of leaf skeletons. Fingerprints caress the face of Dad, blotching his deep-lined smile.

Mum believes in creation, ever more since Dad's death. So do I. Don't I? I create black and white images to make sense of the world. I'm haunted by the thought that once I made the world make sense for her. She created me, and for a moment, she felt connected to some creator force – was it God? In the end the pleasure of creation must have been strong enough to keep her and Dad together. And together they stayed.

What if your creation has already come to an end?

At their end, my parents agreed: life goes on through a continuing, adaptive, life force. Dad said his particles would mingle elsewhere. His skin would help a tree grow;

his last breath would be tasted in a stranger's mouth years down the line and offer a fresh flavour to their life.

The day Dad phoned to tell me the latest drugs hadn't worked – that the cancer had spread, that it was terminal – Pete and I were out walking with friends in the woods at Ponsanooth. I stopped short, losing the group ahead, and sat on the ground. A puff of dusted earth rose around me.

Everything became dark. Summer passed in a second and autumn arrived. A leaf fell and rested on me. I did nothing to remove it. There was nothing to be done. I'd be buried beneath the debris of a falling world.

'How long?'

'They say six months, but at this point it's a rough prediction. Some people continue for years.'

'They can't be more precise?'

'We can't know everything in life, Sophia; some surprises have to remain.'

'There's no more drugs?'

Sat in the dirt my mind whirred names of drugs like a spinning display cabinet. Apparently, there were none left to try.

'I didn't like the drugs, Sophia, remember? They've had awful side effects. It might be better this way. I can live out my days as nature intended. God has chosen, and I can't trick God. That's what your mum's saying.' His laugh coughed from the receiver.

And the tears started. My whole body shook. It was impossible to keep the phone to my ear. I threw the phone to the ground, and began to bury it in the loose earth, then realised what I was doing and scrambled for it, clawing the plastic case and clutching it to my ear as close as I could to resurrect his voice.

'Sophia? I'm sorry, I should have asked, where are you?' His concern relieved me.

'In the woods.'

'With Pete?' He didn't wait for an answer. 'Look up at the trees.'

I choked on tears as they gathered in my throat.

Dad went on, describing the role of the tallest trees, to create shelter, heights to climb and heavy branches to make homes in. I sobbed, held my hand over my mouth.

'But look at the ground, do you see the saplings?' he said.

I looked around, reluctant to acknowledge the spindly sticks poking up from the earth. Dad reminded me how they'd grow to be adult trees one day too; how as the next generation they'd have more resistance to disease and adaptability to the current climate. He pointed out that without the bigger trees dying, the saplings would have no light to grow.

'It's the adults' decay that provides the nutrients to thrive,' he said.

Perhaps Mum agreed to appease his last days. She said, 'Yes, life goes on.' But I knew she had other plans for his life – plans of an otherworld. They're not so different, but now I only hear of heaven, as Mum retraces her steps to understand how she got to this point, hoping to find the moral of the story. And I realise she's always talked to me like this. Only I never minded, because earth was being handed to me by Dad, in dirty, rich fistfuls.

I hold one strip of negatives up to the light. I consider printing my accidental shot of Pete's eye – he'd been laughing, having placed the camera in my hands in the effort to re-inspire. The eye peers from the top corner of the frame, and the sky spreads out behind it. I stare into the eye. It seems to look back at me, unblinking – not going anywhere.

Tap tap, knuckles sound on the door.

'Can I come in?' Pete's voice whispers from outside.

'Come in.'

He's wearing the blue jumper I gave him for Christmas two years ago. The one that brings out his eyes, wet and delicious. I almost want to lick them.

He sits on the chair arm and takes the negatives from me.

'Some of these are quite good. Will you use them?'

'I'm not sure. Pete, maybe I should get a job?' I know what his answer will be. We need to talk, but I don't trust my grief as a reliable voice.

'Hey, don't worry about that, just take your time. You could use some of these for prints and cards if you're bored.' He holds another strip of negatives close to his face and squints. His long eyelashes bow over the watery pools; like a marmoset bending to drink, they shade the craved liquids from sight. Pete's attentiveness hasn't faltered. Despite my moodiness. Despite my not producing what he wanted. Perhaps, like a marmoset, Pete smelt his offspring when it slid out and his nose became tuned to me, the mother of his child. Perhaps soon he'll notice there is no child and be off?

'Love, I don't mean to hamper you,' he starts. I imagine myself like a straw hamper packed full of goodies: wrapped ham, grapes, cheeses. What more would he like to pack into me? 'I want you to know there's nothing to worry about. We can manage on my income. I've been talking to Mum and Dad, and they might be able to help with a deposit for a house. And, well, it's probably time we start moving things forward, don't you think, readjust a little?'

His reassurance skims the surface of an ocean of feelings, and dips below, making not even a ripple.

He puts the negatives down on the table beside him and comes in for a kiss. He always puts everything down before he does this. I duck his approaching mouth by nosing my way into the armpit of his jumper, like a dog looking for a smelly crease. I find deodorant. He holds me. Rubs my back. His hand moves up my side under my top; that familiar smooth palm. His fingers delight to find me bra-less. Their tips quiver and draw slow patterns beneath my breast, above my breast, around my breast. Fingers head ever faster to my nipple. Fingers pinch my nipple between thumb and forefinger. I shudder, numb in his hands. My nipple hardens anyway, weary, itself searching for the child's mouth, ready to serve – but finds none.

Babies suckling breasts release oxytocin in mothers, encouraging bonding, I had read it in my *Guide to Postnatal Care*. When Pete and I slept together, he'd tease my nipple and I'd be flushed with devotional pleasure. I never knew it was just nature's game to bond us together.

My nipple awaits, still hard; why doesn't it know the child's not there? My nipple's found Pete's hand, but I feel nothing. Nurse, I'm having trouble bonding.

When I was still pregnant, the tides of my hormones waxed and waned, controlled by my baby's placenta, which instructed my body on what was needed. Or at least that's what Grandma told me happened. Today, nothing's left to instruct me. The placenta is buried in the garden, half-eaten by worms, no use. The hormones that might revive my libido are all damped down, still restoring themselves ready for the baby. They, like Pete, haven't re-adjusted to the baby's absence.

'Pete, should we head in for dinner? I'm starving.'

His mouth's wet around my ear. The sensation of his tongue tickles my ear's edges and makes me nauseous. I feel as if I'm being fed upon, cried upon, hiccupped over.

'We could open a bottle; I'd love a glass of wine.'

My mind's at odds with my body – that responds to Pete's touch, disobeying my thoughts. I'm getting wet, an animal response, ready for the act. Better to be prepared than be injured when pounced upon. I disgust myself.

Thoughts race as I try to regain control: sex releases oxytocin, oxytocin induces labour. I don't want to be in labour. Gentle reminder: I've already been in labour. I can't do this. Arm hair on end, a cat, hissing at this approaching male. Always hissing, until one balmy day, when on heat, I won't hiss. Who can say when that might be?

'Okay.' Pete surfaces from the nest of my hair. A chick coming up for air. He stands and takes the negatives up again, examining them as if nothing had happened. He's grown-up, he doesn't need me. I want him back, my nipples still hard.

'I'm sorry, I just don't feel … I guess I'm still sensitive.'

'It's okay. Let's go open that bottle.' He replaces the negatives and pulls me up from the chair, smooths my hair.

I put on my boots and take my old trench coat from the hook behind the door. The coat matches the age I feel. So, so, old. Never again will our bodies flap desperately against each other, uncaring of consequence, like fish out of water convulsing on the shore in their fight to breathe.

Pete fiddles with the Yale door latch; it sticks. He disappears for a minute and returns with oil. My arm hairs stand on end again. *Hisss*. He doesn't notice.

Pete fixes the latch, turning the Yale knob from side to side to let the oil settle. He runs the hot water at the sink and soaps his hands to clean the grease off. The awkward squelch of soapy palms meeting adds to the tension in the room. We need to talk, but I can't find the words. I can almost hear him thinking, while he washes his hands, 'We can get through this, we can try again, she's feeling sensitive, I'm here for her.' I'm thinking, 'I couldn't do that. I'm broken, we might as well be broken.'

I have a knotty lump in my stomach that I can't untangle. He dries his hands and leads the way out the cabin.

Outside, he pulls the belt of my coat so I move towards him. He gives me another kiss. His warm lips tremble, a little wren putting all he has into his mating call. His nest was attractive, is attractive: cosy, dependable.

4

I spend the morning in the darkroom, printing photos. I've planned to meet Pete for his lunch break. It's his ploy to get me out: he made the sandwiches with the last of our bread and took them with him.

The wooden slatted walls of the darkroom are insulated to block off the outside world. It had been a challenge to fill the gaps between the slats so no sunlight came through. It was like sitting inside a night's sky: black except for tiny dots of shuddering white speckling the walls. One by one I extinguished each of the stars. With the red safety light on, the warm glow illuminates the skeleton of things more than the thing itself. The negatives reveal themselves when held up, but I remain hidden.

From the outside, my darkroom looks like a gardener's shed: black plastic sheets for raised veg boxes press against the windows, crinkling shiny noses at the outside world. Honeysuckle is planted at its edges. Inside is different: the smell of chemicals, a laboratory of art and science. It's like the inside of a person – chemicals and creation – not the pristine exterior.

I pack my camera and notebook into a bag to take with me to Pete's school. Dad is at the door, a proud smile on his tanned face. His thick skin stretches into lines running from his nose, past the corner of his mouth, down to his chin. But that was my first day at school, not today.

I leave the darkroom and walk down the garden path to the lane. To my dismay the world doesn't reintroduce itself with fresh beauty like it used to. I used to see land through the lenses of my photography books. The images warped the lens of my own vision: flowers stood out larger than life, colours distracted me as I talked to Mum, sat in our garden. Today I can't distinguish my legs from the ground they walk on.

I need something to invigorate me: wind on cheeks, movement in legs. A cycle ride – but I'm yet to collect my bicycle from the bike shop. I'd rescued the bike last week, engulfed by a waxy canopy of leaves and looking sorry for itself; maybe it's better now.

I arrive at the shop windswept, hair loose from its ponytail. My reflection in the glass door reveals blotched cheeks – blood rising to their surfaces like a pile of late autumn leaves, all veins.

The air of the bike shop is different to the outside cold; warm and soft, light as if full of fun and games. I have the impression, as I always do when I enter the shop, that the three men working have been whiling the day away with lewd jokes about 'checking her organs' and 'screwing her tightly.' The men whistle while casually dissecting bicycles. Each man's eyes turned down; gentle eyes that give the sneaky sense that between jokes rest wise words of counsel.

One of the men goes to write a receipt. He places small, round spectacles on the end of his nose, and writes in careful concentration, his pen held tight and upright. When he's finished writing, he holds the paper at arm's length in front of him as though he were about to read a speech. I browse boxes of inner tubes and pretend not to watch.

The youngest man, Joe, looks up from the bike he's working on and sees me. His blue eyes light up like a dog wagging his tail.

'Sophia,' He lifts himself off the floor where he'd been kneeling and rubs his hands on his corduroy trousers. I startle at my name, Dad's choice of name, from a story about the moon. Dad explained to me the importance of the moon, why each day passed the way it did and why the tide at the beach went in and out.

'Your bike's just over here, I'll fetch her for you,' Joe says. His long limbs take long strides, agile and eager to perform. 'I checked her over and she's fine. I just oiled her up, tightened her bits and gave her some general TLC.'

I smile at his fond reference to my bike, imagining he feels a friendship with all the bicycles he works on.

Along the wall behind him rests a double-stacked row of racing bikes, weary handlebars all curving downwards. Their pedals are meshed together. Some of the back pedals have slipped in between the spokes of other bicycles' wheels, like hands reaching out between bars.

'Thanks Joe. How much do I owe you?'

'You owe nothing; it took ten minutes. I'm happy to see it ready to go again.' His relaxed smile tells me he means it.

'If you're sure? Thanks, really.' I offer a smile back and push my bike in a wide circle to leave.

The shop door opens and a girl who looks to be in her twenties steps through the frame. She holds the door for me as I weave my way through the assault course of bike parts. The skin on my neck flushes as I sense the men's eyes lift to my back, and their warm smiles as I manoeuvre around their tailor-made toy shop. I pass the girl and lift my chin in thanks. Her blonde curls roll around her shoulders framing her round, freckled face. She's like one of the wildflowers from Dad's allotment: freckles the specks of pollen in her centre; hair the furling, yellow petals.

From the pavement outside, I look back through the glass door and see the girl talking to Joe. She goes onto tiptoes and kisses him with aggressive speed on the nose as he bends his head down. She loses balance and falls laughing into him, stepping on his feet. They start talking to the other men. The girl occasionally pokes Joe in the ribs – perhaps when she says something with significant force. Her body lifts and shifts as she pronounces her thoughts. The conversation looks like a meeting for a revolution; laughs erupt and their volume rises, creeping through the cracks around the door. Their words are sliding perfectly alongside one another, like puzzle pieces forming a clearer and more intricate image as they join.

Pete's school is only down the road, but I fancy a ride out of town. I tug my ponytail free and shake out my hair. Swinging my leg over the frame of my bike – lifting my skirt so it won't catch – I cycle away.

Flash of red. The colour of a warning signal appears as a brightening spark to the grey day. A fox emerges from the hedgerow and I stop to watch it.

This fox is large, head broad with a slight dome – probably a male, smitten and proud, prowling for his mate's meal, his chance to provide and prove that he alone can be all the vixen wants him to be. I remember the tales Mum told, where the fox was a stealthy, sly creature, a trickster of the night, a purposeful player of life. It wasn't this elegant creature I see here.

The fox is beautiful. Lean limbs lead to a curved hipbone. His quivering paw is outstretched. Flamed amber eyes set un-shy on mine – he's in his own world of watching, while I watch him. He pulls his leg back, wary, unsure as to whether to take the next step. 'Nature doesn't only use eyes,' Dad had told me. The moth smells its mate from miles away, the bird awaits its song, and the mole, dim-eyed, places its whiskers to the earth and feels its way towards life. This fox sees me through the sound of my breathing and the smell of my skin and clothes.

Paw forwards. Red ripples up delicate calf. Thick coat slides over rib bones and shakes at the contemplation of a step forwards. His mood is reflected in the markings on his back as they move over his body while he changes

31

posture. His ears rotate in a flicking motion as he assesses me.

It is his vixens' time of year, the time when their intimate parts swell up eager and inviting, their scent lingering around corners leaving a trail of something like violet; the time when they call into the air, night and day, excited, tipping their heads backwards and parting their white upper lips from their lower brown ones. They call for the male they will settle and start a family with.

Within my own body I'm aware of a vague movement: the slight twist and heat as egg breaks and makes its way out with the cycle of the moon. The sensation is uncanny, saying hello like an old friend at the doorstep, returned after a long time abroad.

Pete told me that, once upon a time, human females had been the same as these vixens: putting self on show in one ecstatic season of every year. 'Now you must find other ways to intrigue and infatuate,' he'd joked, shaking a lacy black dress in my direction. 'Go on, wear it out tonight; you look great when you dress up.'

The fox might have reached the first winter of his and the vixen's four-year stint: the perfect time to pair, copulate, bear a kit, nurture it, and regain strength. Pete told me that foxes re-couple after four years, he described this as a genetic arrangement, 'to reach an outcome.'

Grandpa had recalled arranged marriages from his childhood in India. He described how a girl would be partnered with someone of a suitable ability to provide, that they would make a home together, stand by one another out of responsibility to family and tradition.

It's the fox's desire to stay: a lingering knowing in his long body.

I hear Dad's voice somewhere indistinguishable between heart and ear. 'It's in the fox's interest to stay and nurture his child.' Through sharing the same dedicated interest as the vixen, love grows.

The fox steps out onto the gravelled path and takes a moment to breathe fresh air through flared, dark nostrils and a sharp-pointed muzzle.

What if the fox were to die? A sharp pain stabs at my chest. The vixen would find another; they know when not to mess around, make no more mess of love. Don't cry over spilt milk. Instead, lick it up from the ground with the fast, strong, lapping movements of a thick, pink tongue, and pass it from mouth to womb. If the vixen's womb fails, like mine – waters breaking to leave a puddle of broken membranes and a spirit not yet made earthly – the fox would search for another.

The fox pricks his ears and lifts the great bush of his tail. He turns and retreats into the hedge, leaving with a flash of a white tip of fur.

The reality's more brutal. I know it. That fox, a couple of weeks ago, would have clenched his vixen so tight she would have yelped and howled, stuck in his fierce grip, his back leg bent around her so she couldn't escape. For the survival of her kits, she has no choice but to wait in her den for him to attend.

I've been propped on the side of the pavement, captivated by him. Pete's lunch break will be well over. I resume my cycling, hungry and tired again. The winter's sunlight slips back into the land. The hue of dusk starts its slow journey outwards, grasps its way around the town, and dulls my shadow on the pavement.

I can see by the big, round clock on the school building that I've missed Pete by miles. Irene, the sixth-form receptionist, welcomes me with an unexpected hug. Her heavily creased forehead offers as much sympathy as a human can muster.

'It's so good to see you, Sophia. You're looking so well.' The statement can't be fact – her eyes are too lost beneath her frown to have seen me. 'Pete left these for me to give to you.' She presses some sandwiches wrapped in cellophane into my hands, flattening them in her urge to maintain contact. I take them from her. She goes on, 'Pete says not to worry; he suggested you meet at the pub later instead.' And then she gushes, 'Oh do stay well,' before bustling back behind her desk. Within a blink she is typing away on her keyboard, humming what I think is Britney Spears.

5

The pub is busy: locals already drunk and joking with the woman behind the bar. Her breasts bulge over a strapless top and when she lifts her arms to pull a pint, her chicken wings flap. She laughs, a loud hoot at the clucking locals, and says, 'Oh you boys couldn't manage a real woman if you tried.'

Pete eyes up the scene and says, 'Why don't you go to the garden and find us a bench; I'll get the beers.'

I shuffle my way to the back door, past crowded knees that jut off bar stools.

The pub garden's quiet. One bench is taken by smokers. I head to another in the far corner.

'Sophia.' One of the smokers waves. A tall figure is masked by the smoke from his roll-up. It's Joe from the bike shop, with the blonde, curly-haired girl. She grins and gestures for me to come over.

I join them. 'Hey, how's it going?'

The girl shifts along the bench and pats the spot beside her. I sit down. Her eyes are enormous. Like a fox, they watch me in startling amber.

'Good. How about you?' says Joe. 'This is Isabelle by the way. Isabelle, Sophia.'

'Nice to meet you,' we say, turning to one another.

Joe's smile lifts his beard higher up his face. He looks like a bear stood on his back legs, arms pawing the air to clear the smoke away. He puts his cigarette out on the bench top.

'I'm doing alright. I was trying to get some photography done but felt like an ale might be in order.' My eyes avoid his gaze and dart to a spider's web on the wall.

'I forget you're a photographer. I think Pete said. Pete's your partner, right?'

'Right.'

Joe's shoulders hunch, making him look sheepish. He would stand taller than me if he straightened his back.

'I think Joe fancies himself a photographer,' Isabelle laughs, and rests her hand on his leg.

'Hello,' Pete places a pint of Wherry in front of me. He sits down opposite Isabelle and puts his hand out to shake. 'I'm Pete.'

'Isabelle.' She flicks her hair over her shoulder and takes her hand back from Joe's leg to shake Pete's.

'Pete teaches at the school down the road from the bike shop,' Joe says.

Pete nods. 'What you guys been up to today?'

'We went for a long walk.' Isabelle closes her eyes, smutting amber light. Open, a fixating flame. She holds the bench top with her fingertips and leans back, 'Joe persuaded me we could reach the trees on the hilltop behind the church.'

'And you didn't?' Pete's smiling.

'Oh, we sure did.' Isabelle's laugh is soft and husky.

'It was a great walk,' Joe says, sitting down opposite me. 'It just may have involved jumping several hedges and getting stuck in a bog.'

'But you reached the trees?' All three look at me as I speak. My pulse beats in my ear.

'We did,' says Isabelle, 'and they were great. We had to share the view with the sheep though.'

'That's not so bad; sheep are friendly companions,' says Pete.

Joe shifts position, his long legs cramped under the bench. 'I used to think that too.'

'Now, he hates them,' says Isabelle.

They're working together, words starting in one mouth and ending in the other's.

'I like the look of a field of sheep. I mean, it's nice to feel close to animals –' starts Joe.

'– but reality is we'll never reach ecological stability when our fields are full of grazing sheep,' finishes Isabelle.

Pete groans. I want to place my hands over his mouth, and obstruct this moist den where opinions cultivate.

'There used to be trees all over this island,' begins Joe, as if taking us on a tour. 'Fair enough we needed to build some homes, get some firewood, but now the habitat's fucked. Nothing can grow anymore. And if nothing grows, well, then we're fucked.' His eyes wince, like a wounded animal, while his smile subsides and gaze drops.

'What've the sheep got to do with it? Leave the cute, fluffy ones out of it.' Pete smirks.

'The cute fluffy ones eat the shoots of new plants and trees. They trample the land, compact the soil so it's depleted and—' Joe stops himself, folds his hands and looks at them as if in embarrassment. His hands have dark bike grease burrowed in each line, the nails are bitten and the skin beneath them is nicked down to his top knuckles.

Isabelle's hand finds Joe's knee under the table and gives it a squeeze.

'I was told that because there's no wind cover from trees, any new saplings planted get blown down,' I say, to fill the silence.

'That's right, it means even our 'wild' moorlands are taken over by bracken instead of trees,' Joe's hands raise in the air and stay there, fingers stuck in inverted commas as Isabelle takes over.

'The bracken makes the land stale, like a workaholic human, producing only for its own needs and not thinking of the bigger effect.' They speak like a rainstorm, thunder then lightning. I can tell Pete finds their act tiresome. He can't stand people parading politics.

The pub garden's filling up. A group of young people sit on the bench behind us. Pete passes a glance over his shoulder, uncomfortable. They're probably his students.

Isabelle winks to show she understands, and Pete relaxes. She keeps talking, telling us how sheep mean grazing fields. Grazing fields means less pollen. Less pollen means less birds and less insects.

Pete yawns, probably wondering how a visit to the pub has turned into an ecology lesson – save those for school.

But my ears prick up as Isabelle transforms herself into a storyteller, palms open to read the book at hand.

'Once upon a time the land was full of thousands of bright flowers, plants, and beautiful insects. All these plants and animals helped one another, each different animal serving a purpose for a different plant and vice versa. Then one day some people came along and cut most of the plants down. The animals were sad, and in the plants' absence they withered one by one, until only a few plants were left, and a few surviving animals. Just a few lucky couples,' Isabelle says.

'Just a few plain Janes and average Joes, eh?' Pete jokes, coming back to life. 'But seriously, we've got to work with what we've got. No point complaining.' He hates conflict. He throws me an apologetic look, his eyes saying, 'Sorry, I didn't realise they were full of so much crap.'

'Yeah, we've got to work with what we've got. And that's my point about the sheep – they're working against us,' says Joe, eyes turned upwards again and meeting mine. He takes the last swig from his pint. Isabelle points at the glass and he nods.

She gets up to go to the bar. 'Anyone else?'

Pete passes her a tenner and says to get us both another pint.

Joe picks the debate up. He introduces wolves into the conversation. Pete says, 'You must be joking.' Joe says, 'Definitely not.' Joe says how rabbits and deer are the other culprits. He says how wolves would keep their population down, so we wouldn't need to play hunter and fool ourselves into a sense of predatory control. 'It might seem scary to introduce a species you're not familiar with, but it might be the answer.' He says wild nature can remedy many problems. Pete's getting into the argument now, he says the wolves would kill all the farmers' sheep and destroy agriculture – our biggest industry. Joe doesn't back down. 'Complete opposite,' Joe says. He says that farming is suffering, that supermarkets' competition for lower prices pressurises farmers to take less than they can afford. He says there are higher costs for deer crop destruction than there would be livestock destruction by wolves. 'Anyhow,' he says, 'the soil is so depleted that if we don't change the way we care for it, we won't be able to grow anything.' Pete has a sneer on his face. In my mind the wolves are chasing the deer, who are eating the crops. One pauses to eat a fox, who is lingering at the edge of my imagination with a taste for mutton.

Isabelle returns and I'm relieved.

Pete swigs from his new beer. He looks back at the group of students, and cringes: they're listening.

Joe pushes his chair back, causing Isabelle to move her head. He pulls her to him by one blonde ringlet. 'I'm going to head onto the next bench for a smoke,' he says while placing the ringlet absentmindedly into his mouth and having a brief chew.

'Nice,' she says, her voice deep. 'I'll stay here.'

Joe opens his mouth and lets the curl drop. He moves to the next bench.

'Alright, tell us about your students – any of these the really naughty ones?' Isabelle indicates to the group of students behind us. The group cracks up. We do too.

And the conversation moves on into the breeze of booze.

I'm drunk when we leave and smiling. It feels bittersweet, more bitter, after months of avoiding alcohol. Pete's arm is slung over my shoulder. He steers me down the lane back to our house, occasionally steering us into the hedge. I search out Orion's belt, a comforting base in an endless night's sky. The stars spin.

Pete unlocks the front door and goes to the kitchen. The fridge door squeaks as it opens. Packets rustle as he rummages for a snack. He returns around the corner. 'Those two are deluded,' he says, one hand holding a jar of mayonnaise, the other a slice of bread.

'You've got to admit there's no point ending up starving because there's too many of our species and not enough food.' I nod at his hands. 'You're going to struggle to feed your chickens and grow your wheat if the sheep take away all the pollinators.'

'Whatever,' Pete tries to dunk the bread into the jar and ends up losing most of it to the floor. 'I just want our kid to have a stable life and a solid future, not be eaten by a wolf.' He bends down and picks up the pieces, looking at them puzzled, as if considering whether his starvation deserves him a dirty meal.

⁂

I dream I am inside a lookout hide at Minsmere nature reserve, huddled between wood-panelled walls, raised upon long wooden legs. The open windows are in front of me, slits revealing the lake on the other side. I am peering out, a voyeur of other animal lives. Names spin in my mind: bird species, plant species, insect species. I chant these names into such an intricate web I can no longer tell one from the other.

A man sits beside me. A pair of binoculars hang casually around his neck. He is dressed in practical clothing: khaki shorts and a polo shirt. Noise. There's constant noise. A song that lulls my mind to rest. The sound squawks all thoughts to sleep, but changes pitch in time to stop me becoming accustomed. Instead, my voice too becomes a squawk. The birds are all gathered in this place, safer together. Terns, gulls, geese, oystercatchers. Geese. The geese have babies, fluffy ones, that waddle between their mums and dads from the safety of land to water. A parent goose each side for the rite of passage to learn to swim. They look chirpy. Happy families. I want to ask the man beside me what type of goose they are. But before I can ask, the geese have disappeared behind a bunch of red campion and a mirage of long reeds. They are gone.

6

Field Notes

Honeysuckle, Lonicera

Part of the Caprifoliaceae family.
Honeysuckles are native to the northern
hemisphere They grow as twining vines or
arching shrubs and are recognised by their
bright trumpet-shaped flowers with a sweet

scent. The flowers attract butterflies and hummingbirds. More than one hundred and eighty species of honeysuckle have been identified.

You, my pollinator,

make me blush bright colours.

Touch my petals

and inhale the perfume of the delicate

tissue

between your fingers.

I'm the key,

unlocking the chemicals in your brain.

Twist me in your keyhole,

and never be so bold as to invite someone

else over.

A ray of light casts itself through the window and across the kitchen surface, inviting me to go outside and take some photographs.

A light frost has settled. It strings itself along the cobwebs between the gaps in the garden gate, making little beaded threads with flakes of frosting adorning them. I peer closer – each one is different, just as Dad told me they were. I check the letterbox as I leave; built into the front wall of the house, it was once a sign that not even the postman could disturb our nest. I press sodden lichen aside to pull open its flap. Nothing but bills and bank statements. The toes of my suede boots scuff on the surface of the road, as I don't look where I'm going. My phone rings: a foreign din amidst the cool silence of my surroundings.

'Mum?'

'Sophia, have you talked with your grandma?'

'No.'

'Don't you think you should?'

I stay quiet.

'Sophia, she's asking me how your pregnancy's going. You haven't told her?'

'No.' My tummy twists. 'I will.'

'She also says she hopes your honeysuckle doesn't get killed in the late frost.'

Pause. 'Okay Mum, I'm going to take some photos now.'

'Okay, but do call her.' She clears her throat. 'Bye.'

'Bye.'

What was Grandma doing phoning Mum? Dad's parents never seemed keen on Mum. When they moved to Devon, Grandpa said Dad was welcome to come help plant the new garden and leave Mum to read her psalms. Perhaps death pulls people together – replacing the lost with someone who can talk about them. I look up to find my boots have changed direction and are returning to the house. A wave of fatigue crashes over me, clasps upon my head and pushes down.

I let myself in through the back door and fall onto the hall sofa. My head aches. The wall in front moves in and out of focus. Floral wallpaper ripples and re-forms as new leaves and buds. The illustrations are outlined in a sharp black ink. When in focus this creates an unrealistic separation between each flower and the next. I wait for my vision to settle before deciding which flower buds are blooming. I settle on irises, with the realisation that I hate the wallpaper.

Reaching up to the shelf above my head, I slide the letters into the pile of other unopened ones I keep placing there, forgetting to tell Pete. The pile shifts, and letters tumble down around me. Slumped and bedded in envelopes, I wish I could climb into one and post myself elsewhere. Recognising this is not a possibility, I stand. The letters shed from me onto the floor, a white skin falling.

My hands fumble to place the envelopes back on the shelf and find a book sat dusty where the pile had been mounted: *An Encyclopaedia of Flowers and Fauna.* Taking the book in my hands, fingers sticky from its coat of damp and dust, I close my eyes and feel the weight of it. In my mind's eye stands Mum, holding her Bible and doing the same.

I open the encyclopaedia and flick through the pages. Colours shout at me: disordered, chaotic, mismatched. It's Dad's world – where even the dispossessed are appreciated for the part they play. I search the pages, scouting out wild.

46

Poppies, bloody and beautiful. But I find myself resting on the civilised. Daffodils, reliably cheerful. In between the covers are dying species along with the flourishing, poisonous along with the edible.

One time when Mum was holding the Bible, she broke the silence with, 'Once was an age of peace on Earth, where animals and humans lived together joyously.' Then she returned to her reading, leaving the white noise of a rainy Sunday to take precedence again.

I release a scream. Legs kick out and hit the wall. Face pinches. Something violent within searches to get out. Calm swoops by, on automatic; go kick a ball, release the anger elsewhere. Muddy footprints walk the wallpaper.

Turning to the index, I look up 'Honeysuckle,' and find the page.

I absentmindedly trace the outline of my lips with my finger. When we were on holiday in Florida, Dad had placed me by some magenta flowers, painted my lips with Mum's red lipstick and given me a mouthful of red wine. 'Stand here and purse your lips. Tip your head backwards, but do not swallow the wine,' he instructed. So I did, and a minute later a hummingbird dipped its beak into the warmth of my mouth and drank from me.

I could've sworn it had looked me in the eyes while sipping from the bouquet of fermented grapes.

When I re-emerged from the flurry of flowers, wide eyed, Dad was performing emphatic bows in all directions for an imaginary audience. 'Thank you, thank you – and applause for the humble assistant,' he said as he turned to present me.

Dad explained 'pollinator syndrome': the interaction of my plant-like attributes with that of the hummingbird. 'The colour and smell of the flowers attracts the hummingbird,' Dad said. 'The hummingbird drinks from the flowers, just as it drank from you. It goes from one flower to another, only it gets drunk on nectar, not wine, and it fertilises the flowers as it goes, bringing pollen from the stamen of one to the pistil of the other.'

It is through this successful relationship with their pollinator that flowers can be produced.

I remember the look I shared with the hummingbird: the same look as when Pete and I used to simultaneously open eyes and gasp in the smell of sweat as our bodies locked together. I was wanted. I was beautiful. It was meant to be.

Grandpa told me some men in the Balkans tuck handkerchiefs under their armpits and later offer them to their dance partners as a leaving gift – a desire-soaked remnant of the night.

Grandma said when she met Grandpa it was love at first sight. She never looked back. 'He brought me all I'd ever wanted, and I for him too.'

I reach down and pick up one of the envelopes from the floor, rest this against the one side of the open encyclopaedia. A pencil rests on the cupboard-top beside me; I take it between my fingers and roll it back and forth, mind wandering between people, plants and places. Touching nib to paper, I copy lines from the book's page, then scribble some more, calling from someplace else. An

ode to a flower, an ode to knowledge not yet lost, an ode
to relationships.

7

What comes next depends on what came before. My life combines many stories: ones that Dad isn't present to tell, and that if once told, Mum never listened to.

Mum has her own stories, from the Bible, though the occasional fable creeps in. She phones again. She says, 'How are you?'

A pressing pause awaits me to return the question. 'Yes, I'm okay.' Sigh. 'How're you doing?'

And off she goes, telling me this week's heavenly dream of Dad rising in the clouds, and which passage from the Good Book her neighbour photocopied and slipped into the letterbox, as an act of kindness.

I ask Mum whether she remembers the allotment days. She says she remembers me crying, how I kicked Dad as he piggybacked me there. I say I don't remember that. She says, 'Oh well, then why dwell on it?'

Because in our allotment conversations Dad always said, 'Nature knows how to deal life's cards.' That's why.

She finishes her monologue. I hang up.

Pete and I eat breakfast together. He pours the coffee from the large cafetière. The filter tips at an angle and I watch coffee grains escape. The grains swirl free into my mug.

'I'm going to visit Mum today,' I say.

The visit plays out in my mind. Mum will do the same as she does on the phone. She'll open the door, ask how I am, then she'll begin – to talk of things I can't understand, create a realm I have no place in. As she talks, she'll steer me towards the living room, away from Dad's bedroom. She used to tell me Dad was tired, that I'd better not disturb him. In the living room we will sit, surrounded by family photos: Dad on a windy hilltop, his curly hair blown before his eyes; Grandpa in India, a frowning boy; Grandma, the farm girl in dungarees; me, waving from a treetop with Dad below, his hands on his hips and a smile on his face; and Mum, on our living room sofa, the same sofa as always, with baby me on her lap. Mum looks sad in the photo, like her mind's elsewhere, but she always looked that way.

'How're you going to get there?' Pete frowns, sceptical of this unplanned excursion.

'I'll cycle.'

'It's eighteen miles; you can't do that.'

'It's a beautiful March day,' I say. 'And besides, it'll be good for me.'

Pete crosses his arms, cornered. He looks at me, hesitant. 'I could come with you?'

'No. It's your weekend; time to read the paper and relax.'

'That can change.'

'It's okay, Pete, I'll be fine.' I lean over the table and kiss his cheek to reassure.

'Well, you'd better leave now or you won't make it back by dark. Give me a call if you want collecting – it's really no problem.'

'Thanks, I'll take my lights with me though. I'll be alright.' I get up and begin to clear the breakfast things.

'Leave that. You'd better get going.'

A few miles outside Cranston, the dense woodland on my left reveals gaps between trees. The darkness of the exposed forest floor tempts me in. A rustle comes from the treetops. My face turns up, skull lolling backwards. A shiver of branches, no culprit in sight. I keep walking.

In the past, Pete was the one to take me on walks. He'd lead me out like a pet who'd forgotten what it needed. I'd be drooping on the settee, a forlorn face and a packet of biscuits. He'd take me by the hand, drag me up and direct my feet towards my wellies. Today I'm greedy for a new ability to give myself what I need, rather than have Pete bring me into fruition.

I stamp my feet on the icy leaves. They make a satisfying crunch: the breaking up of particles, the separating of the whole into original components.

The rustle returns. My head tilts back again, an automatic reflex to keep lookout. A bushy tail curls around the thinning top of a tree trunk. The silvery grey blends with the peeling bark of the silver birch. Could I have hallucinated mammal life from the lives of unmoving fungus and moss?

The great oak to my right shudders a sprinkle of brown and yellow. The falling colours act as the speech of invisible lives that pass and surround the oak. Is Dad shaking that branch? He did that – when I was little – me sat on the ground, in my white dress, grass stains across my lap. I watched the apples fall. I discovered gravity and my body as the centre to my universe. Everything revolved around me.

Dad once dressed me as a squirrel for a school play. The play was about the seasons and I was Autumn. From what I remember my job was to sit on stage and eat acorns. I insisted on eating nothing but hazelnuts for the whole two days that we performed. Mum was worried, but Dad understood.

'Leave her to get into character. It's good for her empathy skills and it's not as though she'll keep it up forever – she's an intelligent child.' He said this to Mum in the dining room after the first night's show. I'd been eavesdropping from the stairway, crouched in my pyjamas with a handful of the rounded nuts.

Maybe if I hadn't overheard I wouldn't have stopped, but Dad had said I was an 'intelligent child,' and so after the second night's performance I arrived home and asked for celebratory ice cream.

Mum was pleased. Her face flushed red and she bustled into our tiny kitchen. Her smart shoes (black Clark's worn especially for the outing to the theatre), squeaked on the lino as she bent down to open the freezer. Dad winked and pulled out a seat at our dining table. I was too short for our dining room table, always reaching up to grab a forkful, but I tucked my squirrel tail under me and for once I was the perfect height. Mum returned with the ice cream and my parents both stood, their arms around one another, overwhelmed with pride for their little squirrel. At least that's how I remember it.

In the tree above, the squirrel tail returns and bobs gracefully along a branch. The tail waves – a Mexican-wave from base to tip with each bounce. The squirrel pauses in the crook between a branch and the trunk. A cluster of dead leaves and sticks fill the angled space: her drey. She must be preparing for her baby-to-be.

She's a grey squirrel. Dad told me that twice a year, grey squirrels produce a well-matured scent to attract a mate. I had picked a rose that day and rubbed it on my wrist, feeling like a woman. When he said this, I felt icky: the feminine smell riddled me with fear.

For the one day the squirrel releases her scent, the males come running. Sometimes she'll take one, two, three, or more. *I'm open to my options, so long as one brings a kit.*

The squirrel climbs up the trunk. Tiny claws grip the bark as she shimmies horizontal towards the sky. Her mate, when he finds her, won't be sticking around. He'll rush off to get on with life. His desire will be satisfied until next time.

The squirrel hops to the next treetop – another birch with twiggy branches. She pounces to a thicker branch and hangs upside down a moment. The winter sun catches the ginger tips to her tail hairs. She clambers around and pulls the small twigs free so she can carry them with her.

This squirrel will do everything by herself: carry the foetuses, give birth to up to nine, protect each one, provide for each one, teach each one. Say farewell to all.

Dad said squirrels can live to twenty. She'll get used to goodbyes.

I can't see her. She's probably scavenging more twigs: a busy, driven, lady. I haven't felt that way for months. I could buy a scent on the way home. Dior perhaps, or Calvin Klein – something that might send Pete wild.

I pull my scarf over my nose and breathe in my own scent: exhale on wool. I imagine rearing children alone. But all I can picture is Mum and Dad, their arms around one another as they watch me eat ice cream.

By the time I get to my parents' village, Mum's sent a text to say she'll be waiting in the new artisan coffee shop. She writes, 'I've never been to it before and have been meaning to try it out.'

The last time I hung out alone with Mum was when Dad was on his deathbed. It had happened suddenly, a quick decline of energy as winter drew close. I went to see him every day, to hold his hand and touch his face.

Dad's exhales released more than his inhales took, and I seemed to breathe in the life let out. His skin changed shade like the sun fighting on and off to break through a cloudy day. These continuous changes captivated my attention and the more I looked, the more this tiny world of tones of flesh introduced a universe. He became a door opening and closing and our faces kept looking to see who was behind.

In our eagerness to know what was on the other side, we forgot where we were, and who we were with. I think that's why, in his last month, Mum tried to keep me away from Dad, so she couldn't be ignored as I was drawn in by him. I think she worried I might forget, when Dad closed the door, which side I was standing on, and leave her alone. Her efforts only helped materialise her fears. No one was going to keep me away from Dad. Even my baby, in their liminal home, forgot which side they were meant to arrive into.

When I get to the café, Mum's sat in the window. I see the back of her head first, the grey hair tucked into a neat ball of a bun: an unmoving silver moon. She's wearing her pale pink coat, the one with the surface of a horse's back, coarse and smooth at the same time. I'd like to stroke it, but I don't want to stroke Mum.

'Darling, it's so good to see you.' Her face says so. Her eyebrows twitch up and down. Her mouth's drawn tight and tries to smile but makes at best a straight line.

'Hello. Have you ordered yet?'

'Yes, and I've got you a cappuccino.' She gestures at a tepid second mug sat opposite her.

I might have wanted tea.

We sit, facing each other across the square table, like we're two women crossing the town square, not yet certain we've correctly recognised the other. Her hands rest upon the table, where I rest my elbows. Our mugs face one another, their handles at diagonals.

'How was your ride?'

I feel ten again. Mother and daughter. I don't think Mum was ever comfortable with that relationship. She thought that it meant she couldn't provide for me, because she needed Dad to provide for her.

'Yeah, it was nice, I went for a walk too.'

'You're looking well,' she says, eyeing up my waistline. I glance down at hers, a response I hate. Still, my eyes linger longer than they used to. She's an older woman, and behind the clingy fabric of her top I see her waistline has disappeared under a fold of skin.

She's been woman her entire life, to mother me. But what next? I have fled the drey. The father has too – they always do.

The air between us is intolerable, stuffy and thick. I feel claustrophobic, as if I'm back in Mum's body, her pushing hard to get me out. Neither of us can manage to separate. They'll have to intervene.

I squirm, imagining a cord hanging from her and clinging to my belly button. Mum's belly button had suspended from her mother's. I picture us all walking single file, connected by this rope: prisoners marching one after another. But nobody's standing behind me as we march. I keep checking over my shoulder.

'You and Pete should come for dinner some time.'

'Sounds good.'

We look at each other. Everything's changed. Neither of us knows how to move forwards from this. Except some things hold us together: I have her long nose, but hers sags lower. I have Dad's green eyes; she can't stop staring.

After our coffee date, I walk Mum home. I want to see Dad's room. He slept in the spare room for the last month of his life, the gingham curtains drawn and his body weighed down by a thousand throws. Often, when I went around to visit, Mum was right, he was asleep, but I still liked to go and see him. I would kiss him on his forehead like once upon a time he used to kiss me. This time he isn't present to receive a kiss, to inhale the week's gift of moss and rain from my shoulder. I leave his sheepskin coat on the hard, straight-backed chair pulled up by the bed – where Mum must still sit. I won't be needing it in spring. The coat, with Mum, can wait for him to return.

Belly tickled by a feather. In my sleep I roll onto my side and peck dirt from neck. Scrunching up legs I prepare to jump from perch. I kick at tangled sheets, wings stretching outwards. I dream I am learning to fly. I am learning to trust the wind to carry me in the right direction – for there must be a right direction. My beak parts. Vocal chords wide open. 'Caaawww.'

SPRING

8

The equinox is in motion.

Imagine the equator as a CD inserted into the computer drive of the Earth – exactly halfway up and down between the two poles. The CD plays the merengue rhythm of a vallenato song, then a sub-Saharan jazz, followed by a boduberu which casts a frenetic crescendo of percussion to your ears.

As you travel further afield, away from your central disc, the tunes cool down until you're left with the buzzing reverberation of a song; a deep hum and a subtle harmony of two Inuits throat singing face to face, passing the music from the core of one to another. If you can, imagine the great sun hanging opposite this CD, directly opposite it – the centre of the sun's fat eye staring straight on at the slim edge of the disc, watching it, waiting for it to eject.

That is the equinox.

Today, day is of equal length to night. Here, and everywhere. I'm sharing something with the world – regardless of spring being with me while autumn is with the southern side of the disc. I have the urge to count seconds and give thanks in equal measure to day and night. I have the feeling that I'm part of life again.

I'm going to celebrate by taking photographs of light and dark. The camera's taken to being close to hand. Films stack up as I avoid the darkroom. I want to look forward through the lens, not back. A guilt lingers: of days passing and little done with them.

My child would be three months old today – if I'd given birth to a child, not a ghostly sack. Or at least I didn't find the thing. Sometimes I imagine, if I'd dissected the contents one at a time – blood clot, blood clot, blood clot – I would have found the little foetal body, shrivelling inside a luminous skin. I would have found proof that something was living inside the home of my womb, the home that I never got to fully decorate.

My child is not. No one's going to spend my hours but me. And from today, the lighter hours will begin to outdo the long, dark ones.

I've dressed for spring. The season's not evident in temperature but it is in the daisies on my dress, the orange of my tights, the blue I've dusted on my eyelids. Closing the front door, I look down at my outfit; it looks childish, but I've achieved liberation from adulthood.

The common on the outskirts of town is a riot of dark and light. Clouds pass over long grasses and gorse, making shadows lengthen and shorten. My chest flutters as I leave behind civilisation. I feel ruthless, like I might walk for miles and forget which way's home. My dress gets caught on the first stile, tights nipped by the parted lips of barbed wire.

The common opens out ahead, so anything that crosses is exposed to predation. This is unique land – no longer marsh, not yet returned to forest – semi-precious to recent animal and plant species, not wild enough for the elders.

Meadows lie beyond, with shiny-skinned cows flapping ears to cool down and defend against flies. Flap, flap. Flick, flick of tails – a static in the first of spring heat, that shakes eyesight in shimmering mirage.

Trees line the edge of the common. The shade cast on their bark licks with the wet of mist. The ground's muddy from yesterday's rain. I follow the footpath that runs under the trees. Normally, when light pokes through between branches, it draws lines underfoot, and passes domes of flickering white overhead. Today I find only dark crevices of footprints under a dull canopy. Sorry, did I trick you? You were expecting spring. This is it.

Along the footpath there are fallen bodies from the previous weeks' storms – dead branches heaped across their brothers' arms. A flap of wings explodes the silence that held the field before. The sound of birdsong calls in tiny teetering tones from nowhere to be seen. I hum a song along with all these others. The frequencies vibrate the inside of my throat and I feel like a frog, humming my song to unseen but heard and smelt fellow creatures.

As the sun breaks through the clouds, I have the urge to throw myself forwards, part my hands, and pray, because if the sun burnt up its fuel there'd be nothing left. The sun, ultimate mother – feeding and preceding. I remember holding my stomach and imagining I was fully pregnant, the sun between my hands.

The common is barren. Where many animals used to roam, where people foraged, and insects were rife in pollination – voices laugh, and send birds flying from treetops. The voices break the stream of my hum and the hum of my thoughts. The people aren't visible, existing somewhere below the dip in the land. They pause, perhaps to share a sincere gaze. They whisper, hushed syllables that slur as laughs take hold. I follow them. Below the dip, I see the backs of two people sitting side by side on a low rock. A curly-haired girl and a floppy-haired boy: Isabelle and Joe.

I consider creeping back, but reconsider – it's too late, I'd be caught.

'Hey guys.'

'Sophia, good to see you,' says Isabelle.

'You two got a day off work?'

'Yeah, I have, but Isabelle's life is one long holiday,' says Joe.

'Shut it,' Isabelle mocks a punch. 'I'm an anthropological journalist, so my hours are pretty flexible.'

'Flexible? You mean non-existent?' Joe's smile leaves his mouth wide open, showing a spread of teeth. His two canines point high above the others.

Isabelle shrugs, 'Hey, come join us, we're celebrating the equinox,' she says. Beside her are a pile of books. The top book has an illustration of the sun decorated with Celtic patterns. Its title reads *Sun Mythologies*. Isabelle sees me looking. 'Joe's too tired to read them to me.' She has thin lips that smile with the curvature of a runner bean.

I sit down next to her, our knees touching, the rock not wide enough for three. 'I came out to do the same.'

Joe smiles and passes me an apple across Isabelle's lap. When his arm retracts he leaves his hand resting on her knee, and it lies there, un-noticed it seems, fingers curled a little so the ends touch the kneecap below the hem of her skirt.

'Whereabouts do you and Pete live?' he asks.

I take a bite of the apple and begin to munch. The chewed fruit fluffs in my mouth. I'm eating something's baby, already equipped with the seeds to make one of their own. I swallow. 'We're a couple of streets away from the main entrance into here, so pretty close. You guys?'

'I live on a boat near Beccles,' says Joe.

'And I live in a shared flat on the high street.' Isabelle runs her fingers through her curls, teasing apart knots. 'We used to live in a big house-share together but Joe got offered the boat, and I didn't want to leave communal living.'

'Admirable. It's hard to live with others,' I say.

'Sure. Eaglets find it so hard they eat their brothers and sisters in the nest.' She plaits her hair as she talks. Her legs stretch out in front of her. She lets go of the plait. 'But I've decided to live like a pigeon.'

The sun's come out. Copper and gold streak her hair: a perfect photograph.

Joe finds a stick and draws patterns on the rock. 'She's got a point,' he says. 'Living in a group means if a bird of prey comes, just one pigeon needs to get flustered for the whole flock to follow to safety.' The stick draws circles, then figures of eights. Joe drops the stick and wipes his scratched lines away with his hand. 'Still, what she's not admitting is that she can't swim.' He smiles again. 'Otherwise she'd love the boat. Even Miss Sociable likes to hide sometimes.'

Isabelle nudges him with her elbow.

'A hideaway sounds good,' I say. My face turns away, shy at my revelation of darkness to these bright people. There's no eating the words back up. Entropy has its way; the words are undone.

To my surprise neither of them seems concerned. Instead, Joe says that hiding's probably good for me as an artist. He says that making art is reclusive but really it's sociable, because it helps others to recognise themselves. I shrug, awkward.

'And,' says Isabelle, 'if people identify with one another then they can live together more peacefully.' She looks at me. I try to return the gaze. Her irises have shocks of orange, like the sun's rays, spreading out from each pupil.

'That sounds nice, but I don't really share my photos, I just take pictures for myself,' I say.

She breaks the gaze. 'Same thing. When you look through your lens you experience the world; when you experience the world you share with it. You pay attention to its fabric and in that sense, you attend your consciousness to another. If everyone would pay some attention and share with one another, human and non-human, then we might have some connection and harmony to this cosmos.' Isabelle hugs her knees to her chest. 'Sorry, I didn't mean to get that far out.' She laughs.

Joe tugs on her plait and leans behind her to touch my shoulder. 'She does that.' He turns back to Isabelle, 'Hey, Issy, how'd it go with Mr Archaeology?'

'Mr Archaeology?' I'm confused.

'He's teasing. The name's James, and he's looking for cave art in Scotland. I'm running interviews with him for an article I'm writing.' She flicks Joe on the shoulder. 'It went very well, thank you. We'll meet again when he's next down to help out at Rewild Norfolk.'

Joe and Isabelle explain that they both get occasional work for a rewilding organisation in Norfolk, based at the Wash. They say they help protect the habitat there and are making plans to reintroduce lynxes. 'Or we just sit around talking about wolves, as you and Pete know we love to do,' Isabelle says, rolling her eyes.

I'm astounded by their energy; they keep chatting as I sit there turning my eyes from one to the other. Isabelle says James has incredible stories about cave art he's seen all around the world, early civilisations that drew stories in animal shapes to explain their own ways of life. James doesn't see why there wouldn't be the same in Scotland. Joe considers this, then agrees that anywhere humans had lived closer to nature, they'd be using animals to tell stories and make sense of their place in the scheme of things. I picture Mum's fables.

'It's crazy to get caught in our individual worlds. We need to think of ourselves like mushrooms.' Isabelle nods her pointed chin towards a pile of horse dung. 'Mushrooms live in huge networks. No one mushroom survives alone. They all depend on one another to spread the network further. They feed from one another and pass nutrients to growing things around them.'

Joe stands and offers his hand to pull me up. I push myself, standing alone. He walks over to the pile of dung Isabelle had nodded to. He's quiet and calm. His calves are bare and muscular from cycling. I follow.

'Nail mushrooms,' Joe says, looking at the collection of what looks like little rusty nail heads poking out from the pile of dung. 'They're rare in the UK.'

'My dad's shown me them before.' Dad and I, bending low to poke sticks at dung. 'Don't tell Mum,' he'd said. 'We'll wash our hands when we get home.'

'It's cool how mushrooms work together with the other inhabitants in their environment, isn't it?' says Isabelle.

It's cool how Isabelle wants to be like them, while I've been deep, alone, in my warren. I tell them about Dad's theories on evolution. How he says that nature co-evolves within species as well as with other species, working with everything in order to survive.

'That's cool. It's a shame there's a tendency to stake individual territories and to attack any outsider who enters. I don't get why we don't welcome outsiders to co-habit. We'd have another hand to help out, instead of dying in the fight to defend.'

My stomach tenses. Did I defend my territory too much, with the sheer desperation for something of Dad to continue?

I gather my emotions into a tidier package. 'I don't get it either. My dad would say it's not just a risk of personal loss, it can mean the whole pack suffers.'

'Your dad sounds cool,' says Isabelle.

I've been carried away by their passion, but some of Pete's words now come to me. They recall the risks of making yourself open to others. Like the cost of production of nectar, or the risk of disease from cross-contamination. In a way it makes sense to keep each life contained. 'Work with what you've got,' as Pete says.

Joe's bent peering at the nail fungus. He's got the *Pocket Guide to Mushrooms* in his hand. One knee is on the ground, while his long torso curls to look closer. 'What's everyone up to this weekend?' He changes the subject – I sense for my benefit.

'We're driving to my parents' for dinner.'

'Nice,' says Isabelle, squatting beside Joe to read what the guide says. 'That's cool your folks live near.'

I swallow a lump in my throat, and let it dissolve before speaking. 'They always lived here. I moved back recently. My dad had prostate cancer. He died a few months ago.' I haven't wanted to say anything these last months in case I open my mouth and something indigestible falls out. Here it falls.

'Gosh, that's hard.' Isabelle sucks in her bottom lip, looking pained. 'I'm sorry to hear that.' She stands again and touches my arm. She's short, a miniature frame.

Her uncertainty in what to say leads me to reassure her. 'I'm getting used to it, kind of. We were really close.'

'Wow, Sophia, I'm so sorry,' says Joe, his presence as gentle as my shadow beneath me.

'Yeah, thanks. Actually, I'd better go. Pete will be home from work soon.'

'Well, take my number in case you want a cuppa sometime; you're always welcome at the flat,' says Isabelle. Her amber eyes flash a little brighter.

'And you should come visit the boat. You and Isabelle could cycle out together. It's picturesque,' says Joe, nodding at my camera.

I tap Isabelle's number into my phone as she recites it, press call so she has mine. A message from Pete pops up, saying he'll get some wine on his way home.

'Thanks for having me join your equinox,' I say. 'I'd better get going.'

They both smile – runner bean and bear.

Back on the footpath, below the trees, the sun shines through. The ripples of white light dome beneath my feet and above my head, as if I'm walking in a fishbowl.

⁂

I fly. Frantic. Until I stop to rest on a familiar branch. A nest is close by. I hop towards it. From a twig hangs a sign, with 'Malurus cyaneus' scratched across. Comprehension rumbles in my stomach: this is my nest. I am a Fairy Wren. I lift my tail and spread my abdomen across the hard shells of my offspring. All mine. But are they really? Each has a different father. I giggle; it comes out a long squawk.

9

Field Notes

<u>Nail fungus, Poronia punctata</u>

Nail fungus is a species of fungi rare to the UK and mainland Europe. The fungus has a small, dark brown stem and a flat, white cap dotted with black spores. Nail fungus is found on the dung of horses organically grazed on heathland or acidic grassland. The horses swallow spores as they feed and excrete these in their dung, where the spores germinate. The fungus competes with other dung-growing fungi or bacteria and is a sign of a healthy heathland. Nail fungus is found to have antibacterial qualities.

I'll spread myself, where I please, to meet what I need.

Spreading spores, landing on floors, opening doors.

When I grow, it's not just me, but a whole community.

Our genes are the same, we play our parents' game, no need to be ashamed.

Name any fear, but it won't hurt here: where I degrade the waste, antiseptic land-rape, heal heartache

For I'll survive the desert, the arctic, the
rainforest.
But I won't be alone
I'll share what I bring, receiving something.
We don't live as one, we work together soi:
brothers and sisters, underground whispers,
mind warpers, poison givers, sponge soakers,
food gropers...

Mum greets us at the door, wearing a spotless apron. She dithers on the step, then takes our coats before we enter. As Mum bustles us inside, I notice how I tower over her. She must be five inches shorter than me, but in my head she's up with God.

Dad's seat still rests at the dining table as though he were still sat there, wearing three jumpers – the collars of three different shades of blue folding out around his neck. He smiles, stretching those welcoming lines along his face, and opens his arms for a hug.

Mum scurries around the table. She places bowls in a neat row: roasted potatoes, Yorkshire puddings, braised carrots. Finally taking a seat, she closes her eye in prayer, opens them, and asks Pete how school's going.

'Good, thanks. The curriculum can get a bit repetitive, so it's good being at a new school – it really jazzes things up.'

The two of them keep going – school, exams, Pete – the conversation punctuated by Mum's nasal sounds of agreement. I listen, half-hearted, peeling varnish off the underside of the table – a childhood habit – comforted by the nostalgia of dinnertimes, when grown-up conversation sailed by.

The polite conversation continues between mouthfuls of perfectly cooked vegetables. Pete's careful not to let conversation fall too philosophical and it doesn't take long before the table enters a strained silence, all the usual ground covered. I look to Mum for help. She avoids eye contact and rubs at some invisible stain on the tablecloth. I browse the surrounding family photographs in attempt to converse with someone else present. My favourite is the one of Grandpa. He looks pleased with himself, holding out a hand to show some exotic flower. Behind him are vines and other jungle-like foliage. His mother, my great-grandmother, is blurred in the background, though it's possible to make out a glass in one hand. She's wearing a beautifully cut shift dress, all the trend for the twenties. Grandpa is in above-the-knee shorts, his knees painted with splashes of mud. He looks just like Dad.

'How old was Grandpa in that photo?' I break the silence. Pete slouches in his chair, relieved.

'Nine or ten I'd think.' Mum reaches out to touch the photo. It's just out of reach but her fingers rest in the air as if it weren't.

'And he'd lived in India all those years?'

'Yes, he was born in India. Dad told you that, didn't he?' She flutters her eyelashes as if trying to sweep my questioning away.

'He did. I just never thought what it might be like to raise a child away from home.' I imagine the swallows choosing to rest elsewhere than their usual nesting spots. Would their young ever return to the previous location?

Pete stands to look at the photo, probably to avoid his turn in the conversation.

'I think it was difficult,' says Mum. 'I didn't know your great-granny very well, but when your father and I visited I discovered she had one hell of a liking for gin. Your father told me it started in India.'

'I guess Great-Grandpa was busy with diplomatic affairs.'

'That's right, and I suspect she was pretty busy while he was out.' Mum chews her cheek, irritated. She begins to clear the table, clattering knives and forks.

I ask what she means, but Mum just says, 'Your father said Grandpa first learnt about nature in those years – out exploring the jungle around their house.'

Grandpa had always loved nature, as far as I knew; he'd spent his life as a travelling botanist, forever discovering new plants in some new country I'd never heard of before.

'What about your grandma, Sophia? How did a home-grown farm girl end up with an exotic explorer?' Pete moves over to the picture of Grandma. I'm glad he's finally interested in the origin of my species.

'Grandma loved working with nature, too, on the farm,' I say.

'Yeah, but how did they meet?' He's onto something – how did this perfect couple occur?

Mum gives an impatient sigh, as if it takes great effort to dredge this information to mind. 'Your grandma decided, when she was eighteen, to find work and became a farmhand at a large farm next door to where Grandpa happened to be working on some gardens.'

I remember now: Dad had told me before. These two lovers of nature, finding wilderness to nurture in one another. Grandma didn't keep her job after that. She followed Grandpa wherever he worked. They must have been happy, wildly in love, while still able to meet the domestic expectations of their time.

Mum disappears with the last of the dishes, excusing herself to the washing up. Pete leaves the photographs and leads us into the living room. He picks up the newspaper from the sideboard and settles in Dad's armchair. He doesn't notice when I make my escape to the study.

When I was little, I used to sneak into the study after every dinner – when it was Dad who read the paper in his armchair while Mum washed up. In the study live Dad's natural history books, along with books on countryside management, foraging, natural medicine, and Grandpa's travel books. Where do they think I go each night, I used to wonder, absorbed in pages of picture books: *Wildflowers, Insects, Birds, Trees* ...

I run a finger down the spines of Dad's collection, like playing the keys of a piano. The tune is wild and discordant, the books in no particular order. I seek out the word that plays on my mind, and pull the book free: *Britain's Fungi.* The pages are yellowed, and each one hosts multiple diagrams. Brackets, toadstools, puffballs: they're all there, communicating with one another. The child in me holds her breath; is that Dad at the door? Will I be found out? No one knows.

I don't know where to begin, so I begin where I know. I look up the name in the index and find the page, peer around to check no one is watching, though my adult self tells me this is silly.

I take a biro from Dad's desk and a sheet of paper from the printer. A laugh sneaks out, my inner judge nudging me. 'Love, you're writing as a mushroom.' It sounds like Pete. Soon all of me is laughing, muscles in spasm. No need for my parents to catch me: I've caught myself.

10

I meet Pete at the school gates. We head towards the high street to get lunch out. Pete slips his arm around my waist. My pale legs move in and out of sight as I look down at the cobblestones. Pete's shoulder meets mine and our bones jolt together at each step.

In front, heading down the high street towards us, is the tall frame of Joe. His floppy hair flaps with his great strides. I draw my hand around Pete. Joe smiles and lifts his arms in an exalted hello. Pete lets go of my waist and gives Joe a friendly wave.

'How's it going?' Pete says when Joe reaches us.

Joe's legs are brown and have small cuts across their shins. I scout the cuts, looking for the one with the best shape: I find a kidney-shaped one, catch myself and turn my head back to eye level.

'Good thanks. Where are you guys headed?' asks Joe.

'To Sophia's favourite café – you know Alfalfa at the top, off the high street?'

'Of course. They do a wicked brunch.' Joe turns to me and his gaze wanders my face before he switches his attention to Pete. 'Well, have a good one. I'm off to drop Isabelle at the train station; she's heading to the Wash to work.'

'Cool, well say hello from us,' says Pete.

'Bye,' I say.

When Joe's a few metres down the street, Pete whistles. 'Phew, I thought he was going to ask to join us.'

Pete pushes his empty plate into the centre of the oak table. 'Back to class,' he says, standing up.

I follow his cue and push back my chair and stand. 'See you after.'

'A kiss goodbye?' He takes my head between his hands and presses his mouth to mine.

'See you after,' I repeat.

Pete heads out the door, while I stop at the counter to pay. Outside, a college student in torn denim shorts is bent beside her bicycle, with an impressive scowl on her face. She has a puncture. She moans, aggravated, and reluctantly starts rolling the bicycle down the hill towards school.

I leave the money on the counter and run after her. 'Do you want some help fixing that?'

'Nah, I can't remember how it's done anyway,' she says. 'My dad tried to show me, but we got as far as gluing up the hole and re-pumping the thingamajig, then I got bored.' She shrugs. 'Y'know how it is.'

I ache at the familiarity of how it is. Sometimes, when I was younger, I would take a broken object to my room, and in privacy try to tackle the pieces, but, while I found tiny wonders of my own within these damaged things, I never succeeded in putting any of them back together. Then I'd be pissed off, because I didn't feel I could show anyone what I had discovered – the beauty of the colour of rust, or the wonder of a perfect helical structure.

I had learnt to fix a puncture though, so I ask the girl whether she wants me to show her.

'I guess. I mean, I guess I should learn.' She doesn't sound sure. Her mood lifts with a sideways smile as she adds, 'There's the bike shop around the corner; they'll let us use their stuff and you can show me there?'

We turn the corner at the bottom of the hill, me somehow left to push the bike. She skips ahead, arrives first, and opens the door for me. I push the bike through.

Turns out she is a known face to the men. They greet her with pats on the back. She bathes in the attention, stands taller, and her face glows. The girl explains her predicament and one of the men says he'll show her. He promises to explain it in simple terms but make her do all the work. She looks back at me, apologetic, as she follows him to a bike stand. I'm left hovering at the entrance.

Joe comes out from the store cupboard and sees me. He calls, 'Sophia, do you want a cup of tea?'

'Yes please.' I clear a corner on a table covered in nuts and bolts and hoist myself up. My legs still meet the ground.

Joe disappears back into the cupboard, then returns – a cup of tea in either hand, with tea bags still bobbing. 'Fancy sitting out back? There's a nice sunny spot around this time of day.'

Now I'm the teenager, privileged to drink tea with the grown-ups. 'Sure. How was Isabelle?'

'Beaming; she always looks great when she's off to the outdoors. I'd have gone too, but I had to come back to work.'

He lets me pass, then leans one hand with mug against my back, using the pressure to direct me left and out the back door. I follow, as if he were leading me in a tango. Unpractised as I am in responding to human contact, my body jolts ungracefully against his hand as we move. Grandpa recalled a Buddhist monk he met in India. The monk had told him, 'Life is a dance. Sometimes the music changes, but all you have to do is change your dance with it.'

11

'Sophia, you've got post,' Pete shouts from downstairs. My dress is in my hands, not yet on my body. He calls up again. 'I'll leave it on the stairs. See you later.' Clank of front door closing. Creak of gate opening. Creak of gate closing – all muffled behind the fabric of my dress as I pull it over my head.

I look in the mirror, pull the hem to straighten the material. Turn to the left, the right, peer over shoulder. Yes, it looks good. Fuchsia, bright against my dark hair. I put on a cardigan, a pair of tights. Done.

I run down the stairs, tights-clad feet slippy on the carpet. Three letters sit on the bottom step; I take them into the kitchen. The smooth, curly lettering of one spells out my name in Grandma's handwriting.

Kettle boiling and bread toasting, I rip open Grandma's letter first, lean against the counter surface, my leg in tree pose, and read.

Dear Sophia,

It was wonderful to receive your letter. I must apologise, I believe I'm long overdue in writing. It's difficult being so far away. I sometimes wonder why we ever moved to Devon, and now it's just me. Anyway, I'm glad to hear you're well and are taking care of yourself. Do you know if your father dried any leaves from his raspberry bush last year? When I was pregnant with him, your grandfather bought me raspberry leaves that had come all the way from Asia. He said they'd been used for centuries to make a tea for strengthening uterine walls. I supposed he wanted an excuse to reminisce about his time in India.

I have been looking up foetal growth through your pregnancy, and though I was once pregnant, I still can't believe we have the capacity to grow new beings inside ourselves. How do we find the ingredients? I'm glad to be reminded of this feat. I always saw your father as his own creator. It was his unique ways that inhabited the body your grandfather and I watched grow.

Sometimes it's nice to think how everything is creating and re-creating life – not always in the way we expect. I was looking at the stars from the porch last night and felt aware that they'll also be a light taken from us, and we don't know what their passing will create.

Have you ever watched a ball of elastic bands unravel? I found one of your grandfather's golf balls under the sofa last week. I'd heard they were made of elastic, and so I took off the plastic coating to see. Tension makes the band snake around by itself, and the ball spins mysteriously as if pushed by an imaginary finger. I guess we're all in tension with everything and, in this way, we move among one another and expand, shrivel or adapt, through cause and effect.

Which brings me to your mushroom discoveries. Nail fungus: I've never heard of it. In the cottage in Suffolk, we used to forage field mushrooms from the farm across the way, and puffballs from the woods nearby. We didn't spend much time on the common because your grandfather used to get very upset visiting it. 'No trees left,' he'd say. He had a fear of land being taken over by humans ever since he watched the diplomats disrespect the locals' land in India.

Antibacterial you say? Your grandfather said that lots of his travel books mentioned fungi that could treat cancer. You never know, there might have been a cure for Matthew. Do inform me of any other discoveries you make.

With affection,

Grandma

I hear her voice as if she were visiting for breakfast. I pour water over my chai teabag and think of Grandpa sipping chai from a clay cup as a boy. I smile at Grandma's fond references to him; he still lives on – incarnated in her thoughts.

My stomach rumbles for forgotten toast, and I rub my belly. Should I feel disturbed by Grandma's talk of my pregnancy? I don't. Her words are like warm caramel, comfort food; they make a life that once was, still be. My baby communicated little messages, and I can keep these in a common land where those of us underground feed those of us above.

Outside, spring has taken hold. Hope is delivered in every blink of sight. The ferns along the lanes are unfurling: tiny, furry stems stretch out of foetal positions and open yawning arms. The magnolia trees in the neighbour's garden droop their bud-heavy branches over the wall. I cup my hand around a giant magnolia bud, which points up like a pink birthday candle. When I put my eye to the gap in the petal's lips, I catch sight of a deep yellow centre, one of many colours to come as spring progresses.

The sun is bright and the narcissi a crisp yellow. The flowers' sweetness merges with manure, and my nostrils fill with the familiarity of fields returning to life. The crystal light means avoiding shadows through the lens is easier. Being creative with aperture asks for un-fathomably fast shutter speeds. Images expose themselves for me in the open light. Fantasies linger, of projects that might take off: a book of macro flower photographs, or photo-inkblots from patterns of bark.

Town is quiet. Everyone's at work, creating spreadsheets, or lattes, or – in Pete's case – expanding minds. I worry townsfolk will whisper, if they aren't already, Who is that willowy woman who sniffs flowers and walks an imaginary dog all day, taking photos like a permanent tourist?

I roam the streets. My eyes strain to meet all the light that's been held back for what feels like forever. The bike shop's ahead on my left. The sunlight glints off the glass door and hides the scene inside. I imagine the men working, whistling in the warmth. The radio's probably playing in the background. The glass door swings open and I jump out of my skin and back in again. Joe closes the door behind him and waves, spotting me across the street. He takes something from his jean pocket, a lighter, and places a cigarette to his lips. Smoke rises around his head as he hops off the curb and crosses the road to meet me.

His smile walks the road, eyes set on mine rather than waiting for the appropriate moment to meet.

'Hey.'

'Hey,' I say.

'Nice to see you make time for your art.' Joe nods at my camera.

'Yeah, it's a good day for it. Cigarette break?'

'Lunch break. The shop's super quiet, everyone must be out on their bikes enjoying the nice weather.' He moves his hair from his eyes; the blonde flop falls right back over them. 'Fancy going for a wander?'

'Sure.'

We walk past Pete's school and up the lane out of town. Bunnies jump out of the way, flashing the white underside of their tails like a teasing flash of knickers. Come and get me. They jump into the hedge and leave round portholes into an unseen world. The hedges are flourishing in fresh sprouts that, until now, I'd neglected to notice.

'I swear the hedge grew an inch overnight.'

'For sure.' Joe picks a hawthorn flower and crumbles it between his palms. He lifts his calloused fingers and sniffs the green stains. He asks me about photography. Which is my favourite part: taking photos or printing? I say it depends on my mood. Sometimes I like how looking through the lens makes me see things differently, and other times I like how the darkroom can re-create things to look different once more.

'I forget what things really look like,' I say.

I ask him what he likes about bicycles. He says, 'Focusing on little details until they come to life, and seeing how different things fit together.' We laugh and agree they sound similar.

Birch blossom blows across the lane – the leaves must be ready to uncurl. Joe asks me whether I see myself in my photographs. 'Is something about your personality revealed?'

I think hard before I answer. I ask, 'What's my personality? How can I distinguish between what's me and what's an instinctive response to the environment?' Then I apologise, feeling like an idiot for taking the conversation too far.

But Joe gives a coy smile. 'Fair enough. I was listening to a podcast about gut bacteria the other day, and I guess you could say what's you, or what's the bacteria inside you?'

I picture bacteria sat around my stomach, wagging fingers at one another: a House of Parliament governing my working organs. 'Interesting thought.' My arms are swinging by my sides, relaxed. 'My mum believes everything is created by the same creator, so it wouldn't make a difference in the end.' Another cat out of the bag.

Joe adopts the cat, unfazed. He says, 'I believe everything originates from the same matter, reckon that could be the same thing?'

'I always wondered that.'

His company is comfortable. His thoughts offer gaps to climb in.

Several nests have been built in the trees ahead. 'Have you noticed the rooks are nesting?' I point. Joe's hands rest on his hips as he looks up. His arms are tanned and freckled, his veins draw forked pathways like tree roots. On the edge of each nest perch two or three adult rooks. An incessant shrieking gives away the babies. Feeding time.

'Why are there three parents?' Joe looks to me.

'Maybe two are potential fathers, and they're waiting to see whose offspring hatch? I know that's the case with blackbirds.' I can't remember anybody telling me this. 'It's no family romance. Just one part of the cycle of life that any of the birds might succeed at, but not every bird needs to.'

'There're loads of swan's nests along the riverbank where my boat's moored.' He describes these mountains of twigs that home patient mothers-to-be. He says sometimes the swans are alone and sometimes they're visited by another, but Joe doesn't think it's always the same visitor. 'I've been thinking,' says Joe, facing the nests again, 'isn't it crazy that we think we just need ourselves and a couple of other people when we're actually committed to a load of random bacteria?'

It's a relief not to be the only person asking questions. Pete once told me that one-thirteenth of our bodies renews every twenty-four hours. Our bodies redesign themselves again and again. I imagine the contents of my body like a wardrobe: red dress, green dress, blue dress. I empty the wardrobe, so I know my body's possessions inside out. I possess them. Imagine my garments changing every day. Where do my original dresses go? Whose style am I wearing now? A riddle.

Silence. We've begun to walk in silence, I hadn't responded to whatever Joe last said. He bends to tie the shoelace on his walking boot. Perhaps we're leaving a space for the world to speak. The lambs bleat from the field behind the hedge. A brimstone butterfly flitters by, yellow, landing on white hawthorn before taking off again. Midges make storm clouds around our heads.

Joe checks his phone for the time. 'Better turn back, I've got some bicycles booked in this afternoon. You going to keep heading on?'

'Yeah, I think so, thanks for the company.' We both stop and face each other. A dark patch sneaks from under his armpit where he's been sweating: a strong smell like damp grass rises.

Joe kicks some loose stones into the hedge. 'Sure. Drop by the bike shop for a tea whenever you fancy, if you need a bit of human interaction in your days.' His smile slants up his face like an exercised collie.

'Thanks. Hope your afternoon's good.'

I walk up the path, his footsteps still audible as he walks the other way. Things become quieter, the light less vivid.

※ ※

I dream of opaque feathers. The night's sky. I am a black parrot, a Vasa parrot – Coracopsis – with a line of males waiting in a tree. 'Must we wait?' I meet them one at a time. Each on a different perch. In private. Muffled in the leaves. Take their kisses and take their food. Yes, each is a father. And each thinks he is the only one. They hunt for me, for our offspring. I surprise myself: I don't feel guilty. Pinned by beaks against trunks, wings spread. It doesn't take long. Take their kisses and take their food. I need to feed my brood.

12

'Sophia, we need to talk.' Pete puts down his knife and fork. He looks at me across our breakfast plates. There's a scatter of toast crumbs and specks of scrambled egg around his plate. I clear the table to see the ring left when the plate's missing – a clean middle ground. I return to my seat and stare at the circle, don't say anything. I don't know what we're talking about.

Pete runs his hands over his head, like a cat cleaning itself. 'We still haven't talked about the miscarriage, and I haven't wanted to because you've not seemed well, but I think maybe now's a good time?' His chair squeaks on the tiles as he moves it left to catch my gaze. His shirt sleeve dips into the ring of crumbs as he does so, disturbing their peace.

'What did you want to say about it?' I shudder at the terminology Pete keenly took on. Miscarriage. I miss-carried our child – completely my fault – sorry about that. Natural abortion. I aborted that plan midway. Changed my mind.

'Come on Sophia, don't be tetchy. I've been tiptoeing around you for months. I don't get why you're so caught up in yourself.'

Seeing him riled up leaves me semi-pleased, even a little turned on.

'Look, the nurse said a quarter of pregnancies end in miscarriage. She said it's perfectly normal for a termination to occur.'

Here we go again. Termination. I terminated our baby. Sent it to the airport terminal where it caught its flight, jumped on the soul plane to take off from Earth, and got carried to heaven.

I take my silence to the sink, lean my pelvis against it, roll my sleeves up and pull the washing-up gloves on. A daddy long legs scuttles along the skirting board. Spider season.

'Thing is, I wonder if we can try again.' Pete pauses, waits for a reply, panics when he sees my expression as I look over my shoulder, recoils like a spider, cornered, cup just above its legs. He starts again, flustered. 'We wanted a child, we were going to have one, it didn't work out, but nothing's to say it wouldn't work next time. Don't you still want one?'

The cup now hovers over me – how do I get out of this? I don't have an answer. I don't know. I could say I don't know. 'You still want my baby?' I ask.

'Yes, if you still want mine?'

The first part of his sentence comes with a rush, as it did the first time he told me he wanted my child. I am chosen. The second part hadn't occurred to me. How stupid. In the animal kingdom, it often comes down to female choice. 'Pete—' I stop.

He looks terrified, like the spring bunnies, not yet adjusted to the world and dazzled by my bicycle lights. I fill the washing-up bowl with water.

'Think about it will you? I'd better get to school,' he says, standing.

'I love you.' Instinct leads my words.

He turns me around and cups my face in his hands. He says, 'Nothing's changed, Sophia. I'm still here, we're still in this house, we still love each other.'

He leaves the room. I hear him pull his shoes off the rack in the conservatory, the sound of his briefcase as it falls over: sounds predictable and too close for comfort. I splash the water loudly, and don't hear Pete come back into the room.

'I forgot to say I'll be late back this evening.'

'Yeah?'

'Yeah, I've promised to meet Lily to discuss whether I can help with her thesis.'

'Lily?'

'Lily. I told you, remember?'

The name rings no bells; I turn back to the sink. 'Okay, cool, well, have a nice time.'

The familiar sounds resume: coat off hook, briefcase picked up – and he's gone.

About this time last year, I visited my parents, came up from Falmouth. Spider season. Dad was sat on a patio chair outside the front door when I arrived. He lifted himself up, noticeably weaker in his efforts, and gifted me with a hug.

'Spring is truly here,' Dad said, eyes full of joy.

'I brought sandwiches and a Thermos. Fancy sitting in the garden?' I asked.

'Absolutely. Your mum's gone out shopping, but she's baked some hot cross buns for us. I'll go fetch them.'

We settled on the wooden pew along the back wall of the house. It was crumbling in all its joints. I remembered lying on it when I was a teenager, covered in my duvet, reading. The insects would pop out from between the rotted gaps in the wood and catch my eyes from the page. The smell of spring in my childhood garden hit. Warm dampness. The flowers were out on the magnolia tree. The remnants of their bud's casings scattered the ground, looking like a gathering of miniature, furry rabbits' ears. Dad never maintained the garden like other householders did. He let it grow wild, planting only the magnolia, and otherwise seeing what self-seeded. A lot, was the answer – life happy to take hold wherever it could.

'How are you feeling, Dad?' I'd promised myself to act casual.

'Good. Your mum's baking has been keeping me going.' He whacked his belly, which was shrunken. 'How are things your end?'

'Good. I'm glad spring's here.'

A bee buzzed past, aware of the first spring flowers to feed from.

'How can you tell whether it's a queen or not?' I watched the bee make a round of the garden.

'The queen's probably back at the hive; she doesn't need to hunt for food.'

'Of course, I forget everyone's her servant – even her partner, poor fella.'

'Her partner will be the one bee who isn't around to serve on her.'

'Already out looking for someone else?'

'Not that fortunate. He'll be too dead to appeal to another.'

'You mean she kills him?'

'I don't know if she means to, but she does. She chooses her mate, they copulate, and then when it's over, he dies. The queen's mate was her servant, served, and is no longer needed: just like your mum says we are to God.'

'Harsh.'

I took the sandwiches from my bag: egg mayonnaise. Dad stooped down and pulled some leaves from the ground: wild mustard and nasturtium. He stuffed them into his sandwich. The action was unconscious, his fingers instinctively scouting the food source.

A spider shot from under the pew. With garden spiders – same as the queen bee – the woman chooses a partner, then the partner dies. I'd forgotten.

Other flying insects came out to play, having smelt the same warmth of spring I'd been delighting in.

'Mum's covering the fruit bowls early this year,' Dad said.

We never had a fridge; Mum said the right kind of food for our bellies wouldn't need to be refrigerated. Dad agreed. We kept dairy products with our fruit and vegetables in large bowls. Mum would cover them in nets when the spring came, and I'd watch the fruit flies bash into these again and again while I ate breakfast.

'Do female fruit flies choose their mates as well?'

'I think they do, in a way.'

'In a way?'

'Well, let's just say they won't use the 'produce' right away. They save it for several days in case a better option comes along.'

'And what if a better option does? They can't just poo out the old stuff.'

'No, you're right, they can't. Better options have longer bits, which means the produce is planted deeper, so any old stuff left by someone else dies before it can reach the destination.'

'Brutal.'

'Yeah, but it's what the female wants, else she wouldn't have waited around.'

I considered this, chewing my sandwich slowly.

One of Grandpa's travel books in his library wrote about gorillas in the jungle. It said they live in harems – multiple females to one male. A picture showed a humongous male gorilla with tiny testicles. I had giggled at them. He didn't need large bits to compete because there was no competition. Sometimes Pete's penis had felt intrusive, a pointer continuously directed to me. But there was very little difference between our genital size in comparison to other animals. I'd said this to Pete once and he'd laughed at me. 'Equal sexual dimorphism,' he said. 'It means we've equally chosen one another.'

'It's a shame the insect world doesn't get to experience love,' I said to Dad.

'Perhaps they do; we don't know how it feels to be a fly.'

'You think when the female chooses, she might love her partner? If so, it would be awful knowing they're going to die. I wouldn't commit if I knew that.' I wished I hadn't spoken. 'Sorry,' I said.

Dad continued, unfazed, 'We can't understand what it is to be an insect, but we can ask 'what is love?' and decide if that's what the insect is doing.'

'Love is a connection that makes you happy.'

'Well, in that case, yes, it could be that the queen bee loved her mate. Many animals physiologically change when they mate. Elephants even settle down together after. It appears that making a connection makes them contented.'

'It's true, lots of animals show signs of pleasure at touch – like that piglet from the farm next door: it would roll on its back so I could tickle its belly.'

'That's right, and do you remember watching the horses groom each other? This calms their heartbeat. Most of us enjoy companionship. Maybe most of us love?'

An article in one of Pete's *Biology* journals had talked about a study where scientists tickled female rats' clitorises with a paintbrush. The rats returned again and again for more. 'What if love is just an addiction to pleasure then?' I asked.

'Could be, but so what if it keeps us stable and happy?'

'What's better though: stability or diversity?'

'Impossible to say,' Dad said, 'The human population is high, and if we swapped around it could soar even higher. Plus, our young take a lot of care, so I'd think we need to stick together.'

At that point I'd wanted to ask whether Mum and he were happy together or just sticking together. But I couldn't bring myself to do it.

'What about Grandma and Grandpa?' I asked instead. 'Were they sticking together or were they happy?'

'Their love went beyond having me,' said Dad. 'They both shared an understanding of how nature could protect them from hard times.' Dad's tone had dropped, and he stared into space. 'Hot cross bun?' he offered, changing the subject.

'Yes please.'

We each took one, already buttered. Scrumptious. The cross, not for Jesus, but a symbol of the four seasons, split by each solstice and equinox. It wasn't Mum stuffing us with faith. The sultanas tasted like childhood. Sat with Dad and the smell of spring, I could have been a happy child again, raised by a contented couple.

⁂

I walk to a patch of trees in a large grassy area, and scramble into the one most mossy and rich in texture, scent, and array of acid greens. I climb into its depths until I'm straddled across the thickest branch. Decaying bark crumbles across my jeans. The damp seeps into my crotch. I bend forwards and lean my cheek against the coral-like bed of lichen. Eyes squeeze shut. I repeat, 'I am a damselfly; I am a damselfly; I am a damselfly.' I want to clamber inside a vicious world of non-relationships. Pure sex drive and survival. No more careful considerations.

My body sinks deeper into the branch, until I am a part of the branch. I am a damselfly; barbed cock protruding outwards, angrily pointing this way and that in search for a release, a passing on of DNA. I am ready to scrape out the insides of any female. Ready to remove the unwanted scum of another male and leave only my juices.

'I am a fruit fly; I am a fruit fly; I am a fruit fly'. Tears pry at the edge of my eyes. I land on a crisp leaf and use the bristled sex combs on my legs to grip hard onto the closest female fruit fly. There's a surge of satisfaction as genitals meet, and toxins leak from my body, making the female fly shudder while all other male reproductive cells crack and disintegrate into nothing. I wonder whether this is the same sensation as when a mouse releases a stench so powerful, so poignant, that the nearby pregnant female miscarries – allowing space for him to move in. I don't feel guilty: if I was the last fly to impregnate the female, then I was the strongest, the best suited. Both of us should be happy.

Tears soak into the wood as I open my eyes to the tiny garden in front of them. An insect-eye view of the world.

13

Field Notes

<u>St John's Wort, Hypericum perforatum</u>

St John's Wort is a flowering plant in the Hypericaceae family. The flowers are most often yellow in colour. It is a unique plant in that some form of genus of the St John's

Wort can be found nearly all over the world.
The plant is globally used for medicinal
purposes, including the treatment of
depression.

Change with me
Seasons change, weather changes, the
moon changes, the stars change,
we change.
Work with me
As would a plant,
I adapt, you adapt, I lean, you lean, I grow,
you grow.
We are dancing like this.
But your legs aren't a stem that dances
with the wind.
Your legs you grew to walk away from me,
to turn your back.
If you act like this, you'll miss it.

Dolly Roberts

how I change
I would like to stand like a flower, grounded,
an equilibrium of give and take; committed to
change.

Cow parsley is taking over in the same way parsley overwhelms Pete's cooking. The chestnut trees spread their grown hands, fingers flexed. What am I going to find to photograph today?

The sun has settled its sense of immediacy, no longer overwhelming the landscape in startling brightness. The light has been soaked up by green: fields, foliage and caterpillars. The rain's begun to fall again. Any light struggling to relax into green has been eased by these sudden rainfalls.

My daily rhythms have changed, un-asked. I wake early, I eat late. My energy extends. Winter no longer calls from my bones: every splinter of it, gone. My bones are beginning to forget. The winter is like childbirth. Trauma buried beneath new memory growth.

I haven't forgotten some things though. Some seed was sown over winter and now it grows, only to get bigger. I am restless.

The meadow that runs beside the river is full of blooms. The search is for a new flower to photograph. I stop at a cluster of St John's Wort, not yet flowered, but soon to bring bright yellow between the pink campion. The leaves are different to any other, with a spattering of translucent spots. They're one of Grandma's favourite plants; she gave me jarfuls of the dried leaves and flowers when I was a teenager. 'Good for mood swings,' she said.

I hold my camera up and focus the lens.

The miracle of medicinal flowers. Grandpa was the botanist, Grandma became the herbalist. She explained how plants stand still, unlike animals. They can't run away from their predators, and so they must find other ways to protect themselves. 'They can't have all their communication functions rely upon one central system, like we do, because if something trampled that – they'd be gone in an instant.' We humans can run, walk, duck and move away from the threat, so we work differently. 'Plants,' she said, 'spread themselves democratically and communicate from all over through tiny chemical conversations.'

They are an inspiration of adaptability.

'Us humans have two arms, two legs, stand straight, and sleep lying down,' Grandma taught. 'Flowers can grow new arms if need be; they can turn topsy turvy, stand at thirty degrees, and are welcome to change their minds continuously.'

She told me how a plant's life cycle wasn't dependable like ours: foetus to elderly in a common timescale. No, even metamorphosis was too ordered for a plant. 'A plant,' she said, 'adapts non-stop, because it stays still amid a changing environment, and can't seasonally migrate like animals.'

Is this how medicinal plants work with humans too? Continuing to communicate chemically when the 'environment' becomes our bodies rather than the earth?

St John's Wort. With five petals and small leaves that have the scent of a fox. Can be used to treat depression. These are the qualities I know off by heart, thanks to Grandma.

The sound of a text message pings. I stuff my camera back into my bag and fumble for my phone. The text reads: 'Joe's coming for dinner after work – come join us! 15b High Street. Isabelle xxx' The sentence leaves no room for questions. I stumble over a reply, rephrasing again and again my decline. And then I realise that this is Isabelle. She doesn't need an answer; she needs a movement one way or the other.

I hover on the high street, where 15b is painted in black on the yellow door to my right. The bakery to my left has closed for the day. The workday is over. Joe and Isabelle will be upstairs. I've timed this as casually as I feel comfortable. 'Gone to meet a friend for dinner' read my note left by the kettle. I had rephrased that several times too: 'Seeing Mum', 'Taking a walk', 'Back later, sorry'.

My hands dig deep inside my pockets. I look down: woollen trousers, white shirt. I've dressed like I'm going to a job interview. I lift the door knocker before I can change my mind. The fishtail knocker drops to one side, missing its pad, thudding quieter than I thought and making me do it three times over.

A crescendo of beats tap as footsteps fly down an invisible staircase, escalating in volume and speed. I stare at the door and picture the face behind it as I hear fingers fumble with the lock.

'Sophia, come on in.' Isabelle's face has been graced with more freckles than when I last saw her. She's pulled her blonde curls back and twisted them into a knot, held by a pencil poked through.

'Hello, sorry if I'm late.'

'Not at all, Joe just got in. Welcome to the flat.'

The staircase draws a narrow corridor upwards. The floor is bare pine boards that my shoes play beats on, rewinding the rhythm I heard outside. I imagine being stood on the other side of the door, listening to this sound of me leaving myself behind.

When I get to the top, the flat pans out before me in open-plan. A kitchen borders one side of the room. It is lined with red cabinets and white handles. In the centre of the room two sofas face one another, with a Persian rug lain between them. Over by the window is a table with a surface made of patterned tiles. Four chairs, seated with hand-printed cushions, are pulled up to the table's four sides. Plants hang from woven baskets all around, and potted palms make it feel like I'm still outdoors.

Joe is in the kitchen area, head in one of the red cupboards. 'Anything you don't eat?' His voice muffled.

'Nope, I'm easy.'

'Great, let's make curry.' He begins taking vegetables from the cupboard and placing them down on the counter. Some potatoes roll free and fall on the floor.

Isabelle walks over to pick them up. 'Help me chop?' she says, looking my way.

I take my coat off and put it on the back of the sofa. 'Sure.'

'How was your day?' she asks, and hands me a knife and board.

'It was okay. How was yours?'

'Frustrating. I'm trying to write this article about whether the Western world can stop wanting more than we've got and accept a more sustainable way, or whether this would be denying ourselves a natural desire for progress.' Isabelle launches straight into conversation, oblivious to my nerves. 'It was a mind-fuck, and the editor of the magazine expected me to do it in 800 words.' Isabelle skilfully dices the potatoes, her slender fingers blurring as her hand rocks rhythmically back and forth with the knife.

'Did you manage it?' asks Joe, while pouring rice into a pan.

'I only got as far as this Sanskrit story that describes Sage Saubhan as he meditates by a pond.'

I chop the carrots that Isabelle's piled in front of me. Pete would have specified what shape to cut them into.

'The story goes that this sage was sat contentedly watching the fish in his pond, when one day he saw what he imagined must be a daddy fish playing with its baby fish.

111

The sage thought, 'Isn't that nice: a happy family playing together,' and was suddenly struck with envy, because he didn't have a family of his own. So later that day he went to the king, and said, 'King, I demand of you fifty of your daughters to be my wives.' And so the king provided him with these fifty wives. He then asked, 'Wives, would you please provide me with children?' And so, they did. And soon he had 50 wives and 150 children.'

She looks up and smiles knowingly, then goes on, 'After several months, he decided this was still not enough: his wives and daughters no longer felt new. He wanted more. Luckily, the sage went back to his pond to meditate before making any more requests. As he watched his fish playing with one another, he thought, 'How disgusting this is, a self-perpetuating cycle of desire.' Once each fish had raised one child, they would have another, then another. He thought, 'I don't need to be a part of this process.' And so he left to live in the forest, where he would meditate until the day he died.'

Joe has been dedicated in his tasks, led by Isabelle's voice rather than distracted. He now leaves the frying onions, coloured red with spices, alone, and stares into the simmering pan of rice. I follow his eyes to the white horses of starch rising to the surface. 'That's a great story. Not sure how you've made it into an article though,' he says.

Isabelle groans. 'I haven't. The story alone is about 800 words.'

Joe laughs, then turns back to his pan, serious again, 'So you think the sage can manage to not want?'

Isabelle shrugs. 'I don't know. I guess he's trying to differentiate himself from animals by thinking he can have a choice. That was going to be the premise to my article.' She's already managed to chop all the potatoes and the parsnips. She holds a huge frying pan below the work surface and swipes the pile of vegetables into it.

I offer my meagre heap of carrots to the mix. 'Sounds like a good start.' I can picture this sage, with a long beard wound around his fingers as he ponders the ability of human consciousness.

Isabelle has added a thousand other ingredients to the pan: coconut milk, one spice, another spice, another, some fresh leaves of some kind. She looks like she knows what she's doing. 'Yeah, I thought I'd link it to another story, but I'll tell you that one over dinner, or I'll have no more stories left.'

'Right, time for some wine then,' says Joe.

When the curry's ready, we place plates on the table. I take in the details of the tiles that decorate the tabletop, each one different to the other. I try to settle on a favourite, but I like them all.

Isabelle catches me looking. 'I bought them in Turkey when I was travelling.'

I haven't travelled anywhere, except a couple of trips to France where Pete insisted on shopping in chain stores or supermarkets because he was too embarrassed to speak French. 'It must be amazing to have travelled so much.'

'Isabelle struggles to stick to one line of thought if you hadn't noticed; it's the same with places,' Joe says.

I look out the window and take in the slow trail of cars climbing the high street below. The townspeople have battled for pedestrianising it since I was little, but it's never come to anything. All the punters want is a traffic-free shopping street. The shops say they need car access for deliveries and bin men. It's as though the street leads two lives, both deeply dependent on one another but no longer aware of where the commitment lies.

'Bon appetite,' says Isabelle, with eyes glinting. 'It smells delicious. Thanks guys.'

'It's incredible, when Isabelle returns from her trips away,' says Joe, facing me. 'She speaks of this world, and it seems so foreign compared with here, and then as I listen I realise how tiny actions here are affecting things over there, and vice versa. It's almost impossible to get your head around the mechanics of it. I want to understand, so poor Isabelle has to paint a picture of everything through words.' Joe takes a forkful of curry and places it to his lips; they part, the top lip bigger than the bottom. 'I like to take credit for her excellent story-telling skills,' he jokes.

'Sure, go ahead.' Isabelle kicks him under the table.

Joe chews and swallows. 'It's inconceivable, really, how the bigger space that life exists within – not just the planet, the country, or a town even – anyway, this bigger thing, the whole universe perhaps, is all affected by the tiny actions of each and every living or inanimate organism.'

'Wow. Like we're looking at ghosts,' I say.

They both look at me, expecting more.

'I mean, we're always looking at the effects of past movements, phantoms of another's life.'

'Holy shit. That's true,' says Isabelle, laughing.

The curry melts in my mouth, a strange array of spice-infused coconut making me sleepy. I look at my plate, halfway finished, and wonder what Pete made for dinner.

Isabelle pours another glass of wine for each of us. 'If we're all impacting each other, then I don't think we can really choose to say we'll live by human ethics and not consider animal ones too.'

'This is what troubles me,' I say, 'What are animal ethics? I don't always feel my personal ethics make sense for animals.' I wonder whether I'm going to tell them about the miscarriage, about how if I were really part of the animal world I would have adapted by now.

I don't mention it, and we keep eating, and talking, until my phone goes off, with Pete checking I'm alright. He writes, 'I didn't know you had any friends?'

When I get home, Pete's sitting in front of the television. He asks me how dinner was. He doesn't ask why he wasn't invited. But I can't concentrate on my answer, because the TV presenter's narration has caught my attention.

' … does the bark know where the cancer is, or does the cancer know how to attract the bark?'

'What are you watching?' I break Pete's flow.

'Something about the rainforest. Man, school was tiring today. The kids were being a nightmare.'

' … the relationship between plant and illness is accepted in this tribe. They believe that both can communicate with one another and say what they need …'

I try to listen to Pete tell me about his day, but I can't close my ears to the snippets coming from the TV. We – plants, animals and humans – might instinctively be able to find what we need from one another.

'Anyway, long day, time for bed,' finishes Pete, and he stands up, turning the TV off. The voice shuts down.

I am a bird missionary. I soar above the houses, swoop down and poach the fish from above doorways. The bird messenger. Spreading the word to people who offer fish in return. 'In faith will come new life.' A confused quiver of eyelids. I've remembered something Mum told me as a child. 'Humans work in pairs. They settle down together and start happy families, just as the birds do. Our Father intended us to follow the birds.' She said this while pointing through the window at two magpies conversing in the garden.

An unbearable itching starts at the base of my quills, where they root themselves into the pores of my body. And I'm flying again, with Mum's words fluttering behind, spying on me from the eyes on butterflies' backs – but they can't quite catch up. I'm looking for a different tree to land on – one with a different colour bark – while the butterflies need a new flower.

14

'How come you ended up in Suffolk?' I wanted to ask the question when I first met Isabelle. How does a tropical creature like her survive in Suffolk climes? The soil doesn't seem right. She's more like a seaweed flower, cupped and bright, strewn across a New Zealand coastline.

'Good question.'

I breathe out. She hasn't taken offence. We cycle side by side. The road is quiet and empty. I can smell a sweet mix of pollens and sun-soaked leaves. I don't know the way to Joe's boat; Isabelle doesn't seem sure either. She asks me, at each turning, 'Left or right?' happy to follow instinct and take the slow, winding road of trust.

She takes one hand off her handlebar and leans back. Her chest opens to the sunlight. 'I studied in London and after that I went travelling but at some point I missed the UK. When I lived away there was always some level of miscommunication – tiny cultural nuances that meant I never fully understood or could never be fully understood.' She stops and points at the elder trees in the field beside us. We lean our bikes against the hedge and walk across the grass to reach them. We pull some of the powdery elderflower blossoms free.

'Every time I met someone from England, I was excited to talk with them; they got something integral about me that even I didn't know was missing.'

'You felt like you weren't in your natural habitat?'

'I guess so. But I don't like the thought that we can't communicate across boundaries.'

'Me neither.' I bunch handfuls of the blossom into the basket Isabelle is carrying. 'But we can't expect to get on with everybody.'

'I know, but somehow I can't accept that.' She places the basket on the ground and puts her hands on her hips to talk serious. 'You know what? When I came back, I felt as disconnected as when I was away – despite being surrounded by my 'kin'.' Her pointed chin casts a triangular shadow across her chest. 'But then I went to volunteer with the rewilding project at the Wash, and that's where I met Joe.'

'So, you moved here for him?'

'I wouldn't put it like that.' She smiles to herself. 'I had nowhere else to call home, so I made one here. But now I've learnt I can feel at home anywhere. Everywhere I go there'll be someone who wants to work with me, human or non-human.'

Isabelle hangs the basket of blossom heads around her back with a piece of rope. We return to our bikes and resume cycling.

Dreams have mulled in my thoughts, and want to break into reality. 'I've been having these dreams,' I say. 'In them, I'm different birds, and can communicate to them all – no matter which species.'

'They're probably replacing the humans you want to communicate with but can't get the nerve to – or at least that's what Freud would say.' She lets go of both handlebars, and free wheels – the action makes me burn with anxiety and I cycle extra close in case she falls. 'Freud wrote that when we dream of animals, it is us communicating with the parts of our psyche that are most repressed. He said that if there are emotions we can't bear to express to people, then we project them in sleep onto animals instead.'

This disturbs me. In a second the free landscape of my dreams is snatched away. The bright skies and realms of the wild, the mindless exploration, become dark, dangerous territory.

'Are they sexy dreams?' Isabelle sweeps her curls over her shoulder so she can look me straight in the eye.

'Kind of.'

'Sex is the hardest thing for most people to talk about.'

I stick my tongue out and pretend to be sick at the thought.

'And then we go and kill that animal part of ourselves because it disgusts us.'

I think of Mum's prudishness when Dad first told me about pollination. She hummed to herself and pressed her hands against her skirt fabric, as if to check it was still there.

I haven't seen Mum for weeks; she hasn't called either. We're in stalemate, waiting to see who makes the first move.

'There's this story about Ramayana,' says Isabelle, 'He was determined to have a clean and respectable relationship with Sita. Their sex disgusted him because he saw it as animalistic, and in his eagerness to be rid of this animal side, he hunted anything animal around him. One day, when he was out in the woods, he saw a deer and shot it. He went to collect the meat, and found Sita, shot dead. The animal he'd seen was actually his love.'

It's a sad story. The thought of Rama forgetting his part in the animal world.

'After that he only had language and rationale to connect to other beings.'

Pete's face is in my mind, trying to reason wild grief out of me. A signpost lies at the next turning. It's five miles to Beccles. Nearly there. I stay quiet. My dreams, the flowers, they nibble at my thoughts. I am speaking animal, and I can't tell Pete – else I could lose my human connections.

Beccles quay is busy: Broads cruisers and yachts gathered ready for a weekend break. The water runs slow in the quay and is well directed. The river beyond occasionally channels off into dead-ends, which lead to expensive houses.

The town lies behind the river. The fens in front. We follow the river out of town. The way is winding. Farmland inhabits one side. Horses wander the farmland. The other side is overgrown fen – pink campion and dock leaves. We follow the Angles footpath; long grasses wave at its edges, yellowed by the sun. The big, blue sky soars above our heads and houses a dusty, gentle breeze. What lies beyond the river's edge begins to disappear, us dipped lower than sea level, away from it all – at plant and seed level. Still. Hidden.

Joe's boat is moored as part of a marina. Lines of neighbouring floating homes. The sight of so many people living this way uplifts me. Once the rivers had been lined with gypsies like this, but they had been driven out – not seen as humane. Boat dwellers scatter the pontoons. They chop firewood and work on rooftop veg boxes.

Joe's boat is thirty-foot-long and painted bright red with a cream top. Isabelle knocks on the little wooden door before she opens it. We duck our heads to enter. The inside is sparse. Handmade furniture is built into the narrow frame. Joe is stood ahead, he has to stoop because of the low roof, I wonder if this is why he doesn't stand straight. He gives us each a bear hug. My frame is small in his arms. I am safe.

From the sofa I admire the kitchen surfaces. They retain the bark-edged outline of the trunk of tree they came from and are varnished to a warm glow. Windows line the edges of the boat – little portholes. Looking out of them feels like peeking out of a burrow. The river is rife with bird life. A heron stands stock still, waiting for a fish. Dad told me many native birds, like spoonbills and cranes, are returning to Norfolk and Suffolk. We might be able to return the land to its natural order after all, and then ourselves too.

Isabelle stuffs elderflower heads into a jug of water. Joe sits beside me, places his hand on my knee. 'How's it going?'

A part of me wants to place my hand on top of his and see what his hand feels like beneath mine. Something different. I have a picture from a nature documentary in my mind: a red junglefowl running after its mate. Bright plumage flicks left, right, centre, but the mate won't give in. In the documentary, it turned out the feathers were fake plumage: that's why no one was interested. He was a domestic chicken dressed up to look like his wild cousin. But he'd fooled nobody. The presenter of the documentary had laughed, saying, 'A wild female junglefowl wouldn't settle for a domestic chicken.'

'I'm alright,' I say.

Problem is, if the plumage is too beautiful it creates too much testosterone and the male becomes prone to parasites. Tell that to the advertisement companies. Stop promoting good looks: it will be the end of the human race. Joe's brown eyes are like a puppy's; he's no wilder than any other man.

'Has it been a hard week? Grief takes sudden twists and turns, doesn't it?' he asks. I must be frowning.

'Dad used to go sailing on the Broads,' I say, following his lead rather than explaining my actual thoughts. 'He loved being on water.'

'It's a great feeling.'

What was that nature documentary? After the junglefowl came the natterjack toads, their croaks loud and hollowed. The male with the loudest croak was sat in his waters, ribbuting again and again – long calls to what seemed like nobody. But soon there were females appearing everywhere, each having followed the sound gradients, the sensitive directions to their best mate.

'How's your week been?' I detract attention from me to him. He rests his long legs on a stool, where Isabelle has placed the jug of water. She's busy in the kitchen area preparing the next treat. Joe's knee joints are a little below mine. Taller.

'Good. The evenings are lighter later, so I've been sowing seeds on deck after work.'

I can picture him, hands embedded with soil as it sticks to bike oil. He sings to himself, a soft song, and the freshly spawned frogs listen out. If a male Pacific tree frog has a particularly loud song, the documentary said, the other males can't handle it and they hop away, leaving all the women to this one loud male.

Isabelle has her hands in a bowl, sleeves pulled up. She lifts a floury hand to her face to tuck a curl behind her ear. 'Pan bread?'

'Yes please,' I say. Then to Joe, 'Do you get enough time off to enjoy being on the river?'

'Plenty. It doesn't cost much to live out here, so I don't need to work much. I spend a lot of time maintaining the boat, mind.'

My finger has found its way to my lips, it strokes the top fleshy mound up and down. I pull it away and readjust my blouse so the embroidered flowers hang right. I look sideways at Isabelle, she pounds the dough, muscles rippling along her arms.

'Did you bring your camera?' Joe says.

'I did.'

'Great, let's go on deck, and try to capture my local heron. My camera's not good enough, I've been looking forward to you bringing yours.'

'Okay.' I look sideways at Isabelle again.

'Good luck,' she says, brushing another loose curl away. 'Joe spends hours attempting to photograph that heron; he never gives up.'

We three spend the afternoon on deck eating pan bread with different fillings: hummus, fried tomatoes, goats cheese, honey. The heron flies away. We didn't manage to photograph it. When the time comes for us to leave, my skin prickles – burnt from being outside all day, not used to this exposure. I ruffle my hair; it feels thicker than normal. I feel attractive, excited to see Pete.

Isabelle accompanies me to my door. The cycle home had been quieter, us both enjoying the last of the daylight.

'See you soon,' she says. 'I'm off for a research trip to Scotland next week, but let's have tea when I'm back.'

'Great. I'd like that.'

When I enter the house, Pete is laying the table. His back faces me. His shirt is wrinkled and untucked. I tiptoe up behind him. Hope to surprise him.

He turns around, the smile of a child laps his face, eager. My body flinches an inch back. He wasn't what I expected.

15

Tossing and turning between awake and dreams I summon myself to today. There are no beginnings and ends, is my first thought, no clear dawn and dusk; the cycle is continuous. The same goes for Dad and my baby: every moment before, during and after them is a continuation of their development.

Pete pulls me close. His warm chest presses against my back. He traps me under the weight of his leg, which is flung over mine. Our bodies shift together like this as I try to stir. Our collected heat grows unbearable and finally I throw the sheets off.

'That time already?' Pete groans.

'Yes, sleepy head.'

'But it's the weekend.'

'Isn't there more you want from your weekend than sleeping?'

'Not when it's sleeping with you. Come back.'

I'm already dressing. 'I'll bring you a cup of tea.'

'What's the time?'

'Quarter past ten.'

'Oh shoot, I thought it was way earlier. I'll come downstairs for tea; I've got to leave in an hour.'

'I thought you were spending the day in bed?'

'That was before I remembered I had to be somewhere.'

'First I've heard of it. I thought we were spending time together.'

'Shit. Sorry, Sophia, I forgot.'

So unlike Pete.

'I'll put the kettle on.' Halfway out the bedroom door I ask, 'Where are you going?'

'I told Lily I'd meet her at midday.'

'Thesis Lily?'

'If that's what you want to call her.'

'A lunch date?' I can't see the response on Pete's face because I'm already on the landing. Rain has spattered the window with droplets, but beyond the glass is a clear day, freshly cleansed. I will make my own plans.

'Caught anything?'

Joe squats on the riverbank, beside a tall hazel, with a fishing rod in his hand. His face is tanned from the last few days of sun. 'Not yet.'

'Don't you get bored? I would've given up hours ago.' I press my skirt against my thighs to sit down on the grass beside him, my legs white compared to his.

'Never.'

Dad and I went fishing once. He said it was about listening to the tiny movements of the line. He told me to close my eyes, hold my hand out into thin air and keep it there. 'Can you feel when it moves?' he asked me. My hand tingled in the concentration, as if focusing on one part of my body somehow made it grow. My fingers began to twitch, and each twitch felt like a huge movement. 'Open your eyes,' Dad said. We watched my hand a little longer, and the twitches seemed foreign – occurring on this strange, external digit, disconnected by a vast distance from where I was feeling it. 'Good, now you know how to listen to the line,' Dad had said.

The river by Geldeston lock is particularly still today, the sun's heat relaxing the muscles of everything around. 'Where's your friend the heron?' I ask, taking my camera from my bag. I kneel and lean back to fit Joe in the frame. Freckles have appeared across his cheeks; his eyes crease at their edges.

'Gone fishing elsewhere, I guess. There's been loads of others here though; it's like everyone's returning.'

'Nice.'

'Yeah, I was listening to the radio this morning over breakfast, and they were talking about how the number of new bird residents in Norfolk is growing.'

'Which birds?'

'The spoonbill was one example: there was a new arrival of a small colony about seven years ago, and it's rising.'

'Dad told me about that, but I've never seen a spoonbill.'

'Nor has anybody round here really, but apparently they're growing strong.'

'I wonder why they've returned?' I remember Dad telling me about the day he heard cranes were re-establishing themselves in Norfolk. He was thirty and went out on a week's expedition with a tent and his binoculars, desperate to catch a glimpse.

'Well, the Broads have regained some stability due to protection laws, and the habitats have therefore returned to the spoonbills' preferred state.'

'Does fishing not stop nature re-establishing?'

Joe beckons for me to hold the rod a moment. He stands and heads to the bushes behind us. It takes me a moment to realise he's taking a piss. He continues to talk to me, his head facing along his shoulder. I stubbornly face the river.

He says, while peeing, that for him, fishing is an activity to help us understand nature's balancing act. He says being part of the process of death helps him come to terms with how life must end for some if we are to sustain it for others.

I imagine myself a fish, swimming in the water below, unawares that death might pluck me any minute. Perhaps I'm already expecting it and know this might be the day. How do the fish manage that? If I imagine life might be plucked any moment, me hit by a car on the way home, I no longer see sense in building upon the relationships I have. 'Maybe fish go with the flow of whatever they desire so as not to live the tragedy of an unfulfilled life.' A fish utopia. I burst out laughing.

'You can laugh, but Isabelle's all for that.' He returns from the bush and takes the rod from my hand; a smile rides his face. 'She emailed me her latest article earlier this week: it's about animal desire. Here, she told me to print it off so you could take a read too.' He tugs the strap of his rucksack and scrabbles inside to find a creased sheet of A4 paper.

I try to flatten the creases. 'The Lost Poetry of Desire' reads the typed title. I read on. The article opens with how, in Indian myth, animals speak a more poetic language to humans. 'How can we speak this lost language?' she asks. She writes how Yasodhara, the founder of Buddhism, believed animal poetry came from a place of following desires without instruction. 'Instead of using the language of rationale, animals feel their way towards pleasure. Deer and birds have no need for a guru to learn how to satisfy their desires.'

'Have you got to the bit about genitalia shapes yet?' asks Joe.

'Not yet.'

'It's just like Isabelle to mention that. I couldn't stop laughing when I read it.'

Isabelle writes how animals do not wonder what is 'right,' or wait for a religion to guide them, or follow their relative's opinions. Then comes the part on genitalia shapes. She mentions the Karma Sutra, how it says that the sizes and shapes of genitalia define who is the 'right' partner. She says we can satisfy our desires by following our sensations through these matches of genitalia rather than theorising who is our perfect match. 'Is your man a bull, a hare, or a stallion?' Isabelle asks. 'Are you a doe, mare or elephant cow?' It could, she writes, be the difference between deep satisfaction or a consistent sense of something missing. She finishes the article by quoting a Sanskrit saying that describes the strength of a woman's desire as unquenchable by no number of men. 'Perhaps if we reconnect to our ancestors' poetry, we might follow the course of life without worrying which way we're going, or with whom we're walking.'

I pass the sheet of paper back to Joe. 'Pete jokes about how humans have sex all through the month, rather than only when fertile. He says human desire is un-stoppable.'

'It's a good point. Isabelle's a bit obsessed with trying to figure out why we continually desire more than we've got.'

'Do you think that's true?'

'Absolutely. It's what connected Isabelle and me in the first place. Neither of us believe it's possible to find satisfaction in one human alone.'

'We all struggle to find 'the one'.'

'True, except Isabelle and I don't believe 'the one' exists.' He puts the rod down on the grass. 'We accept that our desires shift and turn and that, if we follow the flow, we might find ourselves elsewhere – and that's okay; that's life.'

'That's petrifying. If I followed the flow of instinct, it would probably flow in the opposite direction to everything safe.'

'Sure, that scares me too. Which is why Isabelle and I are committed to one another; we aren't going to leave one another, but we will go to other places too.'

A wind of abandonment blows over me. I was thinking nature was the queen of match-making, but these two are leaving it to chance.

'Hey, enough big talk,' Joe says. 'How about we pack up and take a swim?'

No more fishing food for thought.

I dither with my camera, pretend to check the settings, adjust the light meter: all an act to buy time for solving the problem of no swimsuit. Out the corner of my eye, Joe's clothes shed onto the grass. I peel back the layers of my own until I'm stood in my underwear. The sensation of wind on skin draws the curves of my body in imagination – a sense of womanhood arises in the awareness of physicality. With this comes the memory that women are faithful in order to bear and rear a child. And this makes Pete stay, Dad stay, and Grandpa. But Joe describes Isabelle as if she were a goddess: someone who bares her own powers to make others stay.

Joe's skinny brown legs step out of his shorts. I look for the kidney-shaped scar that I'd noticed that time on the high street. There it is. My eyes move past those well-worn shins, past the sharp spike of his kneecap, the wiry mesh of hair on his upper legs, the thick muscles of his thighs. He isn't wearing any boxer shorts.

'I don't like wearing underwear: too constrictive,' he says, matter of fact.

'Okay,' I say and unhook my bra. My small breasts shoot outwards. They announce themselves to the outside world and perk up at the chance to touch both cold wind and hot sun at once.

The river feels good. I submerge my body in the cool grip and the water clings to my skin. I am but another animal, not to be looked at, judged or identified as beautiful or not; I am here to be. Joe ducks into the river, water splashing where his body just was. He rises, and little water spirits fly around him in a spray of droplets.

Joe swims to meet me and dives under water, swims beside my legs. His body slides against my calf muscles, they tingle in response. He emerges behind and, grabbing me by the hair, pulls me down. I manage to gasp one breath before I am underwater with him. We slide around one another like the fish Dad told me we once were.

We splash and swim until I'm shivering, then we lie naked in the dregs of the day's sunlight to dry off. The surrounding corn- and hay-fields confuse perspective in their miss-match of long grasses with those freshly cut. All under a clingfilm layer of cloud that distorts and adds a ghostly element to the scene. The land becomes whitewashed in the setting sun, until it is clear. A couple of dog walkers wander past, and eye-up the lines of our bodies. They look down to their toes and stamp louder than need be, to let us know we aren't as welcome as we might feel.

Joe's oblivious. He sits to cross-legged, comfortable to not belong. 'Want to come for something to eat on my boat?' he asks.

'Sounds good.'

The light saturates the corn and becomes thick honey, rinsing the landscape of all detail. The sun sets, a burning red over yellow fields. The dramatic scene fizzles out to gentle lilacs.

16

Joe makes soup from the spinach growing on the deck of his boat and serves it in a mug. I sip whenever a question rises in my mind: Is Isabelle happy with their relationship? Sip. Does she want to be a mother? Sip. Is there no such thing as a perfect couple? Sip. Joe fetches a torch and shows me his vegetable boxes. I fondle the dark compost that surrounds his lettuce heads in an attempt to feel my way back to the present.

We spread cream cheese onto sourdough bread, and pick lettuce leaves to complement our every mouthful. The water, in the moonlight, throws patterns of light against the white edges of his boat – dancing waves of never-ending movement, no time to readjust, ever-changing, like life. I try to explain what Grandpa told me, about how life is like dancing: a flow of movements in response to internal and external surroundings. 'When the music changes, so must the dance.' I smile to myself in the darkness. 'Grandpa often told stories about India,' I tell Joe.

'Telling stories is a nice way to continue a bond with someone we've lost,' he says.

I grieve a child I never met in alive form. Who will I tell that story to? Joe and Isabelle might never have to grieve one another; they get to move on without having to say goodbye.

The questions burn. I say I've got to leave – 'I was meant to phone a friend,' – and cycle home at a fast pace, desperate to out-speed thoughts and leave them to the wind. Too late: the thoughts have flourished, like a mould that stops you breathing easily; the wind carries the spores of questions alongside me.

Pete has prepared dinner. Steak and red wine. 'I didn't expect you to be so late,' he says.

I pull a stool up to the breakfast bar and put together a salad, unable to disappoint him by explaining I've already eaten. Pete compliments my ability to see what's needed. My chopping slows, hands no longer wanting to provide Pete his 'necessary' salad. I sweat with agitation, drowning out Pete's talking without realising.

'The man murdered his wife because she'd cheated on him,' Pete says as I tune back in.

'Really?' He hasn't noticed my absence.

'Really. Apparently, he's told the court that it was self-defence – he said that jealousy kills.'

'That's insane.'

'Right? If he loved her that much, he could have fought to keep her.'

The case of the Pitcairn islanders of 1790 comes to mind. HMS Bounty arrived at the island and, either by enforcement or agreement, was destroyed, leaving six

136

males and thirteen females stranded. Eighteen years later, when they were found, four of the six men had been murdered. It was said they died competing for the women.

Pete's het up and red in the face, he must have started the bottle of wine while he was waiting for me. He's explaining sexual selection, though he knows I already understand. Still, he goes on, 'It's not just for survival but for attraction. This woman must have been seriously attractive for this man to kill her before anyone else could get any.'

It's like Homer's *Iliad*: a whole war fought over the most beautiful woman.

Male birds with the brightest colours fly the fastest. But if I were a monogamous bird, like a puffin, parrot or peewit, then both the male and I would be colourful, because we both must select one another. Pete jokes that if every man who had committed adultery was murdered there'd be no men left. His own raucous laughter makes up for the lack of mine. It's not Joe that commits adultery though, but Isabelle too.

'Sick thing is, he'll probably bag another wife because of this – women love knowing they'll be fought over.' Pete scratches his chin, deep in his debate, not noticing he's debating himself. 'Did you know your friends Joe and Isabelle are unfaithful to one another?' he says, returning himself to two-way conversation.

Their names startle me, the knife slips and I cut my finger. Pete hurries to find a plaster from the medicine drawer, but he drunkenly drops the contents of the drawer onto the floor. I place my finger in my mouth and suck. The taste is comforting, one that's been with me since I was a small child, a little girl with a paper cut, going to Dad in tears with a handful of colouring pens.

'Yes, I did know.' How does Pete? Perhaps Joe is like a bowerbird and wears his stolen feathers with pride.

To my annoyance some of his theories are right: the thought of him competing for me is turning me on, but it's only testosterone rising as I sense the danger. I think it's turning Pete on too: he can't stop talking.

'I'd be fighting if I were Joe.'

Pete's words make me uneasy. I think of moose as they lock antlers and fight until death, all for one woman: a poor helpless female, stood on the side, watching, wondering whether she can give enough to be worth death? Perhaps she sees the fight as proof of her worth.

I could tell Pete that a vole will kill another if the other is unfaithful. To the vole there is no societal ruling upon this. In the exact moment in which the vole kills its partner, he, filled with jealousy, releases the same neurotransmitter as that in a human drug addict. I don't want to be a vole, addicted to someone. Bloodthirsty.

'Will you meet Lily tomorrow?' I ask.

Pete moves his head side to side, like how Grandpa had shown me the men in India do. The question has snapped him out of the topic, and he moves to get two plates for the meat.

The irony of admiring animals' brave fights, to then shoot one down and eat it off a plate without letting it fight at all. Dad said that farmed turkeys in North America have lost their sex drive, they no longer know what to do when placed in front of a mate.

I push scenes of locked horns out of my head and refill our wine glasses.

Tonight, we can play civilised: curl up on our sofa and watch TV, the only fight being who gets to choose the channel.

Grandpa joins me on my branch and puts his arm around my shoulders. He tells me about the polyandrous Pahari people of the Himalayas. 'Their polyandry had been beneficial for the species,' he says.

'Yes?' I say.

'Yes,' he says.

'But is it better for the individual?' I ask.

Grandpa jumps from the branch and flies away. No one's left to answer.

I fling my right leg over, so I'm balanced. Legs dangle together towards the ground. Giving the spongy surface a last stroke, I climb down the tree and let myself hang a moment from the lowest branch. Hands clasp around the rough skin before fingers relax and allow my body to drop. I land on two feet.

17

At Westleton Heath, the heather and gorse are flourishing. They paint the land a mixed palette – moody and sunny all at once – similar to the fast changes of weather above. I walk into the colours – dissipate them as I take the footpath: yellow here, purple there. The heath is flat, unlike the moorlands Grandma wanders in Devon, more like the Indian desert Grandpa once walked.

The woods lie ahead. Tall pines with skinny trunks reach up beyond my sight. Lower branches have broken off, dead from lack of light. The broken branches leave a gasp of empty space before the conifer canopy above – crowded pine needles in the sky. Below is spacious. Deer can walk between the trunks; their hooves can sink into the soft floor. Their urine soaks quickly into layers of shed needles as they mark their place.

Through my lens the scenery is overwhelmed by the pinky-purple hue of the heather. The heath overflows the frame in the photograph I take, as though it never ends – the viewer won't ever know if it did. In the next photograph, paths cut shadows between glowing stretches of heathland. In the third photo, the only end is the sky, which, as I click the shutter, is disrupted by a flock of terns. The terns sweep and spin around one another, returning from somewhere to fly together someplace else — why now?

Visions of locked horns took me here. Last August I'd come with Dad; he wanted to show me something through his imagination. The deer rutting. He'd said, 'I might not make it this year.' He was right. I've returned to imagine it once more. I settle on a bench at the viewpoint. Wrong season means empty seats. The only show is in my head. I replay it.

'Can you hear that?' Dad asked.

'What? I can't hear anything.'

'Green woodpecker. Listen.'

There was a tap-tap-tapping, brought to the forefront of my hearing as if newly arrived in the world.

We sat on a bench at the viewpoint overlooking Westleton Heath. Mum had gone for a walk along the coast to leave us to it. The way she walked off without a look over her shoulder, backpack straps clutched by both hands, was as though she'd already left Dad behind.

He looked sick: thin, pale, tired. His jowls were that of an old dog: floppy, like they'd given up strength.

'Why did you want us to come here?'

'I might miss the red deer rut this year, so I thought I'd at least come and imagine it.'

'The red deer rut?' I'd never heard of it.

Dad tipped his straw hat back so he could meet my eyes. He leant down and pulled a beer out of his bag, 'Fancy one?' he said.

'Sure.'

He looked happy, sat in sunhat, sipping from the green bottle, like a retired man enjoying the best things in life. 'The deer rut happens most years on this heath. It's the event when the males fight to mate with as many females as possible.'

'Sounds like carnage; why'd you want to see that?' I pictured Prince of Wales Road in Norwich, on a Saturday night: men in shorts sleazing their way around girls who totter, like new-born deer, on their stilettos.

'It's incredible to watch the stags risk their life for a woman; well, it's more a risk for the love of life than for the love of their life.'

'So what happens?' I had drunk my beer faster than Dad, anxious Mum might return and tell us off.

'The stags begin to bellow, and the loudest bellow wins.'

'That's it?'

'No, I hadn't finished. The bellows can be heard through the forest, and normally a few stags are of equal bellowing abilities. So these stags walk together, side by side, chests thrust out, to see who's man enough.'

'And then?'

'Then, if there's not a clear winner, they'll fight. Bloody, violent fighting.'

The brutality; all to mate with a bunch of women. 'Just one stag to win all the deer?'

'No, one stag per harem. The hinds come with their young in September to feed and get corralled into initial harems.'

'So how come you never took me to watch before?'

'It's not exactly family friendly.' He laughed, eyes scrunched shut.

The sun was strong that day. Dragonflies lowered themselves into landing, like iridescent helicopters. If there were only one stag, would the women accept him? I read that, in a group of monkeys, if only a few males were present, the women would stay faithful to them. But after a while the women would stop mating with the male monkeys; what would be the point – they'd done their bit for that gene pool. I'd assumed this was why Mum and Dad had stuck with one child – enough was enough.

'At least they've picked a beautiful environment to have a fight,' I said, and rolled my eyes so Dad could see I was joking.

Dad laughed and took another swig of beer. 'Quite. But actually it's true that their characteristics correlate to the wild beauty of this spot. Genes are influenced by the environment, and changes to the environment can determine whether animals remain monogamous or mate with many.'

'Changes to the environment determine their love life, more than individual preferences?'

'That's right.'

I guess, had the forest all burnt down, the deer would cling to whatever chance of life they could. As it is, the land is rich, and the choice of males will be plenty.

We rested our eyes on the heath, both our imaginations whirring.

I returned to the rutting. 'Did Grandpa watch the rutting with you?'

'No, he found the whole event too upsetting. It reminded him of his parents.'

'How's that?'

'Your great grandparents weren't always faithful to one another.'

Dad saw my face wince in surprise. 'I must have told you before?' he said.

No, Dad, tell me everything. Before you go.

'Your grandpa's parents were very unhappy. His dad used to spend a lot of time away, during which he'd meet other women, so his mum made herself acquainted with other gentlemen. She didn't like to be alone, left to care for my dad.'

'But Grandma and Grandpa weren't like this were they?' I was dizzy: drunk or else frightened to hear the truth.

'No, my parents were devoted to one another.'

'That's what I thought,' I said, sobered by relief.

'Grandma said she'd been very sad when she was growing up; I think she probably suffered from undiagnosed depression. She said her only joy came from the flowers on her family farm. She'd wait until spring for the colours to come. One year, Grandpa came as well.'

'I thought their love was wilder than that.'

'Wilderness isn't an easy place to live.'

'Hello.' Mum's voice came from behind us.

Dad looked up and his eyes sparkled for her.

'You two ready to go?'

Dad drank the dregs of his beer. Mum acted as if she didn't notice, turning her head to look at the view as he lifted the bottle. We three headed back to the car; one of the first deer family to roam the heath that year.

A dog walker sits beside me on the bench. Her dog settles by her feet, panting in the hot sun. Collie. The black hair glistens. I smile and push myself to standing, to leave them and my memory to peace.

Dad wasn't showing me the deer, he was showing me my past. 'Wilderness isn't an easy place to live.' My insides squirm like a school child waiting to be picked. I can, I can. Let me, let me. I'm not like my grandparents, or my parents, the domestic has not welcomed me but turned its back.

※ ※

I dream of blackbird, *Turdus merula*. A male partner. I'm kissing him. He's behind me. He's inside me. He moves: quick thrusts. His feet claw into my sides as he holds me in place. He falls back. He wants to tell me a secret. Could it be his male-hood is failing? I press myself upon him, kisses catching him between my beak. Sterile. Dad would tell me to abandon him, 'It's survival of the fittest, love,' I hear him say as we watch a cat dissect a mouse in our living room.

18

It's Wednesday: a Pete and Lily day. They now meet every Wednesday after school, and again on a Friday morning. On Wednesdays she gives Pete what she's been working on, then on Friday he gives her feedback.

A letter waits for me downstairs. I lie on the sofa, relieved to be indoors for once. Everything's been getting too hot. My body is sticky with sweat, my clothes uncomfortable and dirty.

I rip open the letter in the hope that Grandma has something refreshing to say.

Dear Sofia,

It's a scorching spring this year isn't it? I'm exhausted, having done the weeding in the late afternoon sun – it felt just as hot as at midday. To water the veg patch before it gets too warm means waking up at five, and then waiting until nine pm to water it again.

The plants are doing well though. They grow strong and steady. I have far too many greens to eat alone and find myself already looking forward to the root vegetables!

Have you been growing anything this year? I remember how well you and your father used to grow vegetables on the allotment. How wonderful it was that you two fed yourselves like that. I hope you haven't forgotten how; it seems to me this will be a necessary skill in the not far future.

It makes me sad when I go to the supermarkets and see vegetables all wrapped in plastic and packed with chemicals. It is very far from the medicinal plants you told me about in your last letter. If we don't work with the plants, we can only help ourselves. And it's not like all our needs can be met by another human.

I'm sure, however, that you will bring all you can to your baby when it is born. When is your baby due to be born? I await the news as if it could be any day.

Right, it's too hot even to write. I'm going to lie down in bed a while.

All my love,

Grandma

I'm sweatier than before, more than sticky clothes. Guilt. I've been lying to Grandma. How can I tell her that I'm not heavily pregnant, but am instead empty, like my veg patch?

Not empty, I am full of colours fighting for attention, bright invasive weeds and fully-grown leaves.

Sitting up, I take Pete's newspaper and pen from the coffee table; he's halfway through the crossword. I start to form a reply to Grandma on the printed sheets. Try – again and again.

I can't find the words.

Some lingering grief makes me want to apologise or fess up that it was my fault. The grief pesters, scrabbles like rats in my ribcage. My hands rip the page in two without direction from my mind. This is not true – only stale emotions from a place left behind. Pete's sperm once transferred a bag of genes into my body. Then it was up to me to provide the food to my baby, extract the energy from everything. I was strong and stable, ready to kill any intruders, ready to resolve conflicts. I did what I could.

A shoal of reef fish are all women except one big male fish, and when this big fish dies, a woman changes gender to take their place. It is the man who fails, but the woman who steps in.

Women. Reproducers. We are the experts in conflict resolutions.

I draft my letter to Grandma on the next sheet of newspaper, keep it brief and polite. That's all I can do.

The door bangs. Pete calls through from the other room to say he's got sausages for a barbecue; he's invited his colleagues over. He pokes his head around the door and adds, 'I bumped into Isabelle. She said she'd just got back from Scotland. I invited her too.'

Isabelle arrives at the garden gate in Aladdin trousers and a silk kimono, which crosses below her breasts and ties in a bow at her back. Her curls are tumbled atop her head, kept in place by a red scarf, which is knotted at the nape of her neck. I lose my breath. She plants a kiss on my cheek and I inhale – jasmine and thyme.

'I was so happy to bump into Pete and discover I could see you tonight.'

I blush in the force of her presence.

'What a beautiful garden. Will you show me your darkroom?' She touches every leaf in reach and eyes up the honeysuckle, which has flowered beautifully.

I haven't been in the darkroom for what feels like forever, and can't remember what state I left it in. My face must tell my thoughts because she says, 'Don't tell me you've forgotten your art, Sophia?' Her perfect teeth smile. She's teasing, her tiny elbow pointing into my waist.

'Follow me.' I lead her down the path. She moves to walk beside me and slides her arm into mine like we are two schoolgirls.

I open the cabin door. A tinny sound of music starts up from the garden; Pete's setting the scene. The first voices of guests trickle from the gate. I close the door, glad to have an ally for when the teachers arrive.

'How was your time away?'

'Amazing. It's always difficult to readjust when I return, but this time especially. The highlands were just incredible.'

'Well, it's nice to have you back.'

'How're things?' she asks, and browses loose negatives, shiny in their developed strips. 'You still having dreams?'

'Weirdly yes, and, things are okay. I'm—' I bite my tongue, not sure how to continue.

'You're …?' She drops the negatives and digs in her bag. Like a rabbit uncaring of the soil it sprays while making home, she leaves a mess of tissues and cigarette papers: an ode to the search party.

My eyes scan the debris. Isabelle comes up for air, a packet of biscuits in hand. She passes one to me. I take a bite: chocolate caramel. I calm.

'Oh my god, are you pregnant?' Her smile is huge, white. It shrinks quickly as she watches my face. 'Oh shit, Sophia, I'm sorry. What is it?'

'It's okay, just – I had a miscarriage last December.' I writhe. Isabelle's hand presses against mine. The writhing settles.

'Oh Sophia, that's so tough.' Her eyes are all compassion. 'It's very common to take a few tries.'

I stay silent.

'And it's okay to not want to,' she says.

I look at the floor. It needs a sweep: empty film spools and trims of photographs are strewn around our feet. Isabelle's pile of debris is nothing compared with mine.

Her facial features shift into a warm smile, and a lightness is brought to the room, 'Let's join in the celebrations, shall we?'

We return to the bright world outside and follow reggae beats and the smell of burning meat to the bottom of the garden. Isabelle makes a round and introduces herself to people with a hug. Several of the crowd I don't recognise. Some of them are women; I wonder if any might be Lily. Pete's busy talking to one of them by the barbecue, a pair of tongs in his left hand. He's ignoring me or hasn't noticed my return. The woman is a pretty brunette in a modest knee-length skirt and a crisp, white blouse. Isabelle's in deep conversation with one of the younger men, her hip thrust out as she leans against a table dragged out from the house. With gentle footsteps, I pick my way back up the garden path.

19

Field Notes

Bee Orchid, Ophrys apifera

The bee orchid is a small orchid with several
larger pink flowers shaped like wings and of
a furry texture. The lips of the flowers are
dark brown with yellow markings. The plants'

Together We Evolve

main pollinator is the bee, who enters the
familiar looking flowers expecting to mate,
but instead transfers the bee orchid's pollen.

I touch you: dappled fur.
You're the perfect size,
let me climb inside.

I help you become what you are,
return again and again,
until your petals are like the ears of a
domesticated dog,
flopping tamely from my kisses,
wolf no more.

I read your signs,
conclude you are waiting for me
and copulate with your curled petals.

Then when I leave,
turning to blow another kiss,
I realise I have nothing

But a dusting of your sperm
that will make someone else grow,
Not me

On the kitchen table is a letter from Grandma and a note from Pete. The note says: 'Just popped out to get some bits and bobs for dinner'. The handwriting is immaculate: rounded letters in straight lines.

I rip open the letter, wander through to the living room and collapse backwards onto the sofa. Envelope drops onto carpet as legs are pulled up.

Dear Sophia,

I am so sorry to hear your news.

My heart skips a beat, jolted from safety. A few deep breaths. Continue.

It amazes me that you kept this to yourself. However, in horrific times we do only what we can. There are friends I still have not told about your father.

Oh Sophia, how awful it must have been. How has Pete responded? It can be a disturbing event – change everything you thought you knew. I know it did for your parents. They did very well, considering.

Surely she doesn't mean …? I can't be sure.

In kinder news, the flowers in my garden are coming along wonderfully. They remind me of Grandpa in his last spring. He would wander around the garden and try to name each flower that popped up. He couldn't remember most of them, and it broke my heart to watch him struggle. He had always been proud to know their Latin names. For me, the Latin is difficult to remember – such funny words.

She writes about the sunny weather, how it lifts her moods, but the rest of her words are lost to my distracted thoughts.

I toss the pages onto the coffee table. It pains me to imagine Grandpa hobbling around their garden, teeth ground together while he tries to find the drawer in his mind where he's stored the Latin names for flowers. To him this would be a most important task: to be able to identify each individual beauty with a name and description, the season they blossom in, the pollinator they attract, the colour of their petals and shape of their leaves.

I go to the bookshelf and pull out a heavy volume: *The World Encyclopaedia of Flowers*. The pages leave me in rapture. Colours call, just as they call to their chosen pollinator. Flicking through, I repeatedly stop on yellow, my choice of mate a sunny bloom. I could be flicking through memoirs: a scrapbook of lovers past, none free of dilemmas.

I pause to take in their names. The Latin lacks the full story each flower tells, but it does allow them to be kept in order.

The book comes upstairs with me. Men in the Victorian days would choose certain flowers for certain occasions. Flowers allowed them to avoid having to say how they really felt. The men were modern pollinators, second-guessing when and where a flower needed to be delivered in order to manifest another blossoming.

I open the book on a random page. Bee Orchid. I've seen one once, on the coast, with Grandpa and Dad. They were both over the moon, hopping from foot to foot like they themselves were excited bees.

⁂

I open wings and glide an inch above water. Reflected below me are passing clouds and a pair of eyes staring back: mine. Genus *Cygnus*. I'm a swan. Settle on water. Pristine wings fold back to my body like shoulder blades drawn together. Leathery feet move inwards. The rushes are unravelling – candy floss tops wave and part. A hidden swan is revealed. Not yet. My mate's watching. I paddle to him and wrap the white snake of my neck around his sturdy rump. His tail feathers wag and we nestle. Until night falls, and dark blue wraps around my body like velvet. I'm roused. Nearly time. I head to my midnight rendezvous in the rushes. A voice tells me this is natural. It's not true that swans mate for life.

Little do I know my mate is making plans to leave me by moonlight.

I flip back over, knees to chest.

'Promiscuous,' Mum calls into the evening vesper. 'Promiscuous.'

I turn and fly towards the call. It's my name, 'Promiscuous.' Sting of shame.

I stretch out wings but find arms with empty hands searching. I thought in nature females didn't seek sex for pleasure. But a female cow's vaginal muscles contract, same as mine. I consider masturbation: the porcupine and their carefully selected stick: mount it, let it enter, walk forwards, rattle it over stones, feel it vibrate inside.

20

Everything has to end one day. Dad was first, my incomplete child next. Not all cycles can continue. I lie in bed, dreams haunting the outline of my memory.

I think my relationship is ending.

I remember talking with Dad after I decided to leave my last relationship. He told me, 'It's been four years; your cycle of desire is reaching its end. You've had two years of attraction provoked by your brain's natural amphetamine, which prickles infatuation into your limbic system.'

I'd giggled, knowing he meant our groins.

'And then your brain couldn't take it anymore: too much ecstasy playing upon its nerves. So it introduced some replenishing friends: the 'endorphins'.'

'And what do they do?' I was eager to hear I was doing the right thing.

'Endorphins create attachment and dependency. When they come along you find yourself safe from storms.'

'So that's when I settle?' Disappointment.

'Well, that's where you could settle. More likely it's when you'll find your body calling you for another hit of phenylethylamine.'

He didn't tell me what to do. He was responding to my emotional state in his own way: as a naturalist.

I pull myself up to sitting, and stare at the blank wall we never bought a picture for – I was meant to take one.

Being at the end of a relationship feels like standing on a fault line as the earth begins to part. Everything quavering, and I can't decide which side of the line will lead to security. The split grows, and I'm stood on one side with Pete. The other side, with everything else I know, moves away. I forget what exists on that other side – what opportunities, opinions, places – and so I lose the confidence to jump. If I don't jump now, then I never shall. Will my legs then always be shaking? Or will they settle, and this will become normal, the rest forgotten? I've never stood on a fault line as it divides, so I can't say.

I throw off the duvet. Pete left for school hours ago. I heard his footsteps as he crept out of the bedroom – turning the doorknob at an excruciating speed, a squeak a millisecond instead of a single loud one.

Since that day where I sat for hours, feeling life fall from me – slimy and dense, never to evolve – I can't stop replaying the conversations I once had with Dad. I pull my dressing gown from the hook beside the bed, its silky fabric slippery between my fingers; the fabric fondles what I no longer want to have touched.

I'm sorry, Mum, to disappoint you – I know I've abused God's will. I'm sorry, Dad, to disappoint you – I've not partaken in your evolution. I'm sorry Pete, to disappoint you.

I will myself to walk downstairs and start the day.

When I was five, sitting on Dad's knee as he bounced me over the hurdles ('This is the way the lady rides'), I had felt steady, despite the knee-jolting attempts to dissuade me from feeling so. I knew he'd catch me before I fell down the pothole. It's the same with Pete. Pete is the boat on rocky waters that I get to sit within. He's the cosy, sealed vessel that shelters me from the storm. He carries me and, as he does so, I'm relaxed in his cradle. I'm moving calmly to and fro on the sea. I'm floating in the womb.

I flick the kettle on.

These days, Pete's boat feels as if it's trapped in a glass bottle, like one of those ornamental bottles, the ones that hold miniature, replica ships mysteriously caught inside their glass. We're suffocating. If Pete saw that domesticating a wild carrying vessel like a boat would prevent it delivering the goods, then this would be different. Easier.

But I am domesticated, in my silk dressing gown, blinking at the sunlight dappled on our tiled floors as I wait for the kettle to boil. So why do I no longer feel it?

I return upstairs to dress, in the hope that the act will snap me out of my daydreams. I pull a long-sleeved top over my head. Momentum is lost and I pause with it hanging around my neck. I catch a glimpse of myself in the

163

mirror: pale skin loses itself against the white walls, hip bone pushes to break free. My dark hair, still tucked inside the fabric, scratches my shoulders.

I remember being a little girl on Dad's shoulders. He wasn't distressed by my muddy knees tapping against his rough cheeks. We'd walk to the allotment like that, Dad all the while a-whistling. That's where my ad-hoc ecology lessons took place, at the allotment. After meeting me, Pete began to teach biology at home as well as at work. Sometimes the lessons moved into the bedroom, but for a long time they were make-believe: I took the pill from the packet on the bedside table every morning, and my body was left empty, like the clean cup I drank from to swallow the pill down.

Snap out of it. I finish dressing and return to the kettle to make a cup of tea.

Chai. Inhale the spicy aroma; get lost in it. I'm in the streets of India: the smells and noises overcoming me. I submit to being at the mercy of this foreign place. It's good to let go into the unknown, into this life without its points of reference: without Grandpa, without Dad, without Pete.

Yet I can still hear them somewhere, or at least I find myself scouring the throng of people on the street for their heads: Pete's brown curls, Dad's grey. I don't want to be alone.

The smell of freshly mown grass gets me out of the house and back to where I belong. I cycle to the woods on the outskirts of town, with the plan to delve inside and leave everything behind. Instead, my legs stop just outside the fence. The smell of hot pine fills my nostrils and catches me still. Chin points to sky. Delicious scent of sap and dry needles. The birds sing behind the fence: the sound of fun being had. They are having fun because they are free. And those like me live outside their playground.

It seems right to leave the birds to their mysterious whereabouts. They laugh at me as I sit down. The birds cause havoc in shrieks and choruses, overjoyed to be left alone.

I take my shirt off, and my skirt, and lie down in a bed of soft pine, red and brown, to cool down. No shade in my land. My land is human land, and I lie, happy, leaving the wild alone – until passers-by pass by and snigger at, I suppose, my half-dressed self. I don't open my eyes to see. But I realise: I am half-breed. Not in the passion of bird land, but not in the comfort of bricks and mortar. I am the feral woman, misplaced, waiting to be delivered to which family: Dad's nature, or Mum's culture.

I text Pete to tell him to come meet me on my land after work. He asks, 'Where exactly?'

Pete shocks me out of my skin when he arrives. My ears only detect his footsteps when he is right behind my crouched body. Did I detect his body heat or his footsteps first? I spin to face him, camera still clasped in hands, and as if by reflex, I shoot. Another picture, of Pete's face, confused at his paparazzi greeting.

'Don't you think you should put some clothes on?' He sounds pissed off and looks my body over as if it were a dirty dog's. He can't stand to look any longer, so his eyes dart the strip of my land until he spies the heap of my clothes. He scoops the clothes up and throws them at me.

'Hey, thanks for coming to meet me.'

'I didn't know where to park.'

I look up and down the road. There are no lay-bys in view. 'I didn't think of that.' My bicycle leans against the fence, its red frame complementing the bark of the pine behind it.

'What's up, Sophia?' Pete can't do spontaneity. In nervousness, his fingers grip his hips – otherwise they'd be running through his hair.

'I thought you might like to hang out with me in this beautiful place?'

'Hang out? That's all you thought?' He brushes his trousers to sit down. 'I thought something awful had happened.' He relaxes once he sits down, takes one of my hands in his, and grips that instead.

'Sophia, I wanted to ask …' He stops.

'What?' I say, half worried, half excited.

'Have you thought any more about us trying for another baby? I didn't want to have to ask again, but I need to know.'

'I have, sort of.'

'What do you mean, sort of?' His face hardens, every muscle taut.

'I mean sort of. Not directly.' I feel dizzy: too much sun. A pressure rises in my temple. My heart beats fast.

'I need a bit more than that, Sophia. I need to understand what's going on. As far as I knew nothing had changed, but something clearly has. I'm not an idiot.' Beads of sweat roll down Pete's temple. Anger. Heat. Passion?

'I don't want anything to change. Enough has changed. But—'

'But what?'

My eyes meet his, and his soften. Muscles relax around his jaw, his nose, his forehead. And I want to nestle into him, be enveloped in his relaxed body. I lean against him. He lets go of my hand and strokes my hair, begins to plait it.

'But I'm not sure I can return to how things were. Maybe I should stay with Mum for a bit, until I know what I want,' I say.

'Don't be ridiculous; you hate your mother.' Pete presses his mouth to my head and his breathing, hot and cold, reaches my scalp.

'I don't hate Mum,' I recoil, a moment delayed.

However much I don't want the world to fall out of kilter – something else removed from my solar system – I know something's got to change.

21

Mum and I stare at one another across her kitchen table. She hasn't asked why the unexpected visit – she never would.

She fiddles with the cork placemats. I plait and un-plait my hair. I haven't mentioned the possibility of staying a night, or more. The air is fractious, as if a rainstorm could break out any minute – but it's the inside whose pressure is rising.

'Well, thanks for the tea.' I push my chair back.

'Want another one?' Mum asks.

She refills the china cups before I answer. Her face turns a shade of calm, but the air around her remains stuffy with something unsaid. I take up my cup again and lean back in an attempt to shift the weather of the room to a gentle breeze. The liquid tastes thick when it meets my mouth, and I struggle to swallow.

She starts, 'Sophia, remember when you were little?'

'Which part?'

'When you were very little, say before you were two; when the vicar came to the house for weekly visits.'

'I highly doubt it. You surely can't expect me to remember when I was two?'

'You're right; surely you wouldn't.'

'Mum, are you okay?' Fear sends a chill through me, the weather is cold, something is up, Mum is ill too, both her and Dad will be gone, Grandma is dead. Something awful has happened. A shock as each thought chokes me.

'Yes, yes, I'm fine. I was just thinking about those days, that's all.'

'That's all?' My lips quiver. I can't live in this world, where loss hurts so much, where love leads to dependency and where those depended upon might leave any day. Where we are not adaptable, and we cannot accept these pains. No one can live this way.

'That's all.' She returns to fiddling with the placemats.

I drink my tea quickly, stand and say, 'I'd better get going. Maybe we'll have dinner soon?'

'That would be nice.' Her voice is sombre, she knows it won't happen.

'Take care, Mum.'

She rises to give me a hug and knocks her saucer off with the movement. It smashes on the floor. I go to pick it up, but she grabs my sleeve. 'Sophia—' and then she lets go. I look into h   · their grey irises go cold again.

I pick up the pieces of the saucer and take them with me to the car, not able to stay any longer. My overnight bag sits on the back seat, my camera beside it. Back to Cranston we'll go, to see what new angle we can catch on that.

22

'Close your eyes,' directs Joe.

We lie on the grass in the sunny spot behind the bike shop; only it's no longer a spot – the whole grassy bank is lit up. The sun travels high, rearing up as summer takes over the reins.

Spring flew by with the swallows and swifts. I want to embrace everything before it passes. This summer I will pull weeds by their roots and make space for new plants to grow. And I will let go of what doesn't survive – for you always sow more than what comes.

I close my eyes.

'Can you hear that bird?' Joe whispers. 'No, don't open your eyes; you can hear it better with eyes closed.'

We lie in silence and listen to the chatter of a bird in a nearby tree.

'Thrush.' Its song is a stuttered laugh.

'Good job,' Joe says.

The song is of someone with high spirits. 'Has Isabelle gone away again?'

'Yeah, she left last week. It happens every year. As summer nears, her migrations last longer.'

My stomach sinks, like an elevator dropping from a magnificent view to ground zero. 'When will she be back?'

'Not sure. She's returned to the rewilding project at the Wash.'

'Say hello from me when you two next speak will you?'

'I will.'

We lapse into another silence. Around us, the music of the natural world continues: creaks as branches rub shoulders, rustles of leaf against leaf, chirps as other birds join the thrush in its song – as if he'd sang, 'Come on everybody, use all your vocal chords; let yourself go and sing'.

I roll onto my stomach and open my eyes. A dog rose grows along the wall of the bike shop; I've never noticed it before. Delicate pale pink pretties, sensitive and modest in comparison to their heavy bodied relatives. Still, they grow from a bed of thorns.

As a flower I'd have learnt to be wary: full of spikes and poisons to repel any but the right animal. I'm not. Because I don't know what 'right' is. I remember Grandpa's story of the monk, of the dances of life. I hear him say again, 'Sometimes you must adapt your dance.' He used to say, 'You'll know what to do; the rhythm will take your feet.'

SUMMER

23

My muscles are relaxed, warmed through by the sun, which is high in the sky. Today is the summer solstice. In this hemisphere, the sun's the highest it will go all year. The North Pole bows its head to our star, who kisses their crown, and will do so all day long. The South Pole, behind the scenes, curtained in darkness, awaits their turn. For them it's winter solstice.

This is a game of parenting: learn to trust that your provider will return. This is a game of life: learn that after darkness comes light.

Today, this hemisphere has the longest to consider things in the light of day. Expect enlightenments. Expect epiphanies. Change what you must before the sun begins to leave.

My shoulders rotate without their usual click of cartilage. Knees bend with ease. Chest opens, confident to receive any punch.

The river was a short cycle to meet. My legs hang over the bank, and my feet tickle the water, making it shudder and shake in response. The river Waveney. I drew a straight line on the map – Cranston to river, smallest distance possible – and cycled a wayward journey. Water has an ability to play with light, and I wanted to see what images it threw on this day.

Hands cupped, I lean down and gather some of the river to pour over the wounds of my journey: stings from nettles, scratches from twigs. The road less travelled contains unknown pains and pleasures.

River plus light creates a mirror reflecting the scenery around. Below me is an underworld: trees reach downward, branches sway. The few clouds that pass above, pass below. The image is as well defined as any photograph I could take. Nature's done my work. My body twitches at the possibility of a swim in this underwater forest. What a miracle – to travel like a bird – to sweep arms through sky and explore the highest canopy.

One summer I swam in phosphorescence on a Cornish beach. The water was silky that night, and as I dove under my eyes opened to the dots of light, I forgot I was swimming and believed I was in flight. Coming up for air was no longer a priority. I was in air, travelling through a starry sky. Pete had called me back to land; I was swimming too far out, he said. I returned so as not to upset him.

My fingers rest on loose stones that have broken away from the river edge. I choose a stone to throw, a round flat one, and skim it across the water. The underworld wavers. Ripples draw lines across the scene. The forest separates into individual trees. This won't last long. When individuals rub against one another they must learn to work together and become a community. This is the same with human organs, or plant organelles. They don't automatically work together. At first it's a battle, with each stating their needs above the others'. But soon they find their place, and peace is found.

I am a social animal; we fight conflicts to create peace, to survive.

We are also born to adapt, to find what opportunities are to be found. When at battle it can be wise to have back-ups. Grandpa told me an ancient Tibetan would be wedded to two or three brothers, in case one was lost at war.

I lower my body over the riverbank and dunk my legs into the water. The reflection is disturbed, and a rocky riverbed revealed. Disappointment. This is the difference between the world of reflection and the real: the reflection is a two-dimensional image: a very realistic one, but never quite the same.

I push myself back to sitting and wait to see if trees return alone or as a forest. If this year, at Minsmere, a herd of roe deer return, then a harem will be formed. If only a single roe deer returns, she will settle with one mate. The underwater forest returns – one giant forest – no ripples to form smaller pairings.

Perhaps the human story is the same as the deer. Mum believes it's not our environment that dictates us, but our morals. But what if our morals clash with our natural response to disaster?

Beside me are patches of plantain. The end of each stem fattens, and white flecks of seeds grow in a circle around these heads. The grasses look like tiny phalluses, waving in the wind. I picture a Lily flower next to these phallic grasses. Lily. I picture her as blonde, her hair tucked under a neat hairband. She wears tea dresses and smells like peaches. A gorilla might have a harem of women, but he'd be equally faithful to everyone.

I pick up my camera and point it at the water. No flash, or the forest will burn under a blaze of light. Water is difficult to capture, never as magical in print as the original. My favourite images make the ordinary obscure. This time the ordinary is obscure, and if I take the photograph, I'll ruin the real picture. I place my camera back on the grass.

24

The sun has stayed out all week. Pete waits at the school gates, his hands in his pockets. He faces the ground, trying to avoid questions from parents on how their children can revise better. He hates this time of year, when his students are concerned about passing their A level exams rather than understanding the facts.

'Tough day?' I take one of his hands from its pocket.

'Not too bad. Fancy coming in for a coffee? I've got a proposition for you.'

The last time Pete had a proposition was over two years ago, when he got down on one knee at Pendennis Point in Falmouth and asked if I'd marry him.

'Nothing scary I hope.'

'Nothing to worry about.'

We walk through the playground and into the school building. Pete's broad shoulders lead the way down the corridor to the staff kitchen. He's well built. We were built for alternative roles: each to collect different foods and together create a balanced diet. We were built to stick together. If Pete were far bigger than me, taller, like Joe, he'd be built for a harem lifestyle. He'd be able to keep watch on his females. Joe's sharp canine teeth come to mind; they stick out each time he smiles and I want to run my tongue over them, test their ends. He's ready to compete and maintain access to his multiple females. However, if Isabelle lived in proximity to Joe's other partners, their fertility would synchronise, and Joe would be forced into monogamy anyway, like a toad, whose females all lay their eggs in one week. There's not time for everyone.

Pete opens the door to the kitchen. The room's depressing. Uniform grey walls and plastic seats. He fills the kettle.

The kettle boils. Pete says, 'I've been speaking to some people in the office, and I've formulated a great opportunity.'

He spoons granules of instant coffee into two mugs and pours the kettle. He hands me a mug with 'Live for the weekend!' written on it, and says, 'In a couple of weeks, the students return from exams for a taste of next year's work.'

'Poor kids.'

Pete shrugs. 'Anyway, the photography teacher didn't think about this and booked a holiday. She's away for the last day of school, and you're going to substitute.' He holds his mug between both hands, official.

'You organised this without talking to me first?'

Pete takes one hand off his mug and runs it through his hair.

'Sorry,' I say.

'I told the head you spend most of your time on photography field trips.' His eyes twinkle.

'Okay, I just—'

'Don't worry, Sophia, you'll be fine.'

25

I unlock the front door to our house and let us in. Pete's in a good mood. He hums a catchy tune. In the living room he puts one hand on the back of my neck and pulls me to him, as if a mother collecting her children by the scruff when they venture off. He plants his mouth on mine, and I kiss him back, if only to shut up the tune which is now in my head.

The kiss is wet and open, his tongue searching. His hand finds its way between my legs, and brushes under my skirt. A shock runs up my spine, taking me by surprise. I succumb. He walks me backward to the couch and I sit down. He bends to follow me, his mouth still attached to mine and his hand grasped around my thigh, close to my knickers. I pull my head back and break the kiss, Pete begins to kiss my neck. Relax. I am not a vegetable plot needing to be rotated: potatoes last year, something else this year.

His fingers stroke my body. I wish for any tension the summer hasn't yet released to give way. He kisses my shoulders, my chest. He lifts my dress and kisses my belly.

His mouth is near my crotch. I close my eyes. My knickers come off. He kisses my thighs. His tongue arrives, strong and thick, licking the length of my vulva. He licks circles around my clitoris, then strokes back and forth as if stroking a dog's coat. I feel a pressure as I am sucked and tickled by lips smooth and muscular. My chemical body churns, but I can't relax. I'm too aware of what part of me is touching what part of Pete.

My dress peels over my head. I am a fruit shed of my skin. This is my chosen partner. I want this to work. Get closer to my seeds. Enter my juicy body and find what delicious goods lie within. Pete's body presses against mine. He twists me to lying, one hand on the small of my back. He pulls my hair from beneath me and drapes it over the sofa arm. I spread my legs, let his body fall between them.

He enters me, and thrusts fast right away. I stroke his hair, for me as much as him. He reaches climax quickly; it's been a while. He's been storing up. He crumples on top of me, all the strength and power deflated in a moment.

26

On the Monday of Pete's last week of school, I offer to walk him in. I push my bicycle between us. Whenever Pete tries to place his hand over mine on the handlebar, his shin gets knocked by the pedal, and he pulls it back. He has a lunchtime meeting with Lily. It's their last one. They're checking over the part of her thesis they've been working on together. Last week she brought him chocolates as a thank you. I ate the first three. They were my favourites: strawberry liqueur.

'I was thinking that I might visit my parents for a week when school's out. Do you fancy coming?'

Pete's parents live in Sheffield. His mother is a retired primary school teacher whose ever-doting manner makes me feel ill at ease. Pete's father runs a small car garage. His lungs are full of exhaust fumes and cigarette smoke, and his voice has taken on an ancient rasp, yet somehow he's stayed in perfect health. I imagine Pete's father at work. He sits and wheezes while directing his younger, male employees on what to do. He corrects their mistakes from afar and opens his eyes aghast when one of them doesn't put something back in its correct place.

'I'm enjoying the idea of a Suffolk summer,' I say.

'I thought it might be nice to get away.'

Pete knows his family and I don't get on all that well. He goes home every summer and I'm certain he secretly likes to go alone. Alone he can be spoilt and back-patted without my cynicism getting in the way.

'Sorry, Pete, I will if you want me to.'

'No, it's okay. We can enjoy the rest of the holidays together. We could go abroad if you want?'

'Sounds good.'

When we reach the bike shop, I stop pushing my bike.

'Where are you going?' Pete asks.

'I'm meeting Joe for tea.'

'Oh. See you later?'

'See you later.'

Pete continues down the lane. I lean my bike against the front of the building. When I enter the shop, Joe stands tall in front of me. 'Ready?'

'For what?'

'For our walk.' He steps past, back outside.

My skirt swoops around my knees as I follow. 'Where to?'

Joe heads around the side of the building where a cluster of old bike frames lean against the fence. He tugs on a bicycle matted into the bunch, pedals caught between spokes. 'Thought we could cycle to my favourite woods, if you're up for it?'

'Sure.'

He stops tugging and takes a gentler approach, teasing the pedal of the front bike out. 'It's like that game Tetris,' he says. 'Each bike connects to the other, and before you know it you have a web of bicycles holding one another up. Great – until you need to get one out from the middle.'

'Just looks like a mess to me.'

Joe laughs and steps back. The front bike falls free: a vintage green frame with a white saddle. 'Guess I'll take this one then.' He rolls the bike to the front of the shop and hoists his leg over the cross bar.

We speed down the lane and pass a group of middle-aged joggers in Lycra. Joe waves and they wish us a nice cycle. We weave between a group of children playing football in the middle of the road. Joe says, 'Hey.' They smile and bounce the ball on the spot until we pass. A couple are sat on a bench with coffees in hands – they say, 'Cheers,' to us, lift their cups up and watch us go.

We cycle out of town and along a road I don't remember ever taking. A sharp left and we're on a dirt track. Left again, and we're off our bikes and entering a small woodland.

'Follow me; this is my favourite bit,' Joe says. We lay our bikes on their sides and climb a slope to a clearing. 'From here, you can pretend you're in a giant forest.'

It's true. From the clearing no tracks can be seen. Joe sits close to my feet. I join him on the floor.

'I have a terrible sense of direction,' I say. 'One winter I was in Devon visiting my grandma, and Dad sent me to collect firewood. It started snowing, and I was busy watching the snow fall so wasn't thinking where I was going. When I looked around, I was disorientated – all familiar markings were covered in white.'

'It's mad how surroundings become unrecognisable when the weather changes,' Joe says.

I can't bring myself to make eye contact with him. To make eye contact would be to acknowledge familiar markings have been left behind and I'm in deep. 'I'm not very good at knowing which direction to take, even when it's not snowing.' My hand finds a leaf, and I tear it up, eyes focused on the task.

'Don't be silly,' Joe says, and he gives me a little push. I push him back and he forward rolls away. I roll after him, and we race one another like this, until our bodies bump together and we tumble to a stop, snorting and gasping for air between laughs.

'Look at the branches of that tree.' Joe points upwards and we rest on our backs to admire a fan of beech leaves overhead. 'I love how the young branches stem from the bigger branches, which stem from the trunk, which stems from the roots. And they all feed from everything around and share their food with one another.'

He drops his hand down, and it falls on top of mine. He does nothing to move it. I move onto my front. My hand moves with me and starts to fondle some moss.

'All these trees start as small as this,' Joe says, rolling to fondle his own patch of moss.

I rest my chin to the floor and close my eyes. 'It's hard to imagine something so small can grow to be part of a massive forest.'

'It's already part of the massive forest.' The sound of his words is close. I can hear the air that carries them. My body shuffles towards the words and my nose nestles into knitted jumper. I inhale the warmth of his body, before heading up for air. The hairs on his neck bristle my cheek. Fingers run through my hair. I follow sound. My breath: centred. His breath: close. Leaves: above. Moss rubbing trousers: below. My lips come into contact with his mouth, un-searched for. I bite one hot lip, slide my tongue along the smooth skin that homes all this rising blood.

Facing our front door, I tidy my hair into a ponytail. A couple of twigs fall to the ground.

From behind, an arm snakes around my waist.

'Hey,' Pete says.

My hands dart away from my hair.

'Sorry, did I scare you?

'Not at all.'

'Did you have a good afternoon?' he says.

'Yeah, I'm knackered though. I was going to take a nap.'

'Mind if I join you?' Pete steps ahead and lets us in.

'How was your day?' I ask, hesitant to follow his lead to the bedroom.

'Good. Lily's done an amazing job. I reckon it's publishable.'

He lies down on the bed and I don't know what to do other than follow suit.

'That's exciting.' My stomach stirs. She's intelligent, ambitious, capable. Am I jealous? Scared? It's too late. What would I rather? That Pete was one of those worms who seal their mate up after copulation, so no one else can enter.

Pete says, 'Lily asked if I can help her on the next section too. What do you think?'

'What do I think?'

'It's not too awkward for you is it, us meeting?'

'Not at all. It's good you can help each other out.'

Pete's been stroking my arm, now he stops and puts his hand to his face. What's happened?

A lump gathers in my throat. I turn and stare at Pete. His eyes are closed; he could be thinking of Lily, picturing her face, her body. A pied flycatcher would fly three and a half kilometres away from his home to build a new nest where he can't be caught. We haven't been that clever.

I close my eyes and picture Joe, his calves, his shoulder blades dense with muscles.

We could all be dung flies. And these two males will struggle to possess me, and I'll be pushed further and further into the dung, until I drown in shit.

Pete's breathing has slowed down: he's fallen asleep.

27

It's the last day of school and the students appear puzzled by why it doesn't feel as significant as they believed it would. They lean against the walls of the photography classroom and twiddle their thumbs. They are twitchy, on edge, as though any second a momentous sense of adulthood is going to creep over them. Nothing happens.

This is my chance to have a role, a purpose. I attempt to build a vivid nostalgia around the smell of the darkroom chemicals and the shine of red lights. The students look as if they're nodding off. I bring out some pinhole cameras, prepared at home, and say we're going to use these to photograph one another and make a montage of faces to mark the end of year. The kids are reluctant. They hold the cardboard boxes in front of each other with flaccid arms, no enthusiasm mustered for composition. They're aware they'll be seeing one another around town for the rest of the summer. Don't get soppy too soon.

What the kids are eager for is change. A chance to leave Cranston and explore elsewhere. I admit to myself I feel the same. A girl rolls a cigarette with her back turned to me, as if I won't notice. A boy lifts his camera, uncovers the flap taped on for a shutter, and closes it again. The pinhole was pointed at the floor. 'Miss, I'm done,' he says. I don't bother to pull him up on it, instead I usher him to the darkroom and ask him to develop the image.

A girl with bleached hair and a hoody touches up her friend's makeup before pointing the camera. 'That's better, now pout a little more,' she dictates.

None of us recognise how lucky we are. We could never be this blasé if we weren't secure. These children long to climb on a wobbly bus in Thailand rather than eat Mum's lasagne. We're all doomed: eyes peeled for something more than what we know. One girl re-adjusts her bra and a boy picks his nose. I'm putting too much on them.

The students find their rhythm. Several head back out of the darkroom to take another shot. I poke my head in to see how the others are getting on. To my surprise, once out of daylight and hidden from sight, the chatter and flirtations have died down. The darkroom is full of silent concentration. This is how it was for me as a student. Some plants like to develop in the dark.

The students trickle back into the classroom, and when the last student returns I ask whether everyone is finished. Most students have found themselves a seat and are playing on their phones. 'I take that as a yes,' I say. They nod without looking up. 'Then if you can all go and collect your pictures from the drying rack please,' I say, confidence feigned in a loud voice.

The students groan and chairs squeak across the floor. The students slump their shoulders and head into the darkroom. One by one they return with an image clasped in their hands. They roll their eyes, but each student is smiling, and I can tell they're chuffed with what they've produced.

I hand out rolls of Sellotape and ask them to stick their photograph wherever they please on the classroom walls.

'Miss, who's going to see them? Won't the cleaner just rip them down?' One boy asks.

I cringe at the formal address. 'We'll see them now.' I cross my arms.

The kids follow my directions but scrunch their eyes at me as though I'd spoken Dutch.

I tape the last photo onto the wall: my face. We stand back to observe our work. It's haunting: thirty-two pairs of eyes stare at us, all with an expression of boredom and submission. I blush; this isn't much of a celebration.

'It's quite cool, miss,' one girl pipes up. 'It's like we've already moved on and this is our past staring back.'

Everyone cheers, pleased to finally get a sign that things have changed.

※ ※

I am a female bird, the colours of my feathers changing with every flap. Relief drips down my flank. The responsibility of attracting others is no longer mine. Tails of different patterns and sizes dance around me, mesmerising my suitors. I duck and dive, suffocate in the sexual energy as bottoms wave in my face. I burst free and fly alone. Gasp in the glorious sunny sense of independence. Inevitability. It is my choice, not theirs. One will be chosen.

28

Conscious thought breaks through, until the surreal becomes ridiculous. How can a human have wings? I am not a bird. I am a dreamer. I wake drowning in a sense of mixed-up self. It seeps around my insides, bubbles, nauseates and fills, until my lungs are itching. I can't breathe. I mentally attempt to mop up the sensations. Pull yourself together. But the mop is drenched. Frustration splashes for help. Neediness capsizes. I'm going under. Restless desire comes up for air. Must get out, must get out.

Pete left for his parents' yesterday. He can't reason with me from afar. Nothing can be done but to get outdoors and see what unfolds. Get out, Sophia, get out.

I don't dress but run downstairs in my underwear. I grab my trench coat off the hook by the back door. I yearn for Dad's sheepskin coat. The sheepskin would be soft on my shoulders, but it's too late in the year, and I left that behind with Mum. I close the door and walk. Long strides trip over one another in heat, pace and desperation to escape.

Following feelings means walking fast; a faltered step makes room for a faltered thought. I keep legs moving in the hope that they know the direction they want to go. When body fails, mind directs. When mind fails, body directs. Fails. Mum's word. Mum's sharp tongue, telling me right from wrong. I'll no longer photograph in black and white – as attractive as it is – accentuating features and making the world more defined. It's not the way it goes. Life is full colour: vibrant, mixed up, conflicting.

My legs lead me to the bike shop. My mind only half surprised. My heart thumps.

Hands stuffed in pockets, I walk up to the door. A wired, wide-eyed reflection stares back. The door doesn't budge. Its 8 a.m., nobody's here. I slump against the glass. What an idiot. My head falls into my hands and I try to massage sense back.

The neighbours are probably watching. I don't care. Willowy woman has gone mad. Willowy woman sits in nothing but trench coat at 8 a.m. waiting to be repaired by bicycle mechanics.

'Sophia?' Joe's voice wakes me. His hand grips my upper arm. 'You okay?'

I open my eyes. The other two men from the shop stand behind him. They pat him on the back and give silent nods of understanding. They squeeze past, unlock the door and head inside. One of the men catches my eye as he passes. His smile is soft and kind. He pities me. He shouldn't.

'Yes. I'm fine.'

Joe pulls me by the arm to standing. His eyes are alive but their edges wrinkle in concern. He keeps hold of my arm as if I were a dead rabbit and he were carrying my limp body.

I spark up, come back to life. 'In fact I'm great.'

His eyes run over me, as if I were a bicycle. Have I arrived at my destination or broken down? 'It's good to see you,' he says when he's finished the examination.

'Have you got your car?' I ask, 'Can we go for a drive?' My body buzzes, it needs to move.

We park the car at the entrance to Bradfield woods. Joe opens the door for me and a rush of sanity comes with the fresh air. 'Oh shoot, I'm sorry, Joe, you need to get back to work.'

'I'm not going.'

'But—'

'I'm here with you.'

The buzzing of my body rises: an ecstatic plague, here to stay.

We link arms. Our footsteps meet on beats as we walk into the woods. Joe's mouth opens, but before he can speak I grab him by the hand and run. We dodge tree trunks and twist below branches. We brush our shins with foliage and send earth flying. We stop. He holds me by the waist, under a gap in the treetops. He asks me to look up, to concentrate on my favourite branch. He runs his fingers along my collarbones. I exhale loudly and concentrate on a branch of hazel so as not to topple backwards. I am one of my many birds, in flight through dreams. In search to discover which species I am and how my mate will be.

I untie my coat, let it slip past my hips, and step out as though it was Sita's magic circle of safety. The muscles along my thighs tense. Here lies danger.

Joe kneels and skims his hands over my legs – the brushing of hairs sends shivers through my body. I squint for my branch; I'm losing sight. He stands. Our eyes meet. Blue meets green. Land meets sea. Element meets element and explosions occur. My pelvis presses against his. I pull his T-shirt over his head. His chest is brown and nicked with a constellation of scars. I trace the image they make with my lips. I run my fingers along his shoulder blades, down his spine, explore the muscles at the base.

He leans me against the hazel tree whose branch I'd been watching. He rests one hand behind my head on the trunk, his other hand falls around my crotch. I can smell the damp of the bark and now a new damp – animal, musty – the damp of myself falling into his hand, raining around his fingers. I fumble at the buttons on his shorts. His erection makes the fabric taut, my fingers direct it free. His penis spasms, a snake searching a hole. I move my hand over it, feel the heartbeat, learn the shape. Joe teases the elastic of my knickers down. I lift one leg out and prop my foot against my thigh. He nestles his face against mine and inhales deeply as I direct him inside. My knee goes soft. We're on the ground, legs wrapping around one another. My hair tangles in his beard – black of night, yellow of day. We move to the rhythm of a loudening heart beat: mine? An animal by my side, keeping watch? The Earth's core?

My body burns like molten rock and I scream blessings for being pushed out onto this planet.

Joe opens the door on the driver's side and climbs in. We sit in silence and stare out the windscreen at the woods who hold our secret. He starts the engine. A growl. For a moment I think it's Joe. He's a wolf, adding complexity to my environment, but bringing richness: the predator, arrived to solve the abundance of prey clucking like headless chickens in search for belonging. The predator is their belonging.

I surrender. This is real life. This is the wild at play.

Conflict to create peace.

The car moves and Joe reaches his hand over, rests it on my knee, which has scratches from the forest floor. Dad's voice speaks in my head. He tells me of the thrill our ancestors would have had when fighting large mammals. The thrill of over-powering danger and winning survival. 'It can be fun,' Dad says. It was the urge to fight I felt scrabbling at the edges of my subconscious this morning – an imprint from generations ago. I've given in, and it feels good.

Mum's voice speaks, uninvited. 'You've submitted, Sophia. You've lost.' She says intelligence is stronger than muscle flexing. I take Joe's hand and cup it around my inner thigh.

I will not submit to being pest free, predator free, competition free. I see now that I never was.

The car winds down streets, and with every minute passed and every turning made my nervousness amounts. Eden has fallen – it always would – but how can balance be reintroduced?

29

I've always wanted to visit the ruins of a large farmhouse on the outskirts of town, but somehow never made it. There was a rumour in my family that the building was set alight by an angry farmer's wife who thought the farmer spent more time with the animals than he did her. I don't know how the rumour started.

We would pass the ruins when we drove between Cranston and my grandparents' house, before my grandparents moved to Devon. I mentioned the farmhouse to Joe, asked whether he knew the true story. He said he didn't, but suggested we visit – and so we have.

Most of what's left is foundations. Blackened stones dug deep in pale, green grass. Where did the rest of the house go?

Joe traces the outline of the building, taking careful steps upon the stones, one foot in front of the other. I kneel in the centre and follow him with my eyes until he's out of sight, closing the circle behind me. A bump sounds as he hops off the last stone.

'Did you see the old door?' he asks.

'No. Where's that?'

I stand up – my trousers have grass stains on the knees. Joe walks us beyond the foundations, where the grass is longer.

Nestled in the green is an old wooden door, knocker intact. The door looks odd, rested on the ground, with bits of grass sprouting up between the joins.

'A door into the home of Earth,' Joe says, going on all fours to look closer.

'I don't get how the door can survive but all the walls have gone.' I kick some rubble away. 'A house can't disappear into nothing overnight, surely someone knows what happened.' I bend to look closer. 'It's a shame. This must have been a lovely home before it fell apart.' Around me are fields of wheat, which glisten as if the sun were pouring water, not light. The road is beside us, but wouldn't have spoilt the view. The occupants would have seen sunrise from the front of the house, and sunset from the back. It would have been the perfect Suffolk home.

'It is a shame, but this new house isn't so bad. Come, make yourself at home.' Joe knocks the knocker. A chip of wood comes flying off.

'Don't ruin it!' I sit down and shoo his hand away to prevent more damage.

'Do you have your camera?' Joe's eyes light up.

'Of course, why?'

'I have a photo I want to take.'

'Do you know how to use it?'

'I reckon so.' Joe looks cheeky, his freckles showing up from the sun.

'Then help yourself. The camera is in my pannier, but you'll have to get it; I'm too comfortable.'

'That's because you're at home.' Joe jumps up and runs back to the bikes.

I lie down beside the door and search the sky for clouds to make shapes from. A rabbit, a bird, a tree. There aren't many clouds to play with. Summer has come on full heat.

When Joe returns, he has the camera in his hand. He says, 'That's perfect, just as you are.'

'You want to take a photo of me?'

'Yes. I've got an idea.'

I want to roll on my belly and cover my face. I hate having my photograph taken; the perk of being a photographer is to rarely be the model.

'Just imagine this is the door to your home. I'm going to take the photo from above so no one can tell you're lying down.'

It's an idea worth a model. I cross my legs, as if I were leaning casually against the wall of my house and turn my face to profile.

'That's beautiful. Do you mind if I arrange your hair?'

I shrug. The attention feels good. Do the subjects of my photos feel the same?

Joe stoops and lays my hair out as if it were blowing in the wind. 'It looks great. The black of your hair is so stark against the green.'

I hold back a smile.

Joe stands at my feet peering down through the lens. A bird's eye view from his tall stance. The shutter clicks, and he draws the camera away.

'Finished?' I ask, tingling all over. I can imagine the photo: my hair blowing to the side; my tall frame leaning by my door; the door, chipped and worn like the rubble below; the grass, eating me up from behind. I love it.

'Finished.' He puts his hand out to help me up. 'Bits of the grass are blackened too, so it looks like your hair and the grass are joined together.'

'I hadn't noticed.' It's true, the grass beneath my feet is smudged black in places. Perhaps charcoaled by the mystery fire and never regrowing fresh.

30

Joe arranges to collect me from Cranston, and together drive to the boat. I text Pete to say we can speak later. Luckily, Pete's parents have kept him busy fixing things around their house, and we haven't had much chance to speak. My finger twitches as it presses send, almost missing the button.

I get into the car and my hands reach out to touch. I'm starving for intimacy.

It was Dad who told me stress and anxiety repress oestrogen: this explains why if food resources are low, animals won't reproduce. Pete told me how men calm these anxieties down, the same way a candle and a hot bath can.

I slide my hand back and forth along Joe's leg, feeling calmer with each stroke, hormones regulating at last.

Joe strokes the hand stroking him. My hand coos, like a mother with tunnel vision to her new-born child. This is new-born love.

Mum once told me she'd been searching for paradise when she found Dad. But at some point, the tunnel vision must have worn off, because she'd returned to her previous quest.

At the boat, Joe leads me under deck. We're quiet. Relaxed. The stresses of the last year fall away. A vole would attack a visitor on home turf, but take them away from home, from responsibilities, and they'd seduce the stranger instead.

It's not sadness I feel but regret, for not doing this sooner.

Joe scoops me up and lays me on the bed. A porthole to the outside world by my face. Blue sky, blue water. Blue eyes. Inside exists only this moment. At last.

I wake to white. To nothing beyond the arms of my lover and the sheets of our bed. I blink, and droplets glisten between my eyelashes with rainbows bouncing off. I lie disorientated.

Bleary eyes make out the porthole above my head. Droplets waver, swollen on the window pane, my arm stretches out to caress one. The droplet springs down upon my finger and dribbles along my arm. I flatten my palm on the cold glass, and wipe. The droplets slip together, blurring the world behind glass.

I ease myself from Joe's spider grip and press my nose against the window. Moist and cool, like a dew-dressed tent. Exhale. The glass is veiled again.

My blindness gives the sensation of being held – as though I've slipped into a bubble. I'm invisible to the outside world; the outside world's invisible to me. I can rest. The elements pass by but leave me untouched.

Something urges me to wipe the moisture from my breath with my cheek. So I do; shaking my head left to right. A big 'no' to the outside world, painted by my cheeks on the smeared pane.

The veil lifts and reveals the outside world is also covered in mist. Everything is frozen behind thick air. The shadows of the world's previous self, shine through: glimmering edges as sunlight spells shapes of hills and banks that hold the river. The river: it barely exists. I'm no longer on water but in the clouds. A cloud kingdom burns golden, pink and purple. Valleys emerge in the distance. A far-off fortress points its spire from a haze of colours and shapes. Not so much of those either: more like swirling, changing, shifting patterns of light and air – of scenes behind smoke.

'Come, cocoon with me,' murmurs Joe. 'It's not time to get up yet; the world hasn't finished creating.'

I long to fall back into his arms, into the resting to heartbeats and dreams as we, in sleep, ready ourselves for the day. But I can't turn away from the window. Before me is evidence that waking life has been playing a trick: the world is more beautiful when falling apart or coming together. It's more beautiful when incomplete and meaningless.

I tug my leg from Joe's hand and keep my eyes on this forming world. How will it look? Will it be different? I'm hopeful.

Out of the mist come three white figures. They rise and dip, riding an invisible merry-go-round. They hover and bob towards me. They fly. Silent. Without bat of wings: upright bodies levitating through mist.

They are three swans, also curious about this new world. I push the porthole open so as to join them. Joe shivers and pulls the sheets close, losing himself to their white fabric. I lean my head outside. My face tingles as the mist fingers around me, teasing.

The swans turn their heads up and down, trying to make sense of what is what when no sky or river is visible. We are floating. The closest I've been allowed back to floating in Mum's womb. Safe from floods. The ark.

One swan's long neck twists my way. His beady eye fixes on mine. I flinch and withdraw into my nest. But a black figure appears, and I poke my nose back out to see, curiosity getting the better of me. One black cygnet, timid in the mist. Its ancestor's ghosts lead the way. The cygnet, like me, blends in. We're both easing our way out, trying to find our place.

How curious, he and his three elders. I wonder who they are, what relation to him.

Then they glide past, ignoring my face as it peers out. And I let them go – figments of this perhaps imaginary world – and bring myself back inside.

I climb out of bed, leaving Joe in his white cocoon. Pete's at his parents for another day, but I'm overcome with the sense that it's of utmost importance I get home. I never called him last night. My brain feels like a choked engine; it tries again and again to start a clear and confident thought, but stutters. I need to get home.

'Do you have to go?' Joe's voice is muffled.

'I think I should.'

'How're you going to get back? Let me make you breakfast, and I'll drive you in.'

'No, I'll get the bus; I like the journey.'

'When will I next see you?'

'I don't know. Soon, maybe. I need to see how things are.'

'You know you can tell him how you feel, Sophia?'

'It's complicated. We've had a difficult year.'

'You know best. I'm only saying I want you to do what's good for you.'

He makes it sound easy. My forehead throbs.

'I will,' I say.

'I know you will. You're brilliant.'

'Thank you for yesterday,' I unfold the sheets from Joe's face to kiss goodbye.

31

Field Notes

Bear-claw poppy, Arctomecon humilis

A rare species of poppy found in Washington
County, Utah, with only half a dozen
identified populations. Each stem produces
only one or two creamy white flowers with

yellow stamens. The poppies' seed heads carry around thirty seeds. The rare solitary bee is the single pollinator for the bear-claw poppy, which explains the flowers' scarcity.

I swear allegiance to you.

Together we will survive the dry sands of this desert

and show how love can rise above this harsh world.

I am blind to anything

but your erect body shining in the sunlight.

With Pete returned, nothing has changed. He reads while I go on a field trip.

The grassy verge of the roadside curves up to meet the hedgerow; I hop off my bicycle and my boots navigate the new terrain, occasionally slipping upon dewy grass. The hedgerow brims with life. Shades of green overlap one another. Greedy. My head bobs high enough with every step to see over to the other side. I spy a blur of red. A field of poppies.

The hedge is dense. Solidity. Security. Home to thousands. A twiggy shelter for insects, plants and mammals. The hedgerow is their replacement home – a crowded high rise in return for acres and acres of wild forest and meadow that has been ploughed and cultivated. It is not secure enough for the hedgehogs, who walk from it late at night to find their doorstep is a busy road.

Once, Dad came home with a bunch of flamboyant feathers in hand. He plucked one out and offered it to me – long and pointed, a deep red. I poked its end into the French plait Mum had made me that morning (causing tears as she brushed the hair back tight). Dad handed the glorious bunch to Mum, a loving gift that before my eyes transformed itself into a heavy, dull body as she turned it in her hands. It was a pheasant he'd found dead on the road, recently departed. Mum plucked it and cooked it up for us – a gift from heaven. I pursed my lips and wouldn't eat a bite, stubborn to Dad's encouraging eyes.

An opening in the hedge appears: a metal gate with a latch on the far side. I lean over, pull the bolt and swing it open, eager to see the poppies. I walk through the meadowy headland of the field: a luxurious border planted by the farmer to keep original field-residents away from his crop. Not much could be more luxurious than the royal red of the flowers growing here. I wade through the long strands of golden grasses and slender stems of flowers, trying not to step on them. Their delicate red heads bend against my calves and turn to look up at me. At what feels like the centre of the field, I look back over my shoulder. A flood of red bodies.

One year, an old lady came to my primary school, and in return for the fifty pence piece Dad gave me in the morning, she gifted me a paper poppy. I pinned it to my blouse, ripping the fabric as I did so – Mum would be angry.

In this field, the dead face me from all around. The black centres of the flowers call their bloody petals inwards – little death angels pulling life to what lies beyond. I want the petals to fall, for Dad to be free. I long for his body to disintegrate into the ground. I long for the ground to acknowledge blood, soak it up, and have it be gone. I want to let go.

I bend down and let myself be seated in this field: a liminal space between the alive and dead. A bed of remembrance.

I lie back in the flowers, no longer concerned about whether I'm breaking heads or not.

Poppies are one of Britain's rare flowers: Dad told me that. He used to take me to throw the seeds from the dried heads we'd collected from the allotment. We would stand on windy days – me on top of a stile for added height – and throw the seeds up. They'd scatter from us, dusting the ground with an offering of fertility. Dad would say we were doing the job of nature, of the elements, because, 'We are an element of nature ourselves.'

I stare into the opening of a flower close to my face: the crevices, the dark emerald-green pollen, the whorl of stamens, those red petals. I wish I had a macro lens to capture these details before they are gone. In America, there exists a poppy called the Arctomecon poppy. It can only be fertilised by one type of bee. Only one. The poppy knows its perfect partner and sits passively waiting for them to come.

If we hadn't poisoned their ancestors with chemicals sprayed on fields, produced telephone airwaves that interrupted the pollinators' mapped routes, sending them in circles, then the poppies wouldn't be so desperate for their pollinator to arrive.

A bee buzzes its way over my head and gets lost in the field of red. He's hit jackpot. Then again, he might be too full of sugary syrup – fed to him by the beekeeper so he stays a ready producer of honey – for our tummies, not his brood's.

Pete says the honey business depends upon feeding sugar to bees. 'That way the bees don't stray in search of nectar, they can stay at home and produce enough honey to meet their keeper's demand.'

When this is the case, the flowers forget their partners exist, and the bees forget to pine for them – fulfilled instead by sweet, artificial nectar. So, the flowers disappear. The honey tastes sugary. And we all forget.

The memories of our past loves fade.

I think of the intangible web of life Dad had portrayed to me over the kitchen table as he'd warily examined the 'food pyramid' my teacher had given me. 'What an empty piece of hierarchy! So what? You remove one rabbit, and the humans just eat more chickens?' He looked me sincerely in the eyes and said, 'We are not the king of the jungle.'

My philosophising has led me into sleepiness. I check my watch. I need to keep going. I told Pete I was taking photographs and would be home for lunch. He was going to cook soup. He'll be leaning over the stove, inhaling the oily vegetable steam and stirring the pot with our wooden spoon. Since he's been back he's looked happy, and chubby faced. His mother's a feeder. He hasn't suggested our going away together – his nose is deep in Lily's thesis; she's asked him to provide feedback on the whole thing. Pages headed with her name litter our dining table.

I push myself up. Maybe all of us will become extinct, our partners never finding us because they've been distracted by other sugary delights on the way.

I walk towards the gate, the field a little less surreal – full of flowers, not bodies. The sun's risen and the colours are no longer tinged with the fresh light of morning that brings everything to life.

I pause to inhale the fragrance of the field. Nothing. Grandpa once said, 'The only time you'll smell poppies is when they're being harvested.' He was holding my hand as we walked past a stray poppy in the hedgerow. He swung his arm as he went, and so my arm followed. 'When they're harvested the scent rises; it causes a great euphoria for the farmers.' He laughed.

Dad told me Grandpa tried opium from poppies when he was in India. I could never imagine Grandpa high as a kite, flying out of this world and into another. He was a grounded man.

I'll collect the seedheads of these poppies when their time comes. Whether I'll spread their seeds I'm not sure, but I'd like to hold their heads in my hand, no longer bleeding red, and think of Dad.

32

Pete's out, I don't know where. I think we're playing a game: don't ask, don't know. Maybe it's easier that way. An idea strikes me, so I grab my keys and head out the door. I struggle to unlock my bicycle. My fingers shake with excitement and can't direct the key into the keyhole. I shove the keys back into my jeans pocket. I'll walk.

Not everyone would have a partner if we followed Dad's animal world – but humans don't accept celibacy. If we follow Joe's world, the balance of nature doesn't need to be upset. We wouldn't all have babies, we wouldn't all settle down, but we would all get to love.

My strides get longer as I get closer to the bike shop. Ten steps away.

A green dragonfly lands on my arm as I pull the glass door open. Yes, I am a dragonfly, with multiple males, collecting and partaking.

'Joe, can we take a minute?' I say from the door.

'Sure.' Joe's at the back of the shop, boxes of inner tubes in his arms.

The other men keep their eyes with the bicycles they're working on. Joe puts the boxes down on the floor. He picks up his cup of tea and walks ahead of me out the front door.

'I want to take you away for a night,' I say.

'Away?' He looks amused.

'I mean, if you want to?' I haven't considered this at all.

'Sounds great. When do you want to go?'

'Next weekend?'

'Cool.' His face is close to mine; his hair tickles my forehead.

'Okay, see you then,' I say, and hurry away before he can change his mind.

33

Grandpa told a story of when he had visited Ladakh, India. It took him several days to arrive; the road was bumpy and wound through the Himalayas. Grandpa said the road was so bendy you couldn't see around the corner; if another car came the other way, they had to hang halfway off the roadside – which was a steep drop, tumbling down below his window. He said on that road, high in the mountains, he saw little sign of life.

When he arrived, Grandpa discovered the Ladakhi winters were cold, very cold, and no food could grow. Some people died from the cold, and everyone lived off whatever had been scavenged before the snow fell. In the summer it was hot and the landscape arid. All they could grow was lettuce, apricots and barley. This was what they ate all winter too – dried and rehydrated. It was so difficult for the Ladakhi people to grow and store enough food that only a limited number of people survived each winter. For this reason, Grandpa explained, the women had several husbands. Often, they would marry brothers, and they would all live together under the same roof.

This isn't the case anymore. When I looked up Ladakh as an adult, I discovered that these days it's better connected to the West and its resources, which both eases and strains the livelihood of land and villager. I remember first listening to this story of Grandpa's in my childhood bed. He was perched at the bottom, and I held onto the cuddly hare he'd given me for my birthday. Grandpa's eyes were wide as he reached the end of the story: he looked as amazed as I was. He shuffled forward and gave me a kiss goodnight on the nose. I pulled the covers around me as he left the room. That night, I dreamed of cooking lettuce stew for a line of brothers, before running into the snow in my nighty.

Pete puts his newspaper down and looks up. His eyes are glazed, I guess he dropped by the pub on the way home.

'Did you have a good time at the pub?' I ask.

'Yeah, thanks, it was good to see the other teachers relaxed and out of school; shame you missed it.'

'Pete, I—'

'Can you pass me a glass of water?'

'Sure.' I head to the sink and turn the tap on. My hand is surprisingly steady as I fill the glass.

'Thanks.' He takes a sip and places the glass down on the table. His other hand makes as if to pick the paper back up.

'Pete?'

'Yeah?'

'I'm …'

'Come on – you're not the drunk one.' He lets his hand fall back below the table and snorts a little laugh.

'I'm sleeping with Joe.'

My hand moves to my mouth.

Pete's hands form fists, and he places these on the table.

His eyes blink fast.

I've fucked up.

'Is this because of Lily?' he says.

'No, because nothing's happening with you two. Right?'

'No. Nothing's been happening, because I, unlike you, take our vows seriously.' His voice rises.

'I know; I trust you.'

'But you can't trust yourself?'

'That's not true.'

'So I can trust you?' His voice softens. Pete's passionate about science – the scientist can control participating factors. He's hoping this is still the case.

My chest tightens. I don't speak.

'Why are you telling me? Because you feel guilty? Do you want me to tell you how to make it better? Do you want me to tell you it's okay? What are you saying, Sophia? Come on.'

My chest is like a frayed rope about to snap. What falls apart when the rope breaks? Will my whole web of life give in if I lose this one thread?

I head to the nearest window and open it. I take a breath of fresh air. 'I'm saying that I'm sleeping with Joe.'

Pete moves behind me and places his hands on my hips. I jump at the unexpected contact.

'Stay with me,' he says.

I wait until Friday to tell Pete I am going away for a night. When I do, he walks to the bedroom and slams the door.

34

I wake on the sofa with the sound of that door slamming still reverberating in my ears. I fold the blankets I've been sleeping under and place them on the arm of the sofa. Pete isn't up yet. It's best I leave before he is.

Outside, I hook my panniers on my bike rack, straddle my tent on these, and find myself telling Dad I won't be seeing him for a while.

Dad looks me square in the face and says, 'What's happened, Sophia?'

'I have an opportunity to return to the wild, that's all.'

He isn't smiling. He looks the other way. 'That's great, Sophia, but I'm worried about you.'

Worried about me? But this is all by his laws of nature. 'You don't need to worry. I've got this under control.'

35

As we enter the village of Covehithe, the old church looms on my left: a skeleton of walls and arches that have lost their outer shell. The stone is chipped and grey. The window frames a lighter tone. The adjoining new-build is but a shadow of what once was, yet still people gather there and are welcomed inside to (like the church) be born again.

The lane we drove on had been narrow and dusty, the sea nowhere to be seen. I'd suggested we camp at Covehithe. Joe suggested we drive. He pulls his car onto the side. The car dips at an angle as though it might roll, but Joe knows its limits.

The old path to the beach has been claimed by a conservation project – or what is left of the path, that is. The rest has fallen to the sea. We walk a cobbled route instead, carrying our bags in hand. Red admiral butterflies criss-cross ahead of us, like a continuous set of opening and closing doors. With each step we take, the door behind us shuts, pushing us into the future.

The path's too slim to walk side by side so I lead, trusting each door that closes for me will open for Joe. We steer to the left and enter a field. Rows and rows of potatoes: a farmer's field, neighbour to the conservation site. The path ahead is a wider, sandy stretch: a yellow brick road to who knows where.

The sea. Huge and spacious below us.

The coastline isn't gradual. It's a straight ridge of path and an expanse of blue. The world's flat after all. Step off and free fall into air masked as deep water.

Will I be drowning or flying in that blue?

Joe and I walk, arms brushing. The salty air takes my breath away, as does Joe's touch. Poppies and ragwort line the cliff edge, daring to peer down. The cliff is red and gold – earth and sand – the shape of a slide. A smooth 'L' spelt out to the sea from where clifftop has crumbled and slipped. The base of the 'L' is flat stone: layers of decay, red, like rust, with puddles of darker brown where it has been worn by the sea as water encroaches upon land and shapes human territory.

We reach a small woodland, mostly sycamore, and to my right I see yet more land succumbing to the climate. Trees have fallen on their sides, torn out by wind and wave. Roots hang limp from red rock – black and peeling from sunburn, with a new skin exposed beneath. Without a parent plant to hold, the roots wave and dangle in air, searching for what they've lost. The fallen trees lie upon the white sand, their trunks made driftwood by the endless rolling tide. Their bark has been stripped and smoothed, and veins can be seen where branches have broken off – rings of years passed, ready to be counted.

A group of walkers wander between these fallen trees. They don't stop to pay respect, as though it's a normal phenomenon to walk among the dead. I guess every day we walk with the memory of someone gone.

One fallen tree has a flurry of roots knotted and wound around its base, like a giant nest. Maybe new life will come and roost.

Another trunk has had every ligament torn out. The stump's shaped like a star – roots divided and broken. The stump has no arms to reach up to heaven with, or legs to ground in nature, only a yonic hole in the middle with folds of wood curved around like soft cushioning. Some pebbles are lodged in the opening, finding home where life began.

The woods take Joe and me down to this white beach. Pebbles have been scattered by the sea. Grey, amber, white. The sea's calm and flat. Little terns bob atop, their fine pointed beaks shriek into the sky.

So many photographs to be taken. I don't begin to take them.

Behind us is Benacre nature reserve: wetlands rolling backward from the coast to another set of woods behind. The wetlands look foreign against the white sand and the woodland we walked through – all three complete ecosystems in themselves. The reserve at a distance is a blur of long, wet grasses and clusters of white birds. The birds might be little terns, avocets, or one of the new arrivals: egrets. These birds, although protected, aren't safe yet. Dad used to take me to Benacre.

The wetlands are barbed off to leave some of nature to reconstitute. Mum would say it's our duty to protect these birds; we are their guardians. Dad would say the change needs to be bigger than conservation sites, that unless we make big changes, both nature and civilisation are headed to fall apart.

Joe's walking towards the small bird-watching hut, a slatted shed with a sloping roof and skinny windows to poke binoculars through. The hut stands on four long legs, disguised as trees. Joe climbs the hut steps to become a bird, in a tree, watching fellow birds. To gain some perspective. Look what we've done.

I glance back at the sea. The terns rule the waters, floating and calling together from where I can't go. I catch up to Joe.

From the hut we watch the sun slip away. We haven't said a word to one another. Together, we don't need to call out any more.

'Our bed for the night?' I touch the bench beneath me.

'That's what I was thinking.'

We unload our bags in the corner. No one's about, no twitchers today, only us, twitching with excitement for our new landing spot – a place we've been blown, or else flown, to.

36

It was the glow-worms who had led our way back to the hut. Once the summer sun had exhausted itself, the worm's bellies shone a luminous green amid the reeds, signalling the direction for mates to follow. We bent to look closer. Joe picked one worm up and held it in the curve of his palm. I tried to photograph it, knowing all that would transpire would be a white squiggle on black.

After making love we agreed to sleep in our separate bags – the bench too thin for both. Now I want for touch again.

'Good morning.' I slide myself into Joe's sleeping bag.

'Good morning. I was deep in a dream,' Joe says, unzipping his sleeping bag to make more room.

'What was it?'

'You were with me at the Wash, and I was showing you around the Rewild Norfolk site.'

'Sounds nice.'

'It gave me an idea.'

'Yeah?' I'm dreamy, blown on shore, wondering where Joe's taken me and whether I'll remember my way back.

'I think I have some work for you.'

Work. That wasn't where my mind was.

'Rewild Norfolk needs support. We need to promote ourselves, spruce up the website, create pamphlets – make the project look as good as it is. Maybe your photography is just the trick.' His eyes brighten.

'You haven't seen my photography.'

'I know you're good. I just know it.'

'What if I don't want to share my photos?'

Joe doesn't listen, he continues, 'You could join Isabelle at the volunteer site. She's going to stay on for the autumn; I spoke to her the other day.'

I prickle at her name. 'Do they want someone, or is this your idea to get rid of me?'

'They, and I, want you.' He nuzzles my back. His beard scratches against my skin.

The sleeping bag is too tight. I struggle to roll around to face him. He has his eyes closed.

'I can come and visit. You can go for as long as you want. You're free, Sophia,' he says.

As long as I want. I hadn't considered leaving. Last night I left. Yes.

'You'll visit?'

'Definitely.' He runs his fingers through my hair, twists a bunch around his index finger and lets it slip, loop by loop.

'Okay. Yes.'

When I return to Cranston and turn my phone on, a number of messages from Pete are waiting. The first says he misses me, the second that maybe we can make this work. Another message reads, 'Fine, you can do what you want', and the last says to please come home.

37

I stretch out on the cream carpet by our sofa. Pete sits on the armchair and leans forwards, staring down at me.

'Sophia?'

'Yes?'

'What're you doing?'

'Trying to find a relaxing position.'

I'll be leaving in a week. The thought alone makes my shoulders ache. My neck is tight. I haven't told Mum I'm going.

Pete moves from the sofa to lie on the carpet next to me. 'You remember Lily?' he says.

'Yes.' I'd found the perfect position but now my leg hurts. I take my foot in my hand and straighten the leg towards the ceiling.

'She called yesterday. She told me she'd handed in the chapter of her PhD we'd been working on, and her supervisor wants to submit it as an article for a journal.'

I breathe out, tension relieved as if the conversation were a yoga class. 'That's great. Wow, congratulations!' Pause. More's to come. I sense him hold his breath. He's still holding a pose. 'So, does she need to work with you some more?'

Still no exhale.

Release god damn it. The pose is over. Time's up. Time is up.

'We're having a meeting to discuss it. But what I wanted to say is I'm going to ask if we can make it a kind of date too.'

Breathe out. Long, drawn, shaky.

A new tension forms, this time in my stomach.

I open my eyes, expecting to see Pete's face scrunched and pained, the way he looks when he can't finish the crossword. His face is peaceful, a smile forming a boat – smooth sailing.

I want to start another conversation but find none. 'Are you trying to stop me leaving, Pete?'

'No,' he says. 'I just thought you should know.'

'Good, because I'm leaving.'

'I'd better go phone Lily.' Pete stands abruptly, knocking the TV remote from the chair arm. He doesn't attempt to pick it up.

The phone rings before he reaches it. He turns back and looks at me, both of us hesitant. Do we want to know who's calling the other? Pete lifts the receiver, says a hello and smiles. He makes a joke I can't hear and holds the phone out to me so I have to stand to retrieve it. When I take the phone, he walks away without looking back.

'Sophia, your grandma tells me you're going away.'

I bite my nails at the sound of Mum's voice. 'Only for a little bit, Mum. It's no big deal.'

'I hope everything's alright.'

'It's fine, Mum, don't worry. I've been offered some work.'

'I've been wanting to tell you something.' She clears her throat. 'I'd been waiting until I next saw you, but you've not been in touch. And now you're going.'

I wait through an awkward silence. Nothing she will say can affect me. I'm done with her holy propaganda.

'You once had a sibling.'

I choke on a non-existent mouthful.

'But I lost them.'

I can't speak. Mum stays very quiet. The line could have cut out and I wouldn't know.

I wish Pete were in the room, someone to hold my hand. I'm dizzy. 'What do you mean, 'lost'?'

'Lost – like you lost your child.' She sniffs, an uncomfortable sound of mucus and emotion. 'I never told you, because I felt I'd let you down.'

The word 'lost' loops in my mind. Hearing someone other than me say it is much worse. 'It wasn't your fault, Mum,' I say. The words send a rush of calm over me.

'Perhaps not.'

Why tell me today? I suppress a rising shout, which turns into a sob.

'Was it a brother or sister?' I ask, not sure why.

She clears her throat again. 'Does it matter?'

Siblings are closer genetically than any other family member. Would this make it more difficult than losing a dad, than losing my own baby?

Anger pounds. 'Alright, Mum, thanks for phoning. I'd better go pack.'

'Sophia—' she starts. She stops.

'Bye, Mum.' I hang up before she can say more. No more guilt. I want to be free of all the losses. All these people who hold me.

38

Dear Sophia,

The poppies sounded wonderful. They're nearly finished here in Devon. We used to take your father to collect their seed heads when the season was over. Come to think of it, that's where the poppies in our garden came from – seeds we'd collected a previous year, we broke open the heads and scattered their seeds by the back wall of the house. Do you remember those poppies from when you came to visit?

I fold the letter from Grandma in half, then half again, and tuck it into my trouser pocket. Enough news.

I have a couple of days to wait before I leave, but I left my house this morning impatient to get on the road and headed to Walberswick.

Pete's going over to Lily's.

A *Biology* journal was on the bedside table when I woke up. A page had been dog-eared, so I flipped to the marked article. The article said in nature, females who mimic other females are more attractive. Males habitually shop for the sexier version of what they have; same as how Pete's always on the hunt for a better computer system.

Everyone wants to be with the winner.

If this is the case, I could be Joe's better version of Isabelle. Except, Isabelle isn't competing. I could be the failed new version. How long will I be in shops before I'm recalled?

I bite my lip to stop the thoughts. It's not true. Joe will visit.

I jump off the bus at Southwold and begin to navigate streets towards the beach. Colourful bunting hangs between shopfronts: a surviving decoration for the final trickle of tourists.

I hurry on my way. Thoughts of kissing Joe settle my mind; sex beginning a new circuit of chemicals to distract from the feelings of rejection.

Southwold beach is busy. It spills with tourists soaking in the still-cold waters. I march along the concrete walkway: garish bright beach huts to my right; choppy, grey water to my left – with fat, red Englishmen edging like crabs into the depths. The row of huts comes to an end and is replaced by a low sand dune. Keep walking. Enjoy the time it takes to arrive elsewhere. I turn off the beach and walk Ferry Road until I reach Southwold Harbour.

The harbour. A whole new world. Dirty and run-down. Bustling with everyday life. The harbour looks as if it might have not changed for centuries.

Wooden posts stick out of the estuary with gulls perched on top. Fishing boats come in and out, with men in overalls sweeping the decks of bloody water. Buy your fresh fish here. The smell, it reeks into any open pore.

A tiny row boat waits to carry people across the estuary to Walberswick. This ferry service has existed since the thirteenth century. Today the boat is rowed by a wild-haired woman with strong arms. I climb aboard. She recalls, to us passengers, stories of the sea, offering a sentence per stroke of the oars to build tension. 'I asked them lifeguards if they wanted to test the tide.' Stroke. 'See how strong it is.' Stroke. 'Thought they might like to know what chance a person had if caught out.' Stroke. 'I said if they wanted, I could throw myself off and we could see what happened.' Stroke. 'But they used a dummy instead.' Stroke. 'She never came back.' A mother stares aghast at the wild-haired woman, and holds her toddler close. The woman beams, pleased with her effect. An old man says how as a boy he'd throw himself off the estuary wall for dares – wouldn't dare now.

Dark brown huts line the edge of the estuary where she drops us off. Fishermen's belongings hang off the hut edges: nets, overalls, crab hatches. Industrial. This is a country of its own, for the men who fish no man's land. Lawless. Chaotic. Cut off. A contrast to the crabby Englishmen and the primary colours at Southwold. I feel at home.

Off the boat, I trail past these fishermen's huts to the end of the estuary. A corner turned, an estuary crossed, and habitat has changed – untamed. I like it better this way. Shingles and pebbles roll down to the shore. Grass breaks through beach. Broom and brush, rough around the edges. Only nature and nature's folk.

Five steps and I'm distracted by a flicker in the waves, something a shade darker than the grey of the estuary water below. I squat on the concrete that provides a man-made definition to the estuary opening. The water looks the same as before – choppy, unfriendly. Then again, something silky, black headed, smooth skinned. Smaller than a seal. The object has left a swirling circle on the water's surface where it floated. Disappeared.

Again, look, look. An otter, tiny lithe body briefly visible below me, like an apparition. Slick and graceful, speedy in movement, then gone again. I take my camera out and hold it to my face. I wait, moving the frame left and right, up and down, wanting to capture this evasive character. No luck. The otter slips to the surface, and quick back below. Probably hunting for dinner. They'll take the catch to their home in the woods behind the river Blyth. They're probably a female: frisky and determined, impossible to pinpoint on temperament or movements. Was she the one who all the males went to, and now has children to show for it?

This otter's territory could be as much as ten square miles from this spot. She will wait here for someone to court her, though she must agree once asked. A nip of the nose here, a roll around there; hormones rising from the activity. Her mate will present himself and be impossible to resist. He might take her to the water, this same space she now hunts. They'll roll around one another across the surface. For this moment she will be the chosen one. Making love under the stars, a great romance. And then he will be no more, another female having come along. And this otter will be left pregnant, unwanted.

Perhaps she'll only have one kid, I wonder, birthed in this sea – child lungs huge and ready to breathe underwater. A water birth: I had imagined one of those, once. A flush of bubbles as life slips in. And they won't be likely to survive: only a third of pups make it past one year. There are predators here.

If her child is lost, she'll return here looking – desperate for someone else. But even if she finds a new mate she will have to wait. Eager, ready. *Will he pick me?* But this otter hasn't lost a pup, yet. She's still hunting. Still likely to be the chosen one.

She ducks again beneath the surface; how far down dare she go? To the bottom, my love? You could dive as deep as 300 metres if you wanted. A crab! Crack it open with your claws; I know you're tough. If that's not enough, grab a rock, smash it against the shell. Cause death in order to support the new life you birthed. Vicious lady: not as innocent as you appear. A winner. Not me.

She rises again and has something in her mouth. I try to spy what it is through the camera lens, zoom in. Looks like fish – dangling loose, lifeless. She swims inland, off to hide in the wetlands. If I lose sight I can follow her perfume, the perfume of a winner: a strong stench of droppings. The same tone as freshly cut hay, but finer.

I stand and begin to walk along the estuary beside her, no longer interested in Walberswick beach. This is what I came to see: the ultimate woman, evolved from over twenty million years of adaptation. Good for land and good for water. A tough and sensitive creature, following the vibrations of her whiskers to track her prey, then snap, a thrash of retractable claws. She leaves my sight to enter long grasses, unseen by any other human but me: sure of herself alone.

39

Joe and I lie naked in his bed. I can smell his scent, pocketed in beads of sweat hanging from the hairs of his armpit. I pull my hand from under him and hover my finger above a droplet; it jumps to meet me.

The droplet seeps into my skin. 'This is like us,' I say. Hydration.

'What?' Joe slurs the question, half asleep. We've been dozing – like two cats fallen heavy on their sides, purring after a bowl of milk. I was meant to be dropping by for a cup of tea.

'Your sweat as it jumps to my hand,' I say.

Joe rolls to look me in the eyes. He reaches both arms around my body until he has hold of my bottom and pulls, drawing us closer together.

I push a lock of his sandy hair across his eyes.

'A magnetic force to be reckoned with,' he says, yawning.

'You produced it, and now I'm hydrated, and all the better for both of us.' I look over Joe's shoulder and remind myself of the objects in his boat: globe, toolbox, chessboard, fishing rod. I re-collect my bearings. This week, I meant to walk to Walberswick beach, and instead I followed the estuary. When least conscious of my whereabouts, I was exactly where I was meant to be.

'I love you,' Joe says.

Sharp intake of breath. Teeth grind. Tongue ties.

I love yous with Pete are an old walk: Southwold to Walberswick, as planned. Sightings of I love yous are no longer recorded because they're too common a species.

Joe cups my chin with his palm. He rests his fingertips on the mound of my cheek. My eyes scour his for a sign this is a false alarm: a flicker, a blink, a darkening. Nothing.

'I'm not saying anything need change.' Joe takes a mouthful of my hair and begins to chew. He did this to Isabelle's hair when Pete and I joined them at the pub. When this all began.

'What ifs' fill my mind, like what if he loves me as a Mother Earth, when I am her infertile sister. I struggle not to sink in them, reach for the buoy; my arms won't let go of Joe. I'm squeezing too tight: fingers tense with fear that, after all, I will lose this person.

40

I left my house today. Is it still my house? Today is the last time I will leave my house for three weeks, until I return from the Wash – only then will I find out.

Pete was already out by the time I woke up. We'd shared an unsaid goodbye: a quiet night watching a film and holding each other close. He must have gotten up early on purpose. He left me to leave our house. Our house.

Birdsong comes from all directions. Dad would know whose song it is, but I don't. The song finds its home in tiny badger-like birds. Flying badgers, poked faces. Tiny, shrunken faces. Faces with detail – like a cardigan shrunk in the wash, a photo minimised and printed. Unreal in detail. Long-tailed tits.

The land around Horsey Mere has been reconstructed for farming. Joe wanted to show me this before I head off to the Wash. He said it was a good place to begin to understand how Norfolk's landscape and habitats have been shaped.

'This whole area was marshes,' he says, 'but the marshes have been drained by water pumps. The water pumps have sucked the water out of the fields and along low dykes.' He shows me these dykes: skinny ditches either side of the fields. 'These dykes,' Joe says, 'are channelled into purpose-cut riverways: this being one of them.' He gestures to the waterway we're stood beside. This river starts at the bottom of the pump. The pump looks like a windmill, with a white wooden base and broad paddles. We follow the river a short way to reach the mere. Boats are moored along the bank.

'Happy holidaymakers enjoying an outing in what they think is the wild,' Joe sneers. 'I'm glad they're enjoying the outdoors, but they don't realise this isn't what's natural.'

The mere is huge, like a lake. A shimmering lake bordered by waving golden grasses. The far side of the mere is beyond view. 'On the other side,' says Joe, 'the mere joins other rivers which carry all this 'excess' water from field to sea.'

The whole process used to be energised by wind and water; today it relies on electricity. Now that all the water has been drained, the land lies below sea level. If the electricity runs out, Norfolk will drown. By means of sea levels, Norfolk is drowned.

I pick some flowers to keep me company for the last leg of my journey. Little purple flowers. Miniature capsules draped like grapes along the stem. Tongues of darker purple poke out from lilac casings made of the same delicate flesh. They are extraordinary: colours hung in light.

I paw at Joe for more kisses as he presses me to get on the bus that will take me to Isabelle and the Wash. We've picnicked all day until the last bus was due. I have become addicted to him, but it can't last. I give him what's meant to be the last kiss. This desire, this heroin desire. A euphoria I would fight for.

'Sophia, you'll have an amazing time, I know it,' Joe says between kisses.

The bus driver scowls, trying to look anywhere but at our public display of affection. The dopamine has muted the part of me that cares. I climb onto the first step, Joe laughs at my shy progress. 'You can do it; get on.' He nudges my back with his fist. When I reach the second step he hasn't let go of my hand and I have to tug it free so as to move inside. I release a snort; we're ridiculous. The stress of the distance will keep us returning for our reward. This was the trouble with Pete: we were never apart. I'd forgotten the craving – how I can crave. I find a seat and watch Joe from the window. He presses his nose against the glass.

I leave: to miss, to stress, to desire, to need, to love.

41

Isabelle collects me from the bus stop in a battered pickup truck and drives us to the Rewild Norfolk site. I'm introduced to a small team who are eating dinner together in a stone barn. They wave with spoons in hand and say it's nice to meet me. 'That's the communal kitchen and dining area,' Isabelle says, leading me back outside to give a whirlwind tour of the rest. 'That wooden cabin is our office; this is our tool shed; over there's the dorms and showers; and here is my cabin, where you can sleep too.' The site is modest: a cluster of four cabins and the barn. 'A base from which to work,' Isabelle explains. 'The real work goes on outside the site.'

She opens the door to her cabin and tells me she has it to herself because she's staying through autumn to lead the volunteers. 'The other paid workers head home at the end of the day; no one else wants to stay.' The space is basic: a sofa, a kettle, her bed, and a mat on the floor for me. 'Now, time for some wine and a catch-up.'

The 'catch-up' continues until 3 a.m., when Isabelle forms the slurred plan that I should see the landscape as soon as possible. 'You'll love it, Sophia. Let's wake up early.' She clutches me in a great hug goodnight as I try to gather myself. What have I done?

It's seven in the morning and she's stuck to her plan. 'Wake up sleepy head,' she says, handing me a cup of coffee. I take the mug and attempt to open eyes sticky with sleep. Giving up, I drink the coffee eyes closed. Isabelle bangs some cupboard doors, and says she'll wait outside.

At the last sip, I challenge myself to get up and dressed. When I open the door, Isabelle's leaning against the outside wall smoking a cigarette. 'Ready?' she says, and off we go.

The initial path from the cabin is sandwiched between corn fields: farmland, but no farmers. All is quiet and empty.

Signs of life are subtle, and when they come, they taunt: tiny pools, puddles, streams of water appear – hints of the sea creeping inland, taking over.

Despite this, the land looks willing, fertile, ready to serve and produce for man. Until land falls away. Gradually. Not a cliff edge like Covehithe. The land gives up slowly: one side of the path still field, the other marsh, and then neither. Mud.

Succulents take over, but they are dried and withered – flattened instead of full.

Isabelle leads me across a huge mud plane and towards the coastline. We're running on four hours' sleep, and either delirium is responsible for the drama of the landscape, or this is the Wash. The sky is heavy, and the grey weight of water looms from the heavens, promising floods, but not saying when.

Isabelle's abandoned her usual ethnic get-up, and instead wears walking sandals, a pair of cargo shorts, and a Greenpeace T-shirt. My culottes and blouse make me a city girl in comparison. She walks a fast pace and her ponytail bounces with each step. She's far sprightlier than me, considering she also was up late, drinking.

Here on the mudflats – whatever I've done – feels good. We stand together, paused for a moment to hold fort in the winds.

'Rewild Norfolk was started ten years ago by a group of activists, conservationists and scientists,' Isabelle begins her tour, and we move onwards again. 'We began in response to rising sea levels – which are obviously a huge risk to Norfolk, since much of the county already lies below sea level.' She speaks fast, trotting across the slippery flat as if it were her natural terrain.

My footsteps are careful, but soon become accustomed. I spread weight across my feet as though they were the broad paws of a lynx.

'The team works with other conservation groups to help preserve the natural landscape and reconstruct habitats.' She brushes away some curls that the wind has thrown before her eyes; her hand leaves a muddy streak. 'But our project specialises in rewilding, which works on the understanding that a habitat returned to a natural, un-cultivated state will self-manage – unlike most man-made environments, which need constant attention and whose habitants are continuously under threat.' She takes a little skip, pleased with her explanation.

I ask, 'What's your part then? And why here?' I could ask myself the same.

'You'll pick it up, but the basics are: we have a conservation team who preserve the reed beds, the marshes, the mud flats and the fens in general. Our participation team organise volunteers and work on making the site a tourist attraction – human friendly as well as animal friendly. And our office team campaign for flood defences and policy changes in farming laws.' She drops her pace. 'Not much to remember.' She laughs.

The land looks opposite to how busy the project sounds. Washed out.

The dried mud beneath my feet begins to crack, as if it were the top of a brownie. The texture of the moon. 'But why here?' I say.

'There are loads of reasons. Europe's largest colony of common seals live on the banks of this estuary. This is the UK's second largest area of intertidal floods. There are reefs here, sand, water, mud, fen – a huge variety of habitats for a huge number of species.' Isabelle sighs, her peachy skin bruised by thought. 'But also, it's harder to rewild woodland in England because there's little left, whereas the wetlands have started the process themselves.'

I've never seen Isabelle look defeated before. 'This place sounds like it's thriving though. It all sounds amazing.'

We've nearly reached the sea. The end of the earth. Nothing to be seen for miles. Mud slides our feet towards the waters. Mud sinks us under, inside itself, inside the belly of the beast.

'It is amazing. But like the Broads, the fens have been drained for centuries. People just want to access fertile soil, but they don't get that the water's got to go somewhere, and so it goes back to the sea. But the sea levels are rising, and the man-made channels, dykes and riverways are too shallow to hold the recent heavy rainfalls.' She stops walking. 'And some fields are so blocked with silt that water habitats struggle to take hold.'

'Surely that's only bad news for the farmers and villagers who are doing the dredging though?' I say.

'Well, it's complicated.' Isabelle gives up on her ponytail and lets it loose; a flood of yellow curls splashes across her face, whipping this way and that in the wind. 'People will fight to keep their land, and so us conservationists have to fight to ensure existing natural habitats are protected, and that space is reserved for the lost habitats to be reconstructed.'

We turn and walk the beach alongside the waterline. Even the beach is mud, feathered with long grasses blowing in the breeze.

Isabelle tells me Rewild Norfolk believes both farmers and conservationists can work together. For instance, they can both create floodplains, which will draw water away from farmland and, at the same time, provide space for lost species to be reintroduced. 'We've already succeeded with cranes, spoonbills, bitterns and egrets.' She looks cheerier and links her arm through mine.

The sun comes out and my skin prickles as though burnt in an instant. A sudden change from grey to yellow. Cold to hot. I am alien on this land. This land is alien to me. We are spacemen walking the moon. No wonder my ancestors wanted to shape it to accommodate us.

'So there can be space for everyone?'

'You've got it, Sophia. I knew you would. Nature knows how to keep balance. Before all these man-made changes there wasn't the need for conservation workers like us. The lynxes would have culled the deer. The beavers would have directed water flow and created homes for others; but that was when England was forest.' She takes a deep breath. 'The Wash, like I said, has been this way for centuries. It's not like the project's about to return it to forest and wave goodbye to all who made their home here. But at one point our animal ancestors would have sustained the habitat: the reed beds were mown by small mammals, offshore islands could form for nesting curlews, and we would've been surrounded by the calls of sanderlings and harriers.' She pauses our steps and closes her eyes to dream.

'So, you want to do yourself out of a job?' I pull on one of her ringlets. My hand shoots back, my fingers sparking in surprise at their openness.

'I'm running ahead of myself. Obviously nowadays there's the people to think about too, and finding space for them, but I'm not about to let all this go.' She waves her hands around her. 'And I love the work; there are so many challenges.'

In the distance is a small island, beyond this a wind farm. In front of the island are rising mud banks. A second land in the making? A ship is moored on these banks, waiting to discover if this is an island ready to be born or ready to disappear. A bird hovers, preparing to fly upwards, or else dive down. Wings shimmy, keeping them still while they decide. They drop.

'Like what?' I say.

'Like climate change – it's already occurring, so we can't simply introduce natives who suit this current climate, because by the time they're settled, the climate will be changing again.' She lets go of my arm and bends to take her sandals off. Looking up she adds, 'The reintroduced natives will need to be adaptable.'

'So not everyone's welcome after all?' I don't want to challenge Isabelle in case I'm seen to be one of those unwelcome, but this is an immense feat: to try to imagine who is a native and who isn't anymore. Will we be creating borders to determine who's allowed in? Will we be preventing species from exploring – restricting them from trying new lands and foods and friends?

'Everyone who can manage to sustain and keep balance is welcome. I hope space is found for everyone.' The sun disappears behind a cloud again and the shadow of this cloud travels across the sand, passing over Isabelle's bare feet.

'And will you introduce wolves?' I say, remembering her conversation with Joe in the pub, months ago.

'Wolves are easier to introduce to Scotland – more space. Wolves in Scotland would drive the red deer away from the rivers, allowing other species to rehome there. The trees would grow better without the deer eating them when they're young, and this would provide shade for the river life and shelter for animals.'

'So water's important to rewilding?'

'Hugely.' Isabelle allows the coming waves to run over her toes. 'Water habitats have rich ecosystems because they're 'edge' ecosystems and edges have more opportunity for diversity.'

I take my shoes off and we paddle into the water until it reaches our knees. 'So even more can live here than anywhere else?'

'Sure, though we could entertain a lot on land too,' she says, bending to drag her fingers through the dark water. She tells me how beavers would naturally coppice the trees to build dams, which in turn would prevent flooding so other fauna and flora could thrive. She says wild boar would have left wet puddles where they'd stomped, and these would have been ideal environments for wildflowers like bluebells to grow.

It's as if I'm being told magical fairy tales. But this is not forest. This is grey, cold, swallowing waters. What can I offer to this dire space, a land that's disappearing and a weather that whips and burns, a land that asks for more water, that never asked for less? Salty. Salty and sinking.

Isabelle continues to describe the work she's doing, but a speedboat passes and blocks out her words. Waves begin to form around our knees, splashing stronger and stronger, higher and higher. I want to climb out, but the mud has clasped my feet, hands holding me fast. The water explains it is not kind when being meddled with. Nature figures these waters out.

The waves crash around me, slapping against the mud banks like slapping thighs. The man on the boat looks back over his shoulder, watching me quiver and lose my footing. The devil.

The clouds pass back over the sun and this is it. This is the moment when the sea takes back what's hers. This is the apocalypse. I believe it could be, having heard of all these lost species – what roaring madness to think our own extinction is impossible. We have no control.

I think of Rewild Norfolk's visiting tourists, taking paths to this beach. One day, they'll be left to take paths without choice – whatever path is left. They'll gamble at each turning because they can't look back. Will the tourists reach a dead end? Or will they manage to wiggle their way to join me at the end of the earth? The question is, if they do, can we sit on this beach and enjoy what we've found until it is no longer? Or do we want it forever, to know it lasts for generations to come?

The waves subside and Isabelle looks at me, exhilarated, her eyes aflame. We pull our feet free, limbs breaking the clutch of the beast, and wade to shore. Back on land I watch as insects appear and disappear into the cracks on the earth – they've found a hiding place.

Back turned away from the insects, I watch waves roll in. Clouds go soft and bunch together; Pete, Joe, Mum fade and shrink with them. A group of people are in the distance, walking along the land edge opposite me. One person following the other. This is it. They follow. Lemmings, on a truce to give back bodies as compensation for those they took. Everyone is washed out here.

Isabelle's left me to my own devices. She wanders down the mud beach, examining grasses and any speck of curiosity she finds at her feet. A fighter plane flies overhead – playing tricks, spinning around – its motor revs then slacks as it shoots downwards. This is it.

Dad and my baby are waiting. The end's come for me too.

For me – not the marsh birds who have re-found a home they'd lost elsewhere. Not for the crabs who sunbathe ahead.

For me.

I take my camera out of my bag.

42

Fossil, Fossilis

The impression of a plant or animal of
prehistoric origin. Fossils are found embedded
into   rocks   and   preserved   through

petrification. The word 'fossil' can be used to describe somebody or something that resists change.

I am me, you are you, and we were together.
I was beside you, Rock,
when my body gave way.
You offered a resting place,
allowed my form to take hold, solid. Secure.

I left you the ghost of me
and, sometimes, you might want me back
because I look so good in this glorified form.

But I am petrified.
As scared as you are —
wishing you could rid yourself of my memory.

A week in, working with the project, and I've found my place. I jump stones across a marshy section to the back of the mudflats and reach where Dan, one of the volunteers, is working. He's cutting back a patch of reeds with a scythe. The reeds have had a growth spurt over the summer, Dan told me last night at dinner. He said that certain species, like the great reed warbler, prefer open reed beds, while avocets prefer to nest within long marsh reeds. He's making sure both are happy. I focus the lens on him. I'm comfortable to disappear into the scenery, an animal observer set against the grasses. Still, even by heartbeat.

When I press the button, take the shot, Dan is caught, scythe over shoulder, looking away from the camera, unawares. His torso is in focus. The sharp edge of the scythe. The quiet concentration of his manner captured in the softness of his posture. The marshes behind him are a blur through the lens, a watery gleam reflecting the blues and greys of the sky. Dan and the marshes, set against one another.

He gets back to work, and notices me behind him. 'Hey, Sophia, get some good photos?'

'I reckon.' I want to know more of what he's doing, but the photos look better when I don't – the revelations of a subjective viewpoint.

Dan grabs bunches of reeds and cuts them below his hand at the base of their stems. He says this bed hasn't been cut for five years. The beds are cut and cleared on rotation, so none get too old or neglected. 'Too old and they'll return to forest, too neglected and debris will build up causing the fens to dry out.' His T-shirt is soaked, coloured by muddy waters the same beige as the reeds in his hands. Later he will bunch the reeds, stack them and carry the load back to base on his back.

A few more shots of Dan at work, and I return to the stones I hopped across. They are rounded rocks, worn and tired from the water's flow. The stones are used by us to walk across, the water to be directed by, the plants to grow upon, the fish to hide beneath, the insects to settle on. Not allowed to be alone.

I pick up a rock the size of two fists – fistfuls of history. The rock has a spiral fossilised into its edges. I'm holding the outline of a creature. My camera won't focus on the spiral; it would need my macro lens. The spiral is jagged, where a shell once held life inside. The imprint lasts; past and present combined.

'Sophia.' Isabelle calls my name. Her slim legs are wrapped around a fence post ten metres away. She's studying the foliage growing at the post's base and waves for me to come over. 'Photograph this,' she says.

Black bindweed. The flowers are nestled close to the stem, a stark white in the dank marsh. A black and white image ready to take. The leaves are the shapes of aces; I recognise them as weeds from Dad's allotment.

'Weeds,' I say, letting my camera drop on its strap around my neck.

'Wildflowers,' Isabelle says.

Dan joins us to take a look. He asks if we're ready to head back to the cabin for a cup of tea. His eyes are bright, as if they have soaked up colour from the sea.

The kettle boils in Isabelle's cabin. She, Dan and I are collapsed on the sofa.

'Who will pour our blessed water?' Dan says, in mock Queen's English.

'Blessed water indeed. Water's the only thing that is blessed around here,' Isabelle says.

'Not if you want your water to be clean – that's another matter,' Dan retorts.

'What do you mean?' I yawn, tired of asking questions.

'I mean that draining the water has ruined the marshes' ability to keep water clean. They used to filter and store our nasty excess carbon, but not any longer.'

'My god, give us at least a tea break.' I get up to pour the kettle. Isabelle and Dan give me playful kicks.

'Hey, don't be mean,' says Isabelle,

'She's got a point,' says Dan, 'We're allowed to get off our soapboxes sometimes.'

'A moment's peace, please.' I hand them their cups of tea before taking mine.

We nestle together on the sofa, relaxed like family.

Like a fossil, I'm held. Yet I'm free to fall away.

43

Our days are full, as if we could be shrews; our heartbeats thrust faster making each day feel longer. But the clock ticks on usual speed.

Isabelle wakes me with our usual cups of coffee. We sit, mugs between palms, and talk about lynxes, cranes, alders and ants. Isabelle's eyes shine at each organism mentioned – each her 'absolute favourite,' until the next is brought up. Her enthusiasm vibrates the sofa in laughs and judders as she shakes on the spot in her joy. My body mimics hers, arms flailing as I talk about what it's like to work with animal friends we rarely get to see.

She says, 'I feel like we can communicate on a different level to these animals.'

'You sound like my mum.'

Mum. This week her philosophies have felt as constructed as the farmers' fields. Controlled. At the Wash we can manage, but we can't control.

'Mum talks about angels,' I tell Isabelle. 'She believes Dad went to meet them.'

At the end, conversations with Dad were as if he were dreaming aloud. Mum thought this was him communing with the angels – making plans for when they'd meet at heaven's pearly gates.

'Angels and rare species – same thing,' says Isabelle. 'They help us see what's outside our human world.'

The life I've seen at the Wash is the natural world I love. But perhaps looking outside the human world has left some things forgotten – like people. They belong too.

Isabelle jumps up and grabs a book off a shelf. She stands on the sofa, towering above me, and opens to a bookmarked page to read.

'But cloud, instead, and ever-during dark,
Surrounds me, from the cheerful ways of men
Cut off, and for the book of knowledge fair
Presented with a universal blank
Of nature's works, to me expunged and rased,
And wisdom at one entrance quite shut out.
So much the rather thou, celestial Light,
Shine inward, and the mind through all her powers
Irradiate; there plant eyes, all mist from thence
Purge and disperse, that I may see and tell
Of things invisible to mortal sight.'

She calls the words upward, pronouncing each one with care. The hand that isn't holding the book is open beside her, as though she is a preacher.

'What's that?'

'Milton.' She replaces the book on the shelf and drops her hands to her sides. 'He uses angels as characters to explore human questions. He thinks angels experience differently to us, so have some knowledge to impart, but they look more familiar than a crane, so are easier to relate to.' She sits back down and leans against me. The sister I never had.

Isabelle's shoulders rise and fall as she takes a deep breath. She's being carried away with the subject matter. 'I think, in the same way that we forget to notice the birds and the insects and the plants around us, we forget to notice when angels pass us by. We're too distracted,' she says, and smiles as though all has been righted. 'Right, work calls, let's go.'

It takes me a second. Dad's natural world calls, but I'm thankful for this human connection – spirit given words.

I snap out of it. 'Okay, let's go.'

Perhaps communion is possible between Mum and Dad, and their opposing views within me. I pull on the pair of wellies Isabelle's lent me – same shoe size – and we head outside.

A group of volunteers are packing a trailer with potted saplings and a bucket of tangled roots. Upon reaching the group, I take my camera out and turn it towards the bucket. The roots are coated in soil, with patches of white chalk – they must have been grown nearby. The image of the roots is like a pile of worms, a photograph from underground.

Today we're replanting a reed bed. We have bags of seeds collected from local reeds, the potted saplings, and these roots. I turn the camera to the volunteers – a mix of types, some tidy, some scruffy. A young boy with dreadlocks stands at the front, the pockets of his jacket are stuffed full of seed packets. A shiny-haired girl stands talking with him, a plant pot in each hand. The boy takes the handle of the trailer and pulls it behind him. A couple of girls push from the back. I linger behind to get a shot of them leaving. The wind blows corn to the east – the same goes for hair, saplings and coats – all swept to one direction. The sensation of the elements caught.

The strong winds on the exposed fens beat my skin raw. After lunch I trail home to find shelter and peace from the roaring gusts. The morning was a long one. I mingled between the groups of volunteers and used my camera as a pair of binoculars in failed hope that I might capture a crane.

Back at the cabin, the phone rings in my ear, my attempt at communication with Pete silent to the outside world. Ring, ring. I consider hanging up, but his voice comes through the receiver. 'Sophia, how's it going?' Comforting notes of delight.

'Pete, hello. It's great. Glad you picked up.'

'Glad you called. I hadn't wanted to disturb.'

I could ask how he's doing, but he might hear it as 'How're you and Lily doing?'

He talks on, without my needing to say anything.

'So,' he says, after describing his first week back at school: the late arrivals and the eager beavers, 'what have you been doing?'

I tell him about the beach, about the climate, about the talk of lynxes. I tell him about the team and the birds whose habitats we're protecting. What if I tell him I've shed my wings on flight and can't return, like a myrmira rubra ant who has flown on heat, then lost their wings so as to nest and lay. Except I'm building nests so others can lay.

I keep the conversation short, say I love you and mean it, but that I should go. He says he loves me too; to send a postcard.

My eyes have been on the door, keeping watch. I hang up and return inside.

44

The sensation of someone lifting my hand is welcomed into the intimacy of my dream. My hand is shaken, and I startle, snatch it back, 'What are you doing? It's not light yet.' I blink, blurry-eyed. Isabelle's figure is crouched beside me, a pale blue. Daylight hasn't returned the colours yet.

'We're going to my parents' house today.'

'We're what?' My brain tries to join dots but doesn't have dots to join. Isabelle's never mentioned her parents' house. I've never considered the fact that Isabelle has parents.

'I thought it would be nice to visit for a few days. They only live an hour's drive away.' Isabelle's skin has become pinkish-blue, making her look less of a dream wanderer.

'And this only dawned on you now?'

'The best ideas come at dawn.' She stands up and turns on her heel. 'Rewild Norfolk is planning a new project at Wells-next-the-Sea, where my parents live. It would be good to show the funders some photos of the area.'

The sign says, 'Welcome to Wells-next-the-Sea'. We turn the pickup away from the coast, wind a few narrow streets, and enter a gravel driveway with a converted barn at the end. Isabelle's parents are at the door of the barn. They're both barefoot and waving. Envy creeps like ivy around my chest, tightening and spreading. Surprise cuts through as I watch Isabelle hug her parents: not a lone wolf after all.

Her parents take our bags from the back of the truck and lead us into the barn. Isabelle's mum slips her arm around Isabelle's waist and asks how she's doing, while her dad asks me how the journey was. They both have the soft lilt of a Welsh accent.

In the entrance to the barn is a photograph of young Isabelle on a beach. In the photo, she holds a parent's hand either side of her and is lifted above the pebbles. She's laughing and carefree, same as grown-up Isabelle.

Her dad, who introduced himself as 'Isabelle's dad, Gareth,' is slim, a little shorter than me, and has a full head of dark hair. He offers to show me to my room. He's wearing a brightly patterned shirt, tucked into a faded pair of Levi's and walks quickly ahead of me with my bag in his hand.

Sun pours in from skylights. The ceilings are high and the walls white, decorated with wall hangings and paintings. Gareth opens a door to a small room full of house plants, with a bed in the corner. He asks me whether I need anything. A towel? A cup of tea? He lays my bag on the bed, and I fight the urge to hug him. What I need is for him to tuck me in and read me to sleep, but I can't say that. Instead, I say no, thank you, and that if he doesn't mind, I think I'll go to the sea for a walk while they catch up. He smiles, understanding and perhaps appreciative. He goes out of the room for a minute to dig around for a map. He returns, map unfolded, and shows me – drawing lines with his index finger – a lovely walk to take. 'Once you're over the hill at the end of the lane, you'll see the sea,' he says.

I thank him and sneak out, not disturbing Isabelle and her mum's alto flow of conversation coming from the kitchen. Gareth heads to join them, and his voice rumbles off the high walls, partaking in the chorus.

From the driveway I call Joe. He picks up right away. 'Sophia, I'm happy you called. How are you?' His voice rises in excitement, and I'm flushed with joy. I want to ask him whether he still plans to visit, but instead I tell him I'm at Isabelle's house, and ask if he's ever been.

'Oh great, I hoped she'd take you. It's beautiful, isn't it?'

He asks how the project's going. I tell him about the new reed beds, about the fossils. I feel like a child come home from school, telling my parents what I learnt that day. They already know. Dad used to ask questions, make me feel clever. Joe's doing the same, but I feel patronised. I'm on paths already scented out.

I want to ask about his life, but he says he's got to go – he's meeting some friends to go fishing. What friends?

'Well, it was nice to hear your voice,' I say.

'You too, I'm glad you went, I knew it would be good for you.'

We say goodbye, no I love yous.

The minute I hang up I miss him, which makes me wish I hadn't called. I've been sleeping alone on a single mat and have adjusted to the sound of my own breathing, the touch of my own skin, the different ways my body can fold around itself without the assistance of another acting as cushion. My body itches with the memory of what this other body feels like.

I force myself to walk on. Over the hill at the end of the lane lies the town waterfront: the edge before nature takes hold. The smell of fish. I get closer and see the waterfront is not the sea; the sea's miles off, sucked away by low tide. The space between town and sea is sandy beach and grassy islands. Slim waterways and muddy marshes. Lobster bins stack upon one another along the concrete water defence. In the port, sailing boats are tilted on their sides, bottoms sunk into the mudflats.

This space between town and sea looks difficult to navigate. Broken by marsh and water, ready to change pathways depending on time of day. A strange scene is occurring: families are repopulating the islands. People are island wandering. Hands held across stranded beaches. Newcomers wade knee-deep to find a piece of land to claim their own. I could forget it's low tide and believe the sea has risen and taken hold. Civilisation is no longer. All that's left are these humans, sporadically dotted across a shallow landscape, exploring the remains.

The explorers are happy. They're enjoying the waters. They bathe and relax on their wild strip of beach.

I look back to the village. It seems this post-apocalyptic society is divided. Behind me half the population bustle in cafés, determined to sustain civilisation, while in front of me the other half resist the wild no longer, not fearing its takeover but joining in.

Then there are the fishermen. They haul buckets of sea life onto land. They are the go-betweens, the messengers.

The waterfront leads me out of town towards the coastal path, past run-down shacks signposted as artist studios. Taped to the studio windows are fliers advertising the artists' creations. 'Made and inspired from what nature gave us', reads one flier. Maybe art requires things fall apart, so as to have opportunity to re-create. The studios give way to run-down farm buildings. A man in a straw hat, with a pair of braces strapped over his silver-haired chest, fills a pail with water and watches me pass by.

The dregs of civilisation dry out in the heat, leaving me with a huge sky and no trees for shelter.

I walk a little further and am relieved when green fields spring up on my right. The pale mix of marsh, mud and sand continue to pan out on my left. The sea remains far off.

Wooden posts direct me onto a tidy path. I want to turn off onto random footways that might lead to the sea. I'm obedient, and don't. A cluster of trees comes as a surprise amid the open lowlands; they provide a short break from the sun but, once passed, no more are in sight.

In the distance, a grey bird feeds on the marsh. Long legs step gingerly in the long grasses. Tall. Elegant. A crane. I hold my breath, frightened it will fly away. Of course, now I see one I haven't brought my camera.

An electric buzz fills my ears. Crickets. I break off the main path to experience surround sound.

The grasses are high and I can't see beyond. When a new path introduces itself, mud decides my choice of route – some directions too wet to take. I'm in nowhere land.

Until, white beach – damp and unexpected. Pictures drawn upon the sand. Hearts and circles, letters and stars. They give away that someone else has visited, but where are they now? A few steps on, and the path I came from has disappeared.

Cut off.

I seat myself on the sandy shore and delve toes into sand. I wiggle them, allowing tiny granules of the underworld to gradually fall. The wind blows a film of sand across the beach and, just like that, the landscape shifts and rearranges itself before my eyes. I pull my shirt over my head and unbutton my shorts.

Time for a swim.

Walking into the water, I thank each wave as it hits the obstacle of my body and crashes down around me. Salty rivers run along each arm. Water, good to be submerged in.

Dad liked to tell the story of my baptism. He described how Mum was adamant I should be christened and baptised, and so one day, soon after I was born, Dad had driven to the sea, and come back with a bucket of salt water. He placed the bucket in the garden, marched inside to get Mum and me, and much to Mum's anger, dunked little me into the bucket. 'You've been baptised by the holiest water around,' Dad used to say.

I dive under. The water grips my head. My sins are drained as the thrill of cold stills my mind – for a moment.

When my head rises and the water slides down the nape of my neck, I feel renewed. Falling backward I allow legs to float upwards. The sea decides which way my body floats, and for how long. Water's silken drift cradles me. Weightless. My breasts balloon to the surface and tingle with the touch of fresh air. No part of me need carry itself. No need to think or fend for self.

I float, half above and half below. The water feels colder than the outside air but can't be far off the same temperature. Pete would be able to explain this. How can he, when water is so temperamental, alluring, dangerous, erratic? I bob in the water's hold. It is the clasp of a mother, giving but willing to punish.

I sink myself through the liquid back to standing and walk towards land. The water drags around my ankles, sweeping backward, away from my body. She wants to take me with her. She asks whether I'm sure I want to return to the hot sands of man.

On our drive to Wells-next-the-Sea, Isabelle had told stories of selkies and mermaids. On this shore, in the mystical grip of the sea, with the enticement of her maternal comfort, I believe the stories. Naked, arriving onto sand, I could be one of these lustful creatures. But I am on land and learning to breathe alone.

I crouch, and trail fingers across the sand, drawing lines to be filled with water and rubbed out again.

A few years ago, a whale washed up on the beach near Hunstanton. Everyone was shocked – had he lost his way? Once upon a time, many whales would have been in these seas, eating the plankton on the surface, but the whales were rubbed out like the lines I draw. I recall Dad and me on the beach when I was little. He showed me some of the food that lies on the bottom of the seabed, digging his hands into slippery green and brown. He said this food needed light to grow. He said if the sea was too polluted then the light can't reach it. He said the food could instead be carried to the surface on the backs of big fish. But he said most of the bigger fish have been caught.

If I could make myself into a fish and clear the plankton for the lost whales, I would. If I gave myself over, my body could float on the surface and do this.

Dad said when all the big fish are gone, not only will they be unable to carry plankton to feed the masses, but no fish will be mature enough to lead the species migration. I remember he'd been sad because he said all the lower life normally ate the poo of the bigger fish. I had laughed because he said poo, but he gave me a strict look and said, 'If there isn't enough poo to eat, then what are they going to eat?' Dad's look made me sadder than the fish. I couldn't think about the fish: I was a little girl. 'Nobody wins,' he'd said, 'the big fish have less to eat, the little life has less to eat, and eventually we have less to eat.'

From the beach the sea looks blank. Pete would tell me what lives underwater, but Joe would tell me the significance of this. Joe knows why everybody belongs.

Hands prickled by sand, I close my eyes. Crystalline blue flutters behind my eyelids. The colour of Joe's eyes. How dare he hold her in his gaze.

Instinct rises, to swim again and relinquish these thoughts to the sea. I open my eyes and confront the empty skyline.

45

Isabelle bounds into my room and wakes me from a deep, dreamless sleep. 'Mum says we can go sailing today; have you ever been? It's lovely. You don't have to do anything: Mum and Dad will do all the work.' She dances, slipping on the wooden floorboards like an excited puppy.

I groan.

'Time to get up,' she calls, and closes the door.

Up and dressed, I walk down the hall – wobbly on half-asleep legs. Isabelle's in the kitchen, noisily raiding cupboards for plates and mugs. She looks up, 'You're like a deer learning to walk,' she points at my bare legs, 'and with that pale skin you don't stand a chance before the hunters see you.' She hands me a pile of plates, 'Don't worry, today you can relax and get a tan.'

'I don't tan.'

'Whatever. Sit down before you fall over.' Isabelle nudges me to the dining table. I put the plates down and pull a chair across the slate tiles. The chair legs squeak against slate, and Isabelle shudders. 'Somebody needs a coffee.'

'Yes please.' I sit down and study my surroundings. The kitchen's large and open-plan, designed like a farmhouse with the dining table and chairs opposite the long, wooden countertops and ceramic sink. Spider plants tumble from shelves high-up. Jars full of grains line lower surfaces.

Isabelle pours me a coffee from a large French press. She piles slices of dense bread and croissants onto a plate, and places this in front of me. I eye-up the pile as Isabelle goes back and forth between fridge and table, slowly surrounding the plate with jars of jams and spreads.

'I went to the village bakery to get the bread,' she says. 'It's my little ritual whenever I arrive here.'

'I don't know if I can stomach food this early.'

'Oh, shut it. Mum and Dad said you need fattening up, so I agreed, told them you were worryingly thin, and got myself a whole bunch of croissants on top of the bread.' She purses her lips, a cheeky official.

For her effort I grab a croissant, tear it open with my fingers and gnaw on it, plain.

'Oh come on. A little jam? Chocolate spread?' Isabelle pushes the jars of condiments closer and slumps on the chair opposite me. We sit in silence, feet tucked under bums, and munch on croissant.

Outside the house someone whistles. 'Time to go sailing,' Isabelle says to me. 'Coming!' she calls, voice like a reluctant teenager, while kicking over the chair in her hurry to get out the door. She grabs another croissant from the pile and ushers me out.

Outside, Isabelle's parents are in their car with some jazz blaring out. 'Climb on in,' they call. I open the rear door. A young but balding man, with a kind, round face is sat in the other seat. Isabelle opens the door on his side and says, 'Shove over Callum. You can squeeze in the middle.'

'Hi.' I'm not sure whether I'm meant to know this person or not.

Isabelle's mum looks over her shoulder from the driver's seat and says, 'We just picked Callum up from Sheringham station. You guys have met before, right?'

I shake my head and put my hand out. 'My name's Sophia.'

'Oh shit, I forgot, sorry guys. Sophia, this is Callum – remember, I told you about him – he's doing research on cave art in Scotland.' Isabelle doesn't look at me as she speaks.

I have a faint memory of a story about a man Isabelle was interviewing.

'Yeah that's me, though there's more to me than that, I promise.' He has a thick Glaswegian accent and bats his eyelashes as if to prevent us making eye contact.

I've never sailed before and the sight of land shrinking on the horizon makes me nervous, until I realise nothing is present to trigger thought except blue and sun.

Isabelle's parents direct the sail by pulling on various ropes; I have no interest in knowing what they're doing. Her mother, Meredith, is as strong as an ox. She's short like Isabelle, but of firm build, with a curly, cropped haircut identical to her husband's, but blonde. She wears a pair of dungarees over a shirt with the sleeves rolled up to her elbows and steers the sail with precision.

Isabelle drapes across the deck and sacrifices herself to the sun, letting it grope whichever way it pleases and look at her from every angle. I lean against the bars at the back of the boat, a thin scarf wrapped over my shoulders, and watch the escapade of her parent's dexterous navigation. I'm amazed; we've figured a way to ride upon water. A way to confront the sea's tricks as she pulls us one way and we move another.

I take my camera out of my bag, anxious I might lose it to the water. The boat's ropes against sky blue make a good image. They could be the wires between telephone posts, against empty Suffolk skies. They could be tramlines, drawing a web above a cityscape. I take a photo then turn the camera to Isabelle. A golden-skinned creature, with fine blonde hair glinting along her arms. She is petite, ready to slip in and out of spaces. Her arms are strong, built to carry young.

Isabelle pulls herself upright and looks out at sea. 'Isn't this incredible?' she says to Callum, who's sat beside her, going a slight shade of green.

'Ay, what a gift to be given,' Callum says.

We are gifted, because this body of water is far bigger than us, and we can't drink it, we can't eat it, and we can't breathe under it but, for this moment, we can float upon it, leave the troubles of land behind – even if only for an afternoon.

46

Over my time away, I've watched the moon wax from new to almost full. The sky has been clear every evening, and the display of the moon majestic: an invisible body who has grown to be bright and voluptuous, slow-dancing an arc across the sky.

As pitch of night falls, I go alone to watch the moon over the sea. I want to allow it to perform for nothing but beauty's sake.

On the lane from the barn, I stop at the top of the hill to moon-gaze. The moon's body could be my own. The spine of moon-me rubs against a dark blanket and my newly round stomach casts an almost missed shadow across something spooned beside my breast.

The sun's light is not quite finished. It adds a vague hue of orange to the surrounding dark. But the town is dead. No sounds from houses, no cars, no streetlights. I head down the hill and along the waterfront, clamber over the defence to reach a section of beach. The tide's in, and islands have been submerged to sleep beneath water.

The moon sits on my left, overlooking the skinny peninsula and the silhouettes of Holkham's pines which are visible in the distance. A breath of the sun colours the horizon to my right – a steamy exhale that casts purple above the dark blue sea. The view reminds me of when I first noticed the sun and moon could hang parallel in the same sky. Mum had been reading to me in the garden, but I couldn't follow the story. I was distracted, glancing one way then the other, brow furrowed in self-doubt and confusion. Was I imagining it, or could the sun and moon both be out together? I must have been about seven: mind blown. I'd always believed the sun chose a pale blue home and the moon a dark one. But no; in a second what I thought I knew, had to adapt into something else.

I kick off my sandals and walk to the waterline. The line shimmies forward, then shuffles back. I step towards and away from the moving water, playing games of catch me if you can. Grandpa used to play these games with me when he visited us in Suffolk. On those visits he, instead of Mum, would tell me bedtime stories. He told the stories by heart, and his tales were full of exotic creatures and strange people. They made for good dreaming, disobeying the strict laws of fables and the order of nature.

Grandpa once told me a myth about how the sun and the moon came to share a sky. 'The story goes,' Grandpa said, 'that the sun and moon were lovers torn apart in the winds of a nasty battle.' His voice whispered the story while I sat on his lap, hushed. 'The two lovers were banished from one another, and made to exist alone in their own skies, but in secret they plotted a lingering moment every day when they could catch sight of one another and revel in their unity.' I would close my eyes when he told the story, and an image would come every time, of two eggs, sat either side on Mum's kitchen scales. They were the sun and the moon, keeping the world in balance.

An icy shock as waves catch my feet. I skitter backward until I reach my sandals.

On my way up the beach, I thank the moon for turning the tides and keeping the water flowing. I thank her for how she aggravates the sea's temper; allowing the sea to be so powerful. And I accept how sometimes this power sends things askew. Tips boats over.

Back in the barn, Isabelle's sitting at the wooden counter in the kitchen. She nurses a cup of cocoa between both hands. 'Want one?' she asks, gesturing with an elbow at the pan on the stove.

I take a mug from the shelf and pour myself one from the heavy pan, before pulling a stool up beside her. 'Where's Callum?'

'Asleep.'

'You couldn't sleep?'

'I was waiting for you.'

We both take sips in silence.

My eyelids close until not quite touching. The gap lets in horizontal crescents of light. I open them, catching on. 'What is it?'

Stillness, as though the calm of the night were audible. But somewhere things are taking flight.

'Did you enjoy the beach?' she asks me.

'It's stunning.' I blow on my cocoa. 'What is it, Isabelle?'

She sighs, twists a curl around her finger.

I've never seen her so calm and quiet.

'I'm pregnant.'

Inhale. Deeply.

But I don't know what to do next. I sense with the exhale should come words. But I don't know what they'd be. I hold my breath.

'I think it's Callum's, but I'm not sure.' She looks peaceful, chin pointed up so the spotlight above the counter illuminates her profile. 'It's why I wanted to come home: to tell Mum and Dad.'

'What did they say?'

'They're happy for me.'

I stare at the tiles in front of me: red, white, blue. 'And how do you feel?'

'Happy.' Isabelle turns and looks at me. Her eyes are gentle. Her skin looks softer than I remember – smooth and full of life.

'And Callum?' My heart beats fast, disturbing the night's calm.

She drops her gaze to her knees. 'I told him this morning. He was shocked, but he'd kind of guessed.' She shrugs and looks sheepish. 'I asked him last week to come down from Scotland. I said it was important.' She tips her head back to take the last sip of cocoa, then gets up to rinse the mug.

I remain seated, cradling my cup.

'He says he's not sure how it's going to work. He thinks we're from two different worlds. But he wants to try.' She dries her hands on the dish towel, rubbing palms in the face of a herring gull. Her expression remains peaceful, though a shadow has cast itself upon her eyes.

'And do you want to try?'

'Yes. To be honest I've always pictured having my own family. It's all I know.' Her eyes sparkle, a secret told. 'And things will work out the way they're meant to, if I'm open and follow the flow.'

Follow the flow – a long and winding river ending in an unknown sea of options. She's with faith, like Mum. I open my mouth but find no words.

'I wanted to tell you before, but I thought I should tell them first.' She comes behind me and places a hand on each of my shoulders. She squeezes, and nestles her thumb into the exact spot that holds unrealised tension.

'I understand.' Questions burn. Where will she and the baby live? Will she leave Rewild Norfolk? Who has she told? Will she get a DNA test?

I bite my tongue.

'Right, I best get to bed, it's been a hell of a day,' she says.

'Sleep well.' I touch her hand, before she lifts it from my shoulder, then turn in my seat. 'And congratulations.'

Isabelle smiles, her thin lips curved upwards like the light between my narrowed eyelids. A new moon.

I sit alone and wait for the news to sink in. My response takes a new form every second. Tenderness, anger, betrayal, jealousy, calm. I get up, rinse my mug, and go to my bedroom to lie down. In bed I concentrate on how the weight of my body is grounded to the Earth's surface, how Earth is holding me. I am supported no matter what happens. But the waves of emotion continue to roll in my chest.

Tales twist all night long. Tales revolving around the characters of Isabelle, Callum, Joe and their baby. At one point, Callum is a sheep. He has his own new-born. It isn't Isabelle's. Callum baas and bucks, then rolls over, parts his back two legs, and between tawny brown, presents himself for Isabelle. Isabelle is rubbing and rubbing. At first, she is a sheep too, then she is a person. She rubs, until Callum rolls back over, and licks her cheek, committed. He baas at her, adoring, ready to adopt another new-born – the new baby is hers. Then the same happens again, except this time it's Joe she's stimulating. This time it's Joe who looks up and offers her a wet kiss. And they are all three stood together, happily brooding. While I, the farmer, in tweed jacket and wellington boots, am stooped below a tree with my crook – watching from the outside.

47

I blink, disorientated in dawn light. Thought evades me, replaced by a synaesthesia of colours, sounds, tastes and smells. Senses lap against one another, finding no shape to attach to, or no outline to discern shape from.

Because I am molecules.

I am empty space. Part of a bursting mass of overlapping atoms.

I am a shapeshifter. Whatever I want to be. Whatever I make of the moment.

I raise a hand, wave it between the specks of dust which gleam in the soft light, and grasp the molecules within my reach.

A flurry of confusion. Molecules rush past. I'm not quick enough to seize them. They move away and I can't tell whether the way is up or down, because I have no sense of direction, no sense of whether I'm in sky or water. I grapple for the past and cannot catch the future. This space is shapeless.

Without shape I'm as large as a whale. How could I squeeze back inside the frame of a human?

A whale. I release my sperm into the cool waters and allow it to diffuse into infinite blue. Under water my sperm enters any female cell that chooses to take hold of this moment. A minuscule chance. There are no legs to be opened, no heartstrings to be played. I allow my sex cells to move away into the atmosphere to meet more. Who knows whose?

From bed, I can be as far-reaching as a barnacle, lazily stretching out of my house to feel around with my long penis until I reach a space it fits. Blind, I trust the nerves on my tip to find other nerves to excite. This is beyond me.

I spread myself wide, until my barnacle house disintegrates and I'm caught in the remnants: grains of sand, crystals of salt.

I sit up and rub my eyes. The spider plants at the end of my bed dangle from their pots – molecules too.

As a molecule I can be self-fulfilling like a shark. I'm a realisation of togetherness: my own cells copulating with one another when no other can be found. My shark-like cells drift wherever they please, and when the atoms of my mate perish, I won't miss the other molecular moments that move within this void – even if my own.

The white walls of the bedroom have luminous flecks – sunlight cast between the lace curtains. Specks of light, specks of dust. Specks of pollen. Mobile.

Mobile as a seed of a fruit, molecular me can travel through air. She can cling to the particles of another creature as it explores ripples of space, preferring to gather and share cells of others.

Imagine.

The projection of lace patterns on the walls disappears. Broad daylight has filled the gaps. Sensations lift, one by one, leading me back to waking life. Brain clears and remembers where it is. My head's light, as if someone opened it up in the night and emptied the contents. I throw off the bedsheets.

48

From the corridor outside my room, I listen for Isabelle and Callum's voices. Nothing. The adjacent room is one of several yet to be explored. I pull the handle, and peek around.

'Oh, hi darling, just me in here, come along and join,' says Meredith, her Welsh accent soothing.

The room's set up as part living room, part study. A desk, filing cabinet and set of drawers line the wall on my left, while some comfy seats are under the window. Meredith sits on an armchair, legs tucked beneath her. She holds a pencil in one hand and a sketchbook in the other.

'Isabelle's taken Callum to the station.' Her face loses composure for a second. Muscles pick up again as she says, 'She's going to pick up some croissants on her way home – she can't stop herself. Gareth's gone out too. Come, I'm dying of boredom and could do with a natter.'

Meredith's smile is bright, but her eyes are pleading. A large wicker armchair sits opposite her, I settle on that. It's odd to sit with a mother so close but not my own. I sit up straight, on my best behaviour.

'Do you ever miss Wales?' I say, for the sake of saying something. 'I imagine it was hard adjusting to the change of landscape.'

'Not at all,' Meredith places her sketchbook and pencil down on the carpet. 'I was raised by the sea, and so long as I'm by the sea, I don't much mind where I am.'

'Isabelle never mentioned she grew up in Wales.'

'She didn't? Well, we moved when she was very little. Gareth and I were concerned she'd find the transition tough, but she fell in love with Norfolk. If I had a day mourning the mountains, I'd take Isabelle down to the beach and her enthusiasm would bring me back to loving these flatlands.' Meredith twiddles with her earlobe and looks to the far top corner of the room, as if the memory lives in the cobwebs. She claps her hands together and smiles. 'It made me laugh when she said she wanted to study anthropology – she cared about the birds more than our neighbours. But she's an explorer and an idealist, always on the hunt for people who think like she does. That's why she loves you: you're a kindred spirit.'

I blush. 'I guess after all her exploring, she's figured she belongs here.'

'Maybe. Or maybe she's the same as me – so long as she's by sea then she's happy as Larry. I wouldn't be surprised. It's as if the sea were in my veins. When we moved here, my insides reshuffled, like they were a bookshelf waiting to be ordered, but needing the right librarian. The sea's my librarian.' She laughs, her head thrown back.

'I think it might be mine too.' I smile, comforted by this image. 'How old was Isabelle when you moved?'

Meredith fondles the cloth of a cushion lying beside her. 'About seven. You might think that's too young to remember Wales, but places stay with you. I think Wales is why she likes Scotland, and why she loves to travel so much – she might love it here, but she's still seeking the mountains and somewhere foreign that she's forgotten.'

The clock hanging on the wall says it's nine; Isabelle's probably at the shop, choosing how many croissants to buy today.

'In the end, do you think it was for the best you moved?' I ask.

'Well,' Meredith considers, stroking the cushion cover to tidy the folds she's made in her fondling – perhaps a habit to create disorder in something that can be smoothed out. 'I think so.' Her lips twitch downwards. 'You see, darling, I was very depressed before we left, and no matter how much I wanted to do what was best for my family, at some point I had to do what was best for me.'

Her words punch. The intimacy of a mother's understanding sinks in my stomach. 'I know what you mean,' I say.

'We're pulled many ways, but in the end, we take our own,' she says, her eyes sympathetic.

A loud bang sounds as the front door closes. Isabelle stumbles into the room, her hair blown across her face, and her nose pink, while the rest of her is a brilliant brown. She's wearing a kaftan dress decorated with little mirrors.

The seam of the dress is ripped and threads dangle by her knees ready to catch on passing objects, but that wouldn't faze Isabelle. She heaps herself onto an armchair and tips the croissants from their paper bag onto the coffee table beside her. 'Has Mum been boring you?' She chews on one-she-started-earlier, and her eyes look wet, though she won't fix them on either of us.

'I was telling Sophia about our move from Wales. Come now, you could get a plate.'

I lie on the beach, a belly full of breakfast. My thoughts suspend on the horizon as I muse over an imagination of two eggs either side of Mum's scales. Two lovers: Grandma and Grandpa, Mum and Dad, Pete and me, Joe and me. As with the sun and the moon, I can't imagine one without the other.

Lying on my back, I imagine our bodies as nothing but molecules – one couldn't be without the other, because we'd all be everywhere. Dad climbs inside my nose as I smell the salt of the sea, Mum leans in my ear as I listen to the waves, Pete hangs inside my mouth as I lick my chapped lips. Both Grandma and Grandpa sit in my eyes when a bee lands on a meadow cranesbill. A bird flies overhead with a fish in its mouth, and Joe settles in my pelvis.

I move within their old molecules. I am their molecules. They no longer haunt the space between my conscious and unconscious, because there is no space between. I'm around them, inside them, beneath them.

I pulsate with affection, with the love carried and cross-pollinated between all these particles.

On my back, my body joins the horizon. I imagine I'm floating on the surface of the sea, my breasts bobbing: one the sun, one the moon. Together in me. The world rolls on its axis and I onto my belly, face down in the water, eyes open to the beauty that lies beneath.

I'm soon to return home. I'm at home. No disorder can shake me loose because, like the cushion cover Isabelle's mother fondled, it's all the same fabric, and something, somewhere, is smoothing it out.

49

The tide's out at the Wash, a swim out of reach. I walk the grassy mound of the water defence that runs between Peter Scott's lighthouse and West Lynn – the home of a naturalist and the start of a town. On the other side of the estuary to me, the Rewild Norfolk team are at work. Smudged black bodies sit with arms bent, elbows at ninety-degree angles like wings spread. They're looking through binoculars. Bird-watching day.

My walk is with the aim to cool myself down. Inside. Outside, autumn is making itself known. The temperature's dropped and the sun's forgotten to show its face for the last two days. My last two days. They've been more of the same: bending and moving within a barren landscape. Trying to photograph things that don't want to see my face, on ground that doesn't want to feel my footprint.

A couple of water droplets fall from the sky. My face tingles – an internal tracing of an external force.

Isabelle's at her parents' house. They waved me goodbye from the drive. Like how they'd greeted her days before. Like I was a sister. The muscles in my legs ached to step backwards. I longed to pretend nothing had changed. But I knew it had.

A group of insects hover ahead of me: dragonflies with solid metallic bodies, and a handful of horsefly friends. Their wings beat a steady stutter, which keeps them at eye level. I walk into their gathering, and they rise. I watch them helicopter upward: a smooth flight with still bodies. Upwards and upwards.

My last two days at Rewild Norfolk have been a refuge of simplicity. The team and I shared tea at sunrise. We had a three-legged race along the mud plain. Dan fell flat on his face and wriggled wet and brown like a slug. We howled with laughter and untied our feet. We went for a late-night swim. Tonight is my last night away. Tomorrow I get back to my life.

This time last year everything was planned out. I'd returned to Suffolk to be closer to Dad. I was in a new house on a long-term lease. I was married faithfully to Pete, for the rest of my life. I was pregnant with our first child.

Camera held to eyes, my arms also form wings, but mine are closed. I swivel my body around so it's looking back down the estuary towards Sutton Bridge. Huge ships glimmer as the wet mud beneath them throws light upward. My lens is zoomed in as far as it will go. A strange image: powerful objects that can move, drawn to a standstill. Through my lens it's as though they are still moving – upon a sea of mud. Waves are painted in lines across the brown, marking the various sea levels as the last tide dropped. The estuary looks never-ending when caught like this: the bridge out of view and the sea behind out of frame. I click the shutter, and without thought turn the camera upon myself. A lens, staring into my face. A rounded fishbowl with my reflection moving inside. I smile, allow teeth to show. My hair's blown back in the wind. My wings are stretched forward as I press the shutter. Captured: happy and free, wild and glorious.

Much is still the same as last year, yet I've learnt everything can be lost.

Things can be found too. To be found, something must once have been lost. To create it must once have been in pieces. To be a part, it must once have been apart. Nothing complicated, nothing scientific – nothing my mother hadn't told me.

My bag's packed and stands by Isabelle's cabin door, ready for my morning bus. The other volunteers have arranged a dinner for me. We're to meet at eight on the beach. I walk back and forth along a metre length of the water defence, pondering what to do with my last hours before going to meet everyone. Walk further or return to the cabin? Washing up is done. Sheets are cleaned. Photographs are taken.

My phone rings. Pete's calling.

'Hey, how's it going?' My tummy produces butterflies – unexpected, late arrivals.

'Hey, Sophia, I have some news.'

My insides flip, like fish caught in a net and dragged to break water's surface by no accord of their own. 'What is it? Are you okay?' My voice shakes. Tears prickle. I'm in

Cornwall, talking to Dad, crouched on the earth. What now? Who now?

'It's Lily.'

The fish die down.

'She's pregnant.'

The fish flicker, last twitches. That's it. Nothing.

I wait for everything to fall apart. For the apocalypse. Waves to slap my ankles. Me to be stood, marooned and sinking. Everything flooding around me. Washed out. No one to come to the rescue.

Nothing.

'How?' is all I manage.

'Really? You want to know how?' Pete's tone is sarcastic.

I think I want to hit him, but my insides make a different choice – the net gets dropped back below water, the fish swim free, and I find myself laughing.

'It wasn't planned,' he rushes.

'I've only been gone three weeks. You plan everything, Pete.' I can picture them, Pete and Lily: her sleek blonde hair is combed under her hairband, they're holding hands, they've had a great conversation about the genetics of fungi, and it's made them smile because together they're going to co-evolve. It's an image I've created for months. The perfect tidy couple. I knew it.

But I'm pleased such a photograph can be real.

'I didn't plan this. Look, Sophia,' he doesn't sound pleased; his voice is in teacher mode, like he's having a serious discussion with me about my marks.

I cut him off. 'Pete, congratulations.'

I take my phone from my ear, sparing me the surge of explanations I know will follow. I want to stop at this. Relief.

The screen flashes: 'call ended'. I lift the phone above my head. With a great flap I hurl it into the air. The phone flies towards the horizon, hovers a moment, and then drops down, diving into mud as it hunts for quiet.

I wrap my wings around my body and laugh. Because a John Lennon quote Dad used to say has come to mind. Something about life being the things that happen while you were busy making plans. I can hear Dad's voice, low and wise. What is the life I've created in the folds between my plans, in the space between earthly holdings and the laws of the universe – where all those insects were headed?

I'm walking that space, and whatever lies there, I'm about to find out.

AUTUMN

50

I call from a payphone in King's Lynn. One of the volunteers dropped me here so I could get the bus back to Suffolk. They said it was no problem; they needed supplies. 'Everyone misses Jaffa Cakes.'

The telephone cord is tangled. I untwist it so I can face the window and look at the street. The light is low, the concrete shiny from this morning's rain. The ring reverberates in my ear.

I think of our eyes. Blue and green. Earth and sea. The rich ecosystem that makes itself at home in this meeting point.

'Hello?'

'Joe?'

'Sophia?'

'Hi. I'm coming back today.'

'You are? That's great news.'

Dots connect, stars draw constellations, jigsaw pieces join.

'How's it going?' I say.

'Oh, you know, been working lots. Some old friends came to visit.'

The phone rests in the crook of my neck. I sweep my hair over my shoulder and untangle it with my fingers. I'm ready to offer him a pocketful of gems – the sparkling jewels collected from my time at sea, but his voice is slow, controlled. I bite my tongue, sensing my gems might come out dry and lost of shine.

'How was the rest of your time away?' he asks.

'Great. We had a feast on the beach for my last night,' I start.

'Cool.'

His vacant tone makes me gather that today we're to share other rocks – the bricks and mortar of domestic life. My fingers unpick knots in my hair – untangling, untangling – until they're trapped in black webs.

'You there?' His voice sharpens, concerned.

'Yeah, sorry, I'm here, just tired.'

'I bet you are. Once you're home you can get some rest.'

'Right.'

'See you soon.'

We say our goodbyes and hang up.

What waits for me on the other end of this journey is as blurred as the view behind the wet window of the phone box. It's raining again. Who's going to care for whose baby? And where do I stand in all this?

Some types of turkeys build compost heaps the perfect temperature to hatch eggs in. They don't mind whose.

Male marmosets carry the baby while the woman hunts. Male seahorses give birth to the baby.

But human babies are big and take time and energy to develop. Maybe our bodies have created complex chemical pathways of desire and attachment because without them no one would choose to carry the child.

51

Field Notes

<u>Rose, Rosa</u>

A perennial flowering plant. Flowers of the
rose plant come in many bright colours and
are often large and showy. The stems of a
rose plant are covered in sharp thorns. The
Rosaceae family is native to Asia but is

popular in Europe for their reputation as a
beautiful, tidy plant.

I was scrunched up
waiting to be ready,
when you named me, 'Passive.'

You named me, 'Early bloomer,'
'Late bloomer,'
a 'Blossoming bud of sexuality.'

You named me, 'Flirt' because of my body,
'Tease' because of my scent.
You tore me open and named me, 'Woman.'

I wish you'd stop calling me names.

I'm dressed in the last item in my bag that wasn't caked in
mud. It's a hand-me-down from Isabelle: a blood red linen
dress with a decorative hem, whose skirt reaches my knees

but probably hung at Isabelle's ankles. I linger at the bus stop in Cranston, unsure where to go. Little bronze bells tickle my calves. I'm colourful and jingling and stand out like a flirting peacock.

Me and the dress go for a walk, somewhere we won't be found. The cemetery will do: a few windy paths away and hidden by surrounding trees.

The air is cool and tousles my hair. Goose pimples rise beneath the weave of fine, dark pelt that covers my arms. When I catch my reflection in a window, it's unrecognisable.

I reach the cemetery in record time, thanks to staring at my feet and marching double speed the whole way. Looking up, I gasp at the remembrance of how much exists beside my brain. The bramble berries are fully ripe and spilling juice, the chestnuts are beginning to fall. Everything is laden with fruit. Even the graves look bursting, with fresh flowers covering many a stone. It's Sunday; people must have visited after morning service. Mum used to take us whenever we attended this church; she said it was prettier than other graveyards.

I begin to trail the small footpaths. Memory leads the way: here, Dad showed me a sculpture of a rabbit; here, Mum kissed my knee better when I fell.

I reach a rose bush – familiar, or perhaps like any other. I dive my nose into the folds of red petals. The petals are velvety against my skin and the scent heavy and sweet. I want more. I go to hold another flower, a plumper one, whose petals are more splayed, more mature. My hand accidentally catches on a spike, skin broken fast and a bead of blood appearing. I pull my hand to my mouth and suck up the bead.

I could photograph this rose. Over-done. Think of all the women who've been handed these flowers and expected to love their suitor, or forgive them for doing wrong because of these blooms. What a symbol. In the scientific world a name is merely a handy gift to remember something by, but to be named means much more – it is to be pinned down against a naturalist's cork board.

I need to talk to Pete. My feelings for him – chemical, social, internal, external – can't be examined under a microscope and named.

I walk away from the rose bush. Fast. Following footsteps of the subconscious. Nettles prick my ankles. Pete will want to name us. Pebbles get caught in my boots. Pete will want my love. Lower branches of an elder graze my forehead as I forget to duck. Pete follows the rule book, giving roses rather than facing the music. I yelp at the impossibility of defining him and me. And stop still.

A little stone to my left has drawn my attention. I remember standing beside it, Mum's hand in mine. I remember her weeping. The stone is worn, and blank. A bunch of lilacs tied with a mauve ribbon lie next to it.

I pay my respects from habit, take Mum's hand, Dad's too, and they both lift me up, so I swing between them, elevated and freed from effort by their strength. I reach the floor again, skidding on the pebbly path. And we walk away.

52

Leaving the cemetery, I walk to Pete's house. I walk towards his forgiving eyes; the eyes I've looked into for over three years. I walk to face the music. A craving for croissant has launched a bubbling rocket of hunger, and I hope food will be waiting for me.

'Sophia.' Pete opens the front door before I can knock and grabs me into a strong hug. Astounded by his weight I lose balance. He steadies me with a firm hand, leans back and looks me up and down, taking in my body in the bright dress. My shoulders roll forwards, self-conscious.

'You look well.'

'Thanks.'

'Come inside. Shitty weather this morning, isn't it? Was it sunny at the Wash?'

'Yeah, but it turned to stormy today too.' Of course we're talking about the weather first.

'Are you hungry? Will pancakes do?'

'That would be amazing.'

I follow Pete into the house, hyper-aware this is my house too. I could take my bag to our room and unpack while he makes the pancakes.

'So, tell me all about it,' he says.

'We went sailing. Have you ever been? I think you'd like it.'

'I have.'

We're silent while he mixes the flour, eggs and milk in the blender. He retrieves our large frying pan from the hook above the stove, spoons some butter inside, and puts the pan on the hob to heat. 'I saw Joe around town while you were away.'

'Did you talk to him?'

'No.' He pauses as he ladles some pancake mix into the pan. 'Have you spoken to him?' He looks over his shoulder, too fast for me to read his face, and turns back to his pancake, ready to flip.

'We had a short chat.'

Pete places two plates and some cutlery on the counter. 'Lemon and sugar? There's banana if you like, or strawberries.' He places the first pancake onto the plate nearest me.

'Strawberries, please.'

Pete purses his lips, pleased with himself. He holds strawberries one at a time above the plate and chops them expertly into a line down the pancake. 'I'm glad you're back,' he says.

I take a mouthful, and delicious warmth fills my mouth so I can't reply.

'About Lily ...'

I put my fork down. About Lily – we want to get married. About Lily – she's going to move in to have the baby. I'm ready, I'm waiting.

Cough. Pete massages his head. 'So, Lily and I aren't together.'

'But you're perfect for one another.'

'We're what?' Pete shakes his head, dazzled. 'Sophia, you've never met her. You've no idea what she's like.'

'She's blonde. The type of girl who dreamed of the white wedding we never had but you wanted. She's equal to you in conversation. She's smart, in the intellectual sense rather than the emotional. She's from a nice, traditional family who have a roast dinner every Sunday. She had her ears pierced as a little girl. She loves to cook.' My hands are in the air, painting pictures of this woman.

'Sounds like you've met another Lily.'

We both burst into laughter; it's good to break the tension.

'Lily is a twenty-six-year-old with a nose piercing who likes reggae music. I think you'd like her. But we're not about to move in together.' He looks coy, handsome. Pete never knew he was handsome; I wonder if he does now. 'But we have discussed how this is going to work,' he says. 'We're going to co-parent. It will be complicated for the first year, when the baby will need to be with Lily all the time, but I'll visit regularly. I want to be a part of the child's life.'

Pete's plans soothe, as they always have. Nothing is asked of me; it's all decided. I pick up my fork to eat.

'Sophia, there's just one more thing.'

My fork is put to rest again.

'I don't think we can be together anymore.'

My lips purse. I don't have the faintest idea what to say. I close my eyes and try to hear the sea, but it's gone silent.

'Can I have another pancake?' I ask.

53

Field Notes

<u>Dandelion, Taraxacum</u>

A genus of flowering plants that are part of
the Asteraceae family. Dandelions are
native to North America and Eurasia. In
Europe they are important wildflowers and
accumulate quickly. Their common name
translates as 'Lions Teeth' referring to

their long thin yellow petals. They produce
seeds asexually and without pollination,
resulting in offspring identical in genetics to
their parent plant.

Profusive me
Left alone
while others mate or are mown.
But I'm no 'desperately seeking'
no 'looking for someone well flourished'.

I am complete
Blow my mane, I'm ready set.

My young will be beautiful, roaring
yellow faced and adoring.
They will be more of the same,
and they, too, will shed their mane,
to re-create

My art is prolific.
Paints your lawn bright,
wild and messy.
If you want to tidy my hair,
too bad,
I'll take myself elsewhere

The first thing I notice when I leave the house is the dandelion heads have gone. The observation slows my walking pace. I've been cheated – I never took seed when I was away, but everyone else did. They waited until I wasn't looking.

I head down the lane from our house. The cooking apples are ready, hanging heavy from the trees behind the hedge. They want to be picked. I drop several into my bag and know what I must do next.

The men at the bike shop are kind when I turn up and say I need to borrow a bike. They don't ask questions. Men can be good like that. I leave the shop, an old Raleigh racer by my side, and look back through the window. Once, on a winter's day, I'd seen two figures through that window – a girl and a boy. The girl went on tiptoes to kiss the boy, who was tall. I am okay. The two figures and I had become friends and I'd remembered what it was like to be happy without having to serve a purpose. I made a choice. They made me feel a part of something bigger than my individual life. I am not left behind.

At the bottom of the front doorsteps, my thumbs hook under rucksack straps, as if I'm about to depart, not arrive. Collecting myself, I walk on up, an affirmation each step: I am okay. I made a choice. I am not left behind.

My knuckles rest against the door, but I'm not ready to knock. What would I say to her?

That I might not have a partner, or her grandchild, or a father, but that aphids are born already pregnant, and I, too, can continue to be productive.

I am a flower: beautiful and fertile, wild and spreading. Persistent and alone.

And for today, I am enough. And that is that.

54

It's time to go back to where I started. Not the cosmos, not the sea. Home.

I wait on the doorstep, like a cardboard box labelled 'Fragile'. I've passed many hands, crossed species and counties. It's time to return to sender. I'd like to unpack my contents, check my 'made in' stamp before I make any more.

Knock-knock. Light at first, then heavy. KNOCK-KNOCK.

'About time, Sophia.'

'Sorry. I've been busy.'

'And I've been worried sick.'

I suppress a smile. This is how she loves: the frown lines, the sharp words, the silence. She places her hand on my waist and directs me into the house.

'How are you?' I say, comforted by her touch.

'The women from church and I have been making cordials with the elderberries.'

'I picked some cooking apples on my way; I thought we could make a pie.'

Dad used to admire Mum for how she put nature to practical use. 'Your mother loves to make from all of God's gifts,' he would say, as we sat on the allotment with a slice of homemade pie: one week, blackberry; next week, plum. My mother co-evolves wherever she goes – making something out of everything.

'Wonderful idea,' she says.

I unpack the apples from my bag. Mum bustles into the kitchen to get a chopping board and knife. I take a seat at the dining room table. The photos on the mantelpiece stare back at me. My family. Each our own ecosystem. Continuing to give and take.

Mum arrives behind me and places the chopping board and knife on the table. 'Sophia,' she says. The smell of her breath: nuts and coffee. 'I wanted to tell you some things before you went away, but you left so fast.' Her voice is quiet; it used to sing me to sleep.

'Don't worry, Mum.' She has tales: fables, the Bible, the life stories she never told. There's time left.

'No, it's important. I haven't seen you much this year and it's got me thinking. It's never been easy between you and me, and I don't want things to come to an end before we've talked it through.'

'Things aren't coming to an end.'

'You can't be so sure,' she snaps – and it's true.

She sits down and takes my hand in hers – I'm a child, tucked into bed, and she's holding my hand, and the warmth of her touch makes me want to hold on forever, but it also slips me into sleep, where I must let go. I wake screaming, searching for that hand, no time passed in my mind, but it's pitch-black, and the hand is gone.

She licks her lips, ready to begin.

'When I was in my twenties, I moved to the same village as your dad. He was the popular boy: everybody liked him. I liked him, though I never thought he'd notice me. But after some time, he did. We both got jobs as harvesters at a nearby farm. I fell in love. He was able-handed, knew everything about anything. I told him about the wonders of the gifts of God – things my parents had shown me, like the way water ran around rocks, and the way insects could rise to the heavens – and he told me how these things worked. We found wonder in this world together. We didn't much mind our differences – no one is perfect. But my parents did mind; they used to tell me to find a nice Christian boy. But I didn't listen. Your dad was the best boy I'd ever known. Soon I became pregnant. It was great news; we were happy. We were going to start a family.'

Her speech is fast, sentences tumbling out. This is a story she's been saving up. One learnt to recite by heart. One told to herself many times. But she pauses at this point; does she not want to carry on? I follow her eyes, they are fixed on a rogue apple on the floor.

'Well,' she continues. 'It was a complicated birth, and they ended up rescuing you by caesarean section. I became very sad after the birth. I loved you very much, but I couldn't show it. I felt I'd failed you, then I felt I'd failed your father. I'd failed myself and I'd failed my family. My parents told me I should talk to God, ask him what I'd

329

done wrong. And so I did. Religion helped me survive, but I always loved your dad, and could never believe he stuck by me. But I think it was for you, Sophia, not me.' Her hand shakes in mine. 'I'll never forgive myself.' Her eyes gloss with tears.

A lump forms in my throat.

'I'm sorry.' Mum repeats it again and again. 'I'm sorry.' Words wet with tears. 'I'm sorry.' Her hand clammy on mine.

The lump rises.

She pulls her hand back to wipe her eyes and straightens her body, bracing herself to continue. 'I don't think you ever forgave me. We were a happy family, Sophia. Your dad and I respected one another, and we both loved you. But you always pulled away, as though you knew.'

I swallow the lump down. 'Knew what, Mum? You're not making any sense.'

'But you loved your dad, so I let you two bond. I left you two to one another. I was trying to respect you, Sophia, not neglect you. I was respecting your need to blame me.' She writhes, struggling to soften her posture. 'And there was no one else to blame, so I understood. But now you've done the same and blamed yourself – you're my daughter after all – but I wish I'd set a different example.'

I put a hand out and touch her face. She flinches like a sparrow. 'Mum, you need to tell me what happened.'

'When you lost your baby it all came back. I wanted to help you, but I didn't know how – it was your dad who would have known what you needed.'

'Nobody can provide for all of someone's needs.' My skin itches with anxiety, and I want to get up, go for a walk, shake it off.

Mum makes eye contact; her pupils dilate and her lip quivers.

My heart races.

'She was stillborn.' Her voice is strangled.

'Who, Mum?' I sit very still. I know who.

'You had a twin, Sophia. It was her I lost. She was your identical.'

I sit, pins and needles of shock pricking at my pores.

Together we sit.

And it comes to me: the image of a small, unmarked stone, surrounded by grasses. My sister's grave.

55

The mid-afternoon sun has fought its way through clouds and settles the hairs on my arms. I glance left then right. Nobody. The common is empty. I wait on the outskirts, by the muddy football pitch, the forgotten bags of dog poop and the scum of litter from picnickers who've mistaken concrete as a rubbish bin. My hair falls in my eyes. I sweep it back. My summer of neglect has allowed it to grow beyond the small of my back, and the weight lolls over my wrist as I pull my hand away.

Joe arrives, arms swinging by his sides. His skin looks mottled, tired. But he's whistling. In my stomach a flock of pigeons has been thrown some seeds. The birds flap wings against one another in the fight for the most seeds. They disrupt the quiet air and create havoc. Joe smiles when he sees me, an easy smile. I pinch my thigh below my skirt line.

'Sophia. Welcome back.'

He takes me by the shoulders and holds me. His hands are calloused, oil stained, rough. Hands that make. The pigeons flap, brushing feathers against the walls of my abdomen.

'Thanks.'

I allow my eyes to move to his. They are closed. His head tips back, facing the sun. Heat travels through his fingers to my shoulders. The warmth of attention.

I pinch my leg again. He's like a dog, returned to his owner after adventuring to eat the neighbour's good meat. A word slips onto my tongue. Loyalty. Not fidelity.

He opens his eyes. I lean forward and kiss each one. Maybe I'll taste the salt of the sea. His lashes flutter, defending themselves against my mouth. He runs his hands down my sides and clasps them behind my waist. I shoo the pigeons away, but they're going nowhere.

I walk us into the common and choose a sunny area with a tree stump each to sit on.

'Isabelle phoned last night,' he says. 'She told me you'd heard the news.'

'You already knew?'

'Yeah, I knew. She told me before you left to her parents. That's why I didn't visit.'

He had wanted to visit.

'So, she thinks it might be yours?'

'It might be.' His forehead creases.

'What's going to happen?'

'Well, Isabelle wants to have the baby.' His hair flops over his eyes and shades them from me.

'And you'll be a part of their life.'

'I don't expect so.'

The pigeons slow the beating of their wings.

'It sounds like Isabelle and Callum have things sorted, and she always knew how I felt.' His frown deepens.

'How you felt?' I'm tired of decoding.

'About children. Isabelle knows I don't believe in having kids.' He chews his lip. 'She knows I think that's the worst thing we could do for this planet.' His fingers are linked, knuckles white with tension.

'The worst thing?'

'You know what I mean. I'm aware I sound like an asshole; that's why I didn't want to be put in this position.'

'I don't know what you mean.' My voice comes out abrupt.

Joe cocks his head, taken aback, as if I should have understood. 'I mean environmentally. The choice to have a child has a hugely negative impact on our already dying planet.' He straightens his head, cocksure. 'It's selfish. The planet will suffer, species will suffer and the children themselves will suffer. I can't bring myself to support it.' His teeth grind together. I've never seen him stressed before.

'You mean we should all die out, and leave no one behind?' The words were intended as sarcastic, but once aloud, it strikes me that in winter, when I lost my child, maybe I'd been looking for this.

It's not winter anymore.

'Perhaps.' His face relaxes and he looks at me, hopeful. 'So that's why you can be such a hedonist?'

'You think I'm a hedonist?'

'You enjoy having all the fun on this planet, without having to commit.' I can't look up.

His hand strokes my knee. 'I'm sorry you think of me like that. I saw us as committed.'

'Meant for each other?' Perhaps we are. The two left. Childless. To evolve alongside the rest in our unique way.

'Nature doesn't work like that. People adapt, then they readapt.' His shoulders are broad, open. An unlit cigarette balances between his thumb and forefinger.

Standing, I take his shoulders in my hands and give them a squeeze. The muscles are taut under my fingers. I say goodbye.

The common, as I walk across it, is scraggly and overgrown. Summer's over: no one is out. People are back at work or enjoying their tidy gardens. The leaves on the trees that line the edge of the common are huge. It's hard to imagine they're going to fall.

Tall grasses sway. A movement. I brake.

Black.

Winding across the ground I'm walking. A metre from my feet.

My heart beats.

Slick. Black – no, grey – with a dark zig zag along its back. A 'V' at the nape of its neck. Long. Still going. Smooth skinned.

Gone.

The adder has crossed my way and gone.

I've never seen one before: England's only venomous snake. Predator of shrews, voles, mice – mammals too small to stand up for themselves. Dad warned me about adders whenever we walked heathlands. He said they needed specific habitats. He said if adder habitats aren't joined together then adders are forced to in-breed, which leaves them vulnerable to disease. He told me I shouldn't be scared of an adder crossing my way, I should see it as they're on their way to somewhere important.

My heart continues to beat fast. A mirage of the snake's shape hypnotises my mind's eye. The desire to touch skin so smooth. The fear of the bite.

I nerve myself to step forwards, move onward from this serpent's land.

The red bricks of the house lend themselves to autumn's light. They glow a warm auburn. I knock on the front door and can smell the damson berries.

From the outside, the house looks the same as any other, but inside lived a unique couple, and they were happy.

Pete answers the door in a pair of shorts. His skinny knees poke out, white above the kneecap, brown below. 'Come in – or shall we drag some seats out back? It's nice and warm.'

As we walk through the house I avoid looking too close for evidence of what occurred in my absence. We take two of our dining chairs into the garden with us. Our chairs face my photography cabin. Our hands hang in the gap between. They take hold of one another. I peer sideways at Pete. His hair's grown; the mass of brown fondles the bottoms of his ears. I examine the proportions of his face:

perfect halves, thirds, fifths between facial features. It would make a good photograph, his profile lit by the natural sunlight against the backdrop of red brick.

'How are you?' he says, his mouth bending these proportions and then returning them to place.

'Good. I saw an adder, but it didn't get me.'

'They don't normally.'

The birds sing to one another from somewhere behind the heavy leaves.

'You really don't want me back, do you?' I say.

He relaxes his torso against the backrest of his chair. 'No. You knew before me, but I see it now. We don't work together.'

My hand moves to my neck. 'I'm sorry.'

'Me too.' He runs his fingers through his hair. 'I thought we wanted the same thing.'

'I did too.'

'I'm not sure what you're looking for, but I don't want to try and make it me anymore.'

'I know.'

My legs quiver as I stand. I bend and plant a kiss on his cheek. The familiar smell of his aftershave. I didn't know it would go like this.

56

I lie on Mum's living room floor, arms at right angles to my body as if I were pinned to a crucifix. I'm sacrificed to nobody but myself. And the sea. I imagine I'm floating on my back, allowing her to guide me.

The floorboards creak under Mum's footsteps. 'Are you waiting for the birds to eat you alive?'

'Well, they deserve some food, don't you think?' I roll onto my side and brush the dust off my clothes.

'How are you?' she asks.

'Oh-kay.' The syllables come slow.

'Good. You know you're welcome to stay as long as you need? Are you hungry? I'm going to make some dinner – I'll sacrifice some carrots for a stew if you're willing to save yourself?' I never knew Mum could joke.

'Go on then.'

The floorboards creak again as she leaves the room.

I had been thinking about Isabelle. I let my mind return to her. Does she mind Joe's response to her news? When I arrived at the Wash, I mentioned Joe's and my relationship once. 'You really don't mind?' I'd asked. She'd said no. It was nothing different to what always went on between them, except this time he really loved me. 'And maybe that's why it feels good,' she said. 'Our time together was coming to an end, and you've given us an easy way out. I hope you don't mind my saying that?' I blushed and said, 'You're sure?' And she replied, 'Hey, together we learnt to evolve; doesn't matter how or why. We got to where we were meant to.'

We're all part of the same web of life to Isabelle. Sometimes we hang on a closer thread to someone, and sometimes far apart, but our connection is inherent, not designed, and we don't get to choose where we hang, but move with what moves us.

I go to the front window. An older couple, walking a dog, pass below. The couple are wearing hats, prepared for the cold. Hats to warm their thoughts from freezing. I wonder whether Isabelle's baby will carry Joe's curious thoughts. And will Lily's baby understand things as easily as Pete? I wonder what these babies will look like. What colour hair, what colour eyes?

Do I mind? Isabelle's baby will share the world with me regardless. How will baby and the world work together?

I have faith.

My stomach rumbles, not from desire, but from a basic hunger for food.

57

'Good morning.' Mum fills the kettle. I walk up behind her and give her a hug. She stiffens, then relaxes into me.

From the living room I hear the water come to a boil. It splutters and spits. I'm about to cry. If I start, I won't stop.

Mum places two steaming terracotta mugs on the table and sits beside me.

'I need to do something for myself,' I say.

'In your own time.' She crosses her legs and folds her plaid skirt beneath them.

'I think it might be good to get away.'

'There's no hurry.' Mum takes a sip from her mug. Whatever lies behind her words is hidden by terracotta. But I can guess.

'I'm thankful we're on good terms, Mum.'

'But you need to get away. I understand.' She places the mug back on the table and looks up at the ceiling. 'So, where are you going to go?'

'I thought I'd take a trip to Devon.'

'To your grandmother's?'

'Yes.'

'I think that's a good plan.' She uncrosses her legs and looks to me, readied.

'I'm thinking ...' I bite my nail. 'Dad had his naturalism, Pete has his science and I've written these field notes – more like poems, really. I'm wondering about taking some photographs to go with them.'

'Grandma knows a lot about flowers.'

'That's what I was thinking. And, well, she's alone too.'

'I'm sure she'd appreciate the visit. I haven't seen her since your father passed, but she's been very supportive.'

'I forget you two talk.'

'When will you leave?'

'At the weekend.'

'You must send her my love.'

'I will.'

'And send me some of your photographs. I always love the images you create – when you let us see them.'

They never thought they'd see me again, rare, wild bird that I am. I returned with my family in 1979. How did I find the way? My ancestors lived here, centuries and centuries ago. We cranes have home at heart.

Home. We are at home here. This Broad land. This watershed stretch. The long grasses, the marsh, the deep pools from which we can feed. It's simple: we know what we need. We're rare because of our choice of habitat –

which is rare because of another's choice of habitat. What comes around goes around.

We're glad to be back. Today, marching long-legged through waterlogged territory. Hear us call, like the marching soldiers headed to battle – Homer said that. But how did humans not fear our battle call? Instead they fearlessly dredged this land, until we could live no more.

58

The church is empty except for me. The beams run above my head, dark and foreboding against the whitewashed walls. The pulpit stares at me, blank faced: no one here to tell me what to do but myself. The ornate carvings along the altar tell stories I can't make out from the pew I sit on. I could look closer, try to decipher an answer from these stories, but I don't.

'Hello, Dad.'

My knees touch the pew in front. Why am I here? My eyes close, shutting out the oppressive decor. I'm cramped, herded in like the rest. To be emptied of creative juices and filled with ideas. To be kept away from the wilderness, because in the wilderness we might find ourselves wanderers, malleable to the changing climate instead of malleable to man.

Covehithe was Dad's favourite church – if he had to choose a church. I think he preferred the ruins of the old one outside, where the open air talks down to us, and the wind dictates our direction. Still, he used to come inside with Mum and me when she agreed to visit Benacre reserve. Compromise. Balance.

Dad would walk me around the building, point out the different stones it was built from, tell me how long Covehithe had been settled for. Things I no longer remember. Mum would perch on the pew, like I am now, and pray. I never knew who she talked to; I assumed God, but it could have been anyone. Look at me, doing the same.

The car's parked outside. I asked to borrow it from Pete for a couple weeks, so I could visit Grandma and find my feet (or which direction my feet will point). Leaving Cranston, my hands steered me here, knowing the detour they needed. I know myself better than I think.

En route, it occurred to me the car is half mine. I'm not left with nothing. Objects, personal growth and memories don't get left behind. Independent but connected – how does that figure?

Much to Mum's annoyance, Dad requested to be cremated. She respected his wishes but claimed for herself that he have a church memorial. We held the service in this church. Compromise. Balance.

I look around at the empty seats beside me. The church may as well have been empty on the day of his service. I had sat alone, eyes on Dad's face, which stared at me from the photograph at the front. The photograph stilled creased lines around his wise eyes. He was silver, faded, aged to black and white. He looked older than a week prior, when I'd held him on his deathbed. This wasn't him.

He was an eternal life force to me – he was the spirit and soul of the wild party of life.

'Dad?' I try again, my voice echoing off the walls and into the silence, like bats fleeing into nooks. When I picture him today, I see the urn with his ashes. A surreal image of a father. I'd watched his coffin move along the conveyor belt and into the furnace of hell. I'd laughed watching the coffin roll down that belt. Dad's favourite tree, oak, made a commodity. His wild life a factory line. Mum had given me an angry glance, but I hadn't cared. After, they'd handed the urn to me. 'Here's your dad.'

'Dad, can you hear me?'

It's easier to speak to nothing than to speak to that urn. The urn is nestled in Mum's wardrobe. I'm not sure she'll ever throw him back to nature.

'Dad, I'm going to start a new venture. I'm going to create something from my photography. Dad, I think you'd be proud of me.' I stop, uncross my legs, re-cross them the other way. 'Not that you need to be.' I chew my lip. 'I'm going to move to Grandma's for a bit. I'll say hello from you.' My calf cramps and I uncross my legs again. 'I'm sorry you'll miss what I produce.'

The words knife my chest. This is all wrong. Abort plan.

A pigeon casts a quick shadow across the nave as it lands on a window ledge. Dad? This time it's different. I think of Dad, Mum and me – a pride of lions on the savannah. The women would live together when the men went away.

'Mum's happy for me,' I say, not sure where to go next in my monologue.

I imagine Dad, sauntering on to find another group to join. And I hear his voice. 'Life's hard, Sophia. It takes 3000 copulations to breed a cub who makes it to adulthood. You're doing just fine.'

My hands clutch my belly, sensing my creativity as it grows inside: a miracle seed that might sprout. Will it make it this time? Inside, luck turns. And I'm guarding it in disbelief that, once sown, this seed can grow from dark depths. But it's the dark depths that keep it safe.

'Mum told me about my twin. It must have been hard for you, too, Dad. How did you not need something else to believe in?'

'Isn't life enough to believe in?'

His voice rings in my ears and I jump, certain someone has entered and is clinging to the rope of the church bell, being pulled up and down by the bell's weight. Nothing is constant, nothing is in perfect balance. Life is a continuous to and fro. Trial and error. Adapt and reshape.

You are part of a great experiment.

The last year slips away. It could be September a year ago. I am the same: ready to create, with Dad, in Suffolk. Nothing lost.

Lionesses can't reach oestrus while still in touch with a cub. Until her cub leaves, or another male kills it, the lioness won't return to a reproductive state. There's no shame in this.

I shuffle in my seat, press my hands between thighs.

'Dad, Joe was exhilarating. I wish you could have met him.'

Am I wrong to leave? Palms sweat. I wipe them on my trousers.

'You remember the kingfishers, Dad?'

I do. We watched them on the river in Beccles; the same river I went and had an affair on.

'I can see the kingfishers,' Dad says.

And so can I. Bright. Emerald and red. Sparkling above the water as it falls from my eyes.

'I'm going to make something alone, Dad.'

His voice calls to me from outside, leading me away from the closed walls and down to the beach.

I'm walking Covehithe beach with him this time, not Joe. I always was. Mum's behind, carrying the beach bag with all the goods necessary for me to be carefree and not notice. And then I let him go. He walks away.

I walk with my creativity, with the fens, with the sky. I walk without knowing where I'm going.

59

Grandma wants to go on a Sunday amble. 'Let's talk about your ideas in the outdoors they were born from.' She hasn't asked what's happened.

She steadies herself against the stone wall of the house and lifts one foot at a time into a pair of wellies. Her frame is tall, like Dad and I, and scrawny. Moles and freckles mark her arms, which get swamped by an oversized jacket. I recognise the jacket as Grandpa's. Her hair's long and thick, streaked white and grey. It's pulled back in a clip but insists on falling free.

We leave her house, the semi-detached cottage with a thatched roof, which is familiar in an uncanny way: rooms smaller than I remember from childhood visits, and furniture not quite the way it's been recorded in memory. I understand why my grandparents moved. Dartmoor stretches out from the village, sloping upward on all sides to nestle us safe. The land is painted purple with heather, and areas of dense woodland are spied within walking distance.

We wander through the village. The narrow lanes serve to hold us the same way as the slanting moorland. When between two Devon hills, or two Devon cottages, nothing else can be seen; you must walk with confidence in your stride, assured that you know where you're going. We head out of the village through a field and along a small stream. Autumn has shaded the ground: the yellows of gorse dampened and the grasses browned.

Grandma walks at a brisk pace and I keep up. The water in the stream is higher than last time I visited, or else I remember wrong. A light sputtering of rain refreshes my face. The other villagers have given up on walks today and hibernate inside. They hope this winter won't be the one where floods come.

The birds are fewer than I remember too. Though it was spring the last time. Some bird residents have headed elsewhere for the cold days ahead. I am a new resident to replace them. Grandma and I duck under stray bramble branches as we head into a wooded area. Damp and dark. The smells are rich and earthy. I'm excited to see what plants live inside. Many plants will be preparing for sleep, in the hope that they'll continue the cycle next year. They never know. Life is precarious.

And I'm excited to watch when everything returns: the people, the birds, the leaves, the flowers. Perhaps the clock is rewinding, not ticking forward. Have faith either way. What once was, will be again.

The canopy above rustles in the wind, moving leaves aside for a glimpse of sky. What late autumn light there is takes me by surprise and I'm blinded. When my eyes readjust, the view in front has changed. The mulched earth below my feet is cracked. The foliage is frozen. And walking between the ancient trunks, I see her.

She's slinking, her body swinging. A hypnotic pendulum. Weight transfers from one foot to the next, consistent and smooth. Her belly, solid and round, slides forward and back with each step. She turns her head and fixes on me. Narrowed eyes check me out. She turns back.

Her hair looks soft to touch, a golden grey; she's aged.

What's she doing here? Wandering her homeland, solitary and confident. Free to be. No one searching for her, no one hunting her. No one influencing where she goes.

Will she hunt today? She's a powerful huntress, could grab you by the neck and choke you. She could kiss your lips and suffocate you as she does. She likes the commoners best: roe deer, foxes. Is it revenge? She's held her wild-self back too long.

Is that a gentle mewing I hear? A soft purr. She's comfortable alone, not calling out for company, yet.

The lynx is walking ahead of me, away from me, and it's as if I were walking with her. Scouting forest to make a hide, but first exploring. We have our ears pricked for the sound of life. A mouse hundreds of metres away scrambles in the first fallen leaves. We won't be able to make a hide until next year. But we can paw our way around this winter, solitary.

I can feel my paws touching the ground, thick pads spread out like snow shoes. I am sturdy, balanced on this untidy earth. Let us saunter.

We remember this land. We feel safe. Will others dislike us? We will mark our place and hope they let us stay. They know what it's like to be in danger.

Where are you going? Are you leading the way or me? You say we need to be alone now. Your ears are soft, pointed, I want to nuzzle them. But you're cleaning yourself, like I've seen domestic cats do, and you're turning around; I'm turning around. Pets without owners. The ground is rough, but I am strong. The cool air is sliding through my hair; my belly is heavy beneath me. The fields are behind, the moors are ahead, and we are roaming our woods.

'Sophia?' Grandma says, 'are you okay?'

'Yes. Sorry, what were you saying?'

'What did you see?'

'What?'

'I was saying nothing. You stopped still.' She looks around into the trees, her hand above her eyes as she scans oak, hazel, fern, bracken. 'Was it a bird? Your dad used to stop like that to show me birds I'd never seen before.'

'Yes, I thought I saw an animal, but it's gone now.'

She says, 'Should we head on, or do you want to keep lookout?' Her smile is wry.

'No, no, let's head on.'

'Very good, I'm excited to hear about these flowers.'

Once, we were one of the commonest birds around. They named towns after us: Cranbrook, Cranleigh, Cranston. I was your plain Jane, happily settled, part of the scenery. I could carry out domestic life in peace.

Until our breeding sites were disturbed. No marsh, no water, nothing. Yes, something. Farming, houses – someone else's domestic life.

But I'm back, with my family. Our grey bodies swoop across the waters, wings spread to two metres. You can hear us three miles away; we like to call attention.

Because we flew far. Across air, where everything gathers, ready to emerge. We risked our luxuriant tails. We risked the black plumes from our wings being plucked. We risked our red crowns to be de-throned. Wild. Rare. Back from the dead.

For there are people re-creating our habitat for us, making it safe to come home. They are busy returning the water, the marshes, our everything.

But be careful, civilisation is not so civilised.

We simply want to nest. The wild is our civilisation. We are not dangerous; we are not alien. We want the same as you: a home. A place to carry out our day-to-day. We want to eat and we want to sleep. We want to make sure our young grow old. Is there no way to live together?

Together we can learn new patterns of how to co-exist and create. Together we evolve.

My family come close to me; they are frightened. 'Is it all over?' they ask. I say 'no.' I nudge my white facial streak against that of my young; he hasn't grown his crown yet; he doesn't know if he will reign.

And I wake, feeling tall and at peace.

Acknowledgements

The places, plants, people, and animals to thank for their part in this book, are numerous.

Thank you to a long-ago conversation with Katia Cnop, which introduced me to the Bear-Claw Poppy and its reliance upon one pollinator alone. The fact met us with awe at a time of obsessing over 'the one'. I will never forget my eyes opening to both the finite and myriad ways this web of life survives and thrives.

I must thank George Szirtes, for his enthusiasm in my initial short story and suggestion I expand it into a novel.

Thank you, Wendy Stayte, for our DIY artist retreat in the Canadian wilds where this novel began to grow.

Thank you to my mother, Sacha Jeffay, for providing us the space to make art, and for your endless cheerleading – I needed your faith for the times mine was missing.

Thank you to my partner, Jimmy Marshall, for following me to a houseboat on the river Avon whilst I completed my MA – you created us a home where I could watch the wilds I was writing from, for, and about, and allowed me to get lost in this project without losing you.

Thanks also to my sister, Rachel Roberts, who stood alongside me as we learned about grief. And to my father, Maha Roberts, whose love of the tiny things in nature and whose miniature re-wilding project in his back garden are an inspiration.

Thank you to my friends and colleagues at Bath Spa University, whose insightful feedback helped my writing breathe like the organisms I was intrigued by. Can I thank specifically Stephen Moss, for his joyful nature, kind empathy, and keen interest in this book; and Alexia Wdowski, Joanne Stubbs, Ruby Vallis and Trenna Cormack, whose committed critique and friendship mean a lot to me and my writing.

Thanks to the early readers of this novel – Francesca Ashurst, Heather Holcroft Pinn, Lucy Day, Maha Roberts, John Alton, Sacha Jeffay, and Chris Alton – huge gratitude.

And of course, thank you to Hermitage Press, who welcomed this novel to nest.

Thanks are due to Sarah Dawes for her gentle and astute copyediting (who knew such a combination existed!). Oliver Tooley for taking on the challenge of design and formatting a slightly different book. Dr Paul Taylor-McCartney, for your generous enthusiasm and supportive patience in waiting out my maternity leave before publication. And, Kim Stephens, for her beautiful illustrations and artwork.

Miscarriage is becoming more spoken about, but I feel still not enough. Thank you to the women who shared with me their experiences.

Thanks to Norfolk and Suffolk – the great skies, sand dunes, sea, wind, sun, broads, birds (too many to name here), plants (same again) and creatures.

There are many friendships who have influenced this novel, and rather than name names, I hope you know who you all are. Thank you, Anna Wilson, Wyl Menmuir, Joanne Stubbs and Richard Kerridge ... What can I say? – a writing community and writers' spaces are invaluable.

The research for this novel is too vast to list here, but thank you to the many books, journals, documentaries, exhibitions and more that have fed into this work. Any mistake is completely my own.

Lastly, thank you to my son, Heron. Your arriving earth side is no small wonder. Before even existing, you gave me the eyes to see the magic of this planet and the wish to share it. I hope deeply that there are still wilds for you when you're older.